The Pajama Boy

A Novel by Ginger Mayerson

The Wapshott Press

The Pajama Boy

Published by
The Wapshott Press
An Imprint of J LHLS
PO Box 31513
Los Angeles, CA 90031

The Wapshott Press
www.WapshottPress.com

First printing August 2008

ISBN: 978-0-6152-3547-9

06 05 04 03   4 3 2 1

Wapshott Press logo by Molly Kiely
Cover design by Robin Austin

Author's Preface

I've been reading too much yaoi manga and too many yaoi novels. "The Pajama Boy" was born from the need to kick all those stray yaoi tropes out of my consciousness so they wouldn't end up in something else I was writing. Probably this is a strange reason for writing a novel, but if novels were only written for normal reasons, I suspect very few novels would ever get written. I'll try not to ruin it for you, but although this book is set in contemporary Japan, it has nothing to do with Japan. Or rather, this novel has about as much to do with contemporary Japan as those yaoi manga set in 18th century Europe have to do with 18th century Europe. Or has as much to do with gay sex as, well, yaoi. For those of you who might have wandered in here from reality, yaoi manga is gay porn comics created mainly by women for an audience of mostly women. There are lots of explanations on why yaoi is such a huge hit at this point in publishing history and you can look 'em up yourself. It's one of those why-ask-why kind of cravings. I don't really have a solid hypothesis on the popularity of yaoi. Just when it all seems to be a combination of internalized misogyny, racism, androphobia, the denial or ignorance of the reality of male anatomy (in part due to Japan's censorship laws) and gay sex (again, in part due to Japan's censorship laws, but also because it's messy, sweaty, and can be painful) and my face hurts from scowling at the entire genre, some yaoi manga or novel will make me smile because of its goofy sweetness and the whole crazy circus starts up all over again.

Although "The Pajama Boy" springs from my irritation with yaoi, the genre I love to shake my head at, and my need to exorcise my yaoi demons by writing them out, I can only hope, reader, that this novel makes you smile at least once or twice at its goofy sweetness. And if not, then I hope the bitchy prose and *poco a poco accelerando* plot will keep you reading.

Hey, live it up!

And lest I forget: Many many many thanks to Jane, Lene, Logan, Lynn, and Kris for their editorial and moral support while writing this book. Also huge thank yous to Robin for the gorgeous, and multiple, cover artwork.

Ginger Mayerson
May 2008

Nagasaki

"Sir? Here's your order...Sir?" The boy at the cash register nervously held his take-out order to him. "Excuse me? Sir?"

"Yeah...yeah. Thanks." Still staring, Shimada fumbled for his wallet and shoved money at the kid. He grabbed his take-out order and fled.

Rushing to his room, Shimada couldn't eat his dinner when he got there. "The resemblance...too strong," he muttered. Same soft brown eyes set trustingly in a little pointed face. Same untidy black hair. Same resemblance to a wary kitten with a new toy he's not so sure of. "Too strong..." He splashed some water on his face and looked in the mirror. A man in his mid-twenties looked back, not the callow high school boy he once was. Still young, just tired and thin and in need of a haircut. His youthful phantom slid away and he was suddenly very hungry.

The newspaper Shimada wrote for had recently moved their office to a new building. The café was now on his route home. He'd never noticed it in the neighborhood before, but it smelled good, looked clean and the menu had everything he liked. After his first unsettling impression, Shimada avoided the café for a few days and then gave in. On that second evening, an older man was at the cash register and the boy was cleaning tables. There was no shock that night; the boy was just another teenage boy who looked like many other teenage boys. With a small feeling of disappointment Shimada went home. Even the noodles weren't as good as they were the first time.

The side street café was cheap and cheerful. Shimada only noticed the name, Café Chango, on this third visit when he decided to eat there instead of getting take-out. Eating there afforded him a more leisurely view of the boy. "I really have to get over this," he thought. "That is not Seiji, although he kind of reminds me of him...he's not him."

From behind his menu, Shimada cast furtive glances at the boy cleaning tables and taking orders. The boy was casting his own glances, and occasionally their glances locked before one or the other looked quickly away. When the boy finally came to the table to take his order, neither of them could make eye contact and Shimada decided to get it to go after all.

There really was something about this boy that reminded Shimada of his lost love left behind in Tokyo. He thought Nagasaki was far enough away from all that, but apparently fate wanted to torture him some more. He resolved to avoid the café's street thenceforth.

His work kept Shimada busy for a while. He and his photographer were guests at a new luxury hotel and spa for a week. This soft news story reminded Shimada unpleasantly of advertising. Fortunately, he dug up some disgruntled employees, and exposed some shady labor practices and intimidation, as well as some slipshod construction and kick-backs to local contractors, which put that part of the story in the hard news section. This made him feel better, especially when his friend and editor, Ikoma, got a few threatening phone calls.

"I try to give you a vacation and you find a dead rat," Ikoma said, shaking his head in mock sadness.

"I'm a newspaper man, not a fashion writer."

"We're just a little regional paper, Ryuu," Ikoma said, lighting a cigarette.

"News is news, Jun," Shimada said grimly. "Big, little, local, regional, national, international, it's all news." He walked out on Ikoma's laugh.

"Careful you don't win any awards, pal," Ikoma yelled after him.

Shimada barely heard him. He was very hungry for noodles. But it was late and the café was closed. Disappointed, Shimada strolled on, but stopped when he heard voices in a nearby alley.

"You did it before, you can do it again." A deep voice.

"I paid you back, once is enough." A younger, frightened voice.

There was scuffling and a slap; the deep voice snarled, "Cock tease!"

Shimada stepped into the alley and saw the café boy fighting off a larger man. "Hey."

"You fuck off!" the man screamed.

"I doubt it," Shimada said. He dodged the man's lunge and decked him with a right hook when he came up again.

Grabbing the boy by the arm, Shimada decided a little distance from the situation was in order. They were several blocks away when they finally stopped to catch their breath.

"Th– thanks," the boy panted. "Oh, I know you! Where've you been?"

"Working."

"Oh, um, thanks..."

"You're welcome," Shimada said, enjoying the resemblance/non-resemblance to Seiji in the boy. "What's your name?"

"Katayama, Yoshi Katayama," he said. "What's your name?"

"Ryuu Shimada."

"It's nice to meet you," Yoshi said. "Thank you for rescuing me."

"You said that."

"I'm sorry."

"It's okay," Ryuu said. "I'll walk you home."

"Well, that's a problem..."

"Oh?"

"That guy..."

"Yeah?"

"We live in the same boarding house...and..."

"And?" Shimada's investigative reporter's instincts started to kick in.

"And...I'm not sure what to do," Yoshi stammered. "I guess I could sleep at the café, or...or maybe at your place?"

"You just met me, Yoshi, is it wise to go home with me?" Shimada asked, suppressing a smile. "How do you know I'm not as bad as that guy back there?"

"Because you rescued me from him," Yoshi said logically. "And I know you from the café...sort of."

To buy some time while he thought this over, Shimada asked what was going on back in the alley. Yoshi's story was that he'd borrowed a little money from his neighbor in the boarding house and when he couldn't pay it back, the neighbor offered to let him work it off in hand jobs. Not realizing that one hand job wouldn't be enough, Yoshi had reluctantly jacked the guy off. Yoshi had been successfully avoiding the man until the guy ambushed him after he'd closed the café.

"I was lucky you came along," Yoshi said.

"Yeah...lucky," Shimada said, still mulling it over. "How much did you borrow from that guy?" Yoshi named a paltry sum. "He's going to be mad now, so you can come home with me and we'll deal with it tomorrow."

Shimada's tiny room was a mess. "You can have half the futon," he said when they were taking their coats off. "Unless you want to sleep on the floor. But I only have one blanket, so..."

"I don't take up much room," Yoshi said, looking around. "Where's the bathroom?"

Shimada pointed to a door by the window and loosened his tie. His right hand hurt from punching the creep; the knuckles were red and swollen. It would be okay in the morning, but he put some ice on it anyway. A drink might be nice, but he was crashing from the adrenalin rush so he decided against it. Instead he pulled a pair of pajamas he'd never worn out of his dresser and tossed them on the bed. "You can wear those," he said to Yoshi, who blushed. "What's wrong?"

"Nothing," Yoshi said, blushing harder. "I was just wondering what I could wear..."

"You can wear those," Shimada repeated, puzzled by the turn this conversation was taking. He went into the bathroom while Yoshi changed into the pajamas. Shimada usually slept in the nude, but he put on a pair of sweat pants and a t-shirt that night. He found Yoshi way far over on the right hand side of the futon.

"Is this side okay?" he asked. "I noticed there were books on the other side." He nodded at the pile of books, magazines, newspapers, and junk mail piled up on the left side.

"Yeah, you're fine there." Shimada got under the blanket and turned off the light. "Good night."

"Good night," Yoshi said. "Hey...why did you stare at me that time?"

Shimada turned the light back on, looked at the wide-eyed Yoshi and decided the truth wouldn't hurt much. "Because you reminded me of someone I knew in high school," he said. "But that was a long time ago."

"How long ago?"

"About eight years ago." Shimada watched Yoshi forming another question and decided to head it off. "I'm blitzed, Yoshi, ask me whatever it is in the morning." He turned off the light and fell asleep when his head hit the pillow.

A little after dawn, Shimada woke with Yoshi curled in his arms and a rush of nostalgia for such sweet mornings with Seiji. But this was not Seiji, and it was time to get up. "Hey you," he said, jostling Yoshi, who snarled and burrowed deeper. "It's morning, kid, time to face what must be faced."

"Oh!" Yoshi rolled away and sat up, blinking. "I forgot where I was."

"Who do you usually share your bed with?" Shimada asked.

"No one...now. I used to sleep in with my older brother sometimes," Yoshi said softly. "I was dreaming about that." He looked at Shimada and smiled. "Thanks again for rescuing me."

"Well, I'm not done rescuing you yet," Shimada said.

An hour later, after a hasty wash and breakfast, they were at Yoshi's boarding house. The landlady met them at the door; she'd been watching the street for Yoshi. "You little slut!" she yelled and went on to accuse him of leading nice Mr. Watanabe on and then having a thug beat him up. "Here's your things," she said, waving at a small pile of packages by the door. "Get out!"

"But I'm paid to the end of the month!" Yoshi protested.

The furious woman thrust her hand in her apron and counted out some coins. She shoved them at Yoshi and yelled "Get out!" again. Some of the other boarders were peeking timidly at them from the stairs.

Yoshi was staring stunned at the money in his hand.

"Is that enough?" Shimada asked, watching the landlady lest she attack them.

"I think so," Yoshi said, and told Shimada what he paid a month.

Shimada did some math in his head. "Well, that's robbery, but that's what's left on this month," he said. "Let's go." He picked up a parcel.

"And who are you?" the landlady snarled.

"Me? I'm just a thug who pulls child molesters named Watanabe off little boys in alleys," he said over his shoulder. He shoved the parcel-laden Yoshi out ahead of him before he had to listen to any invective screamed at him.

"Oh, damn, what now?" Yoshi asked. He sounded annoyed and distressed in equal measures.

"Well the good news is you won't be running into your banker, Mr. Watanabe, anytime soon," Shimada said blandly. "I suppose the bad news is you can stay at my place until you find a new one."

"You mean that?" Yoshi said, trotting to keep up with Shimada's determined stride.

"I do. You work at that café, right?" Yoshi nodded. "So if any of my treasured possessions disappear, I'll know where to start looking," he said with a wry smile. "You remember where my place is?" he asked, handing Yoshi his keys.

"I think so." Shimada wrote it on the back of one of his business cards for him. "I read this paper," Yoshi said.

"Many people do," Shimada said. "See you."

That evening, Shimada stopped by his landlord's office to tell him about Yoshi and request a second set of keys. "Oh, that nice young man," the landlord said. "He stopped by to tell me the same thing on his way to school."

"School?" Shimada thought.

"And he did a little shopping and cleaning when he got back from school," the landlord said as if this were the most wonderful thing he'd ever seen.

"Shopping and cleaning?" Shimada thought, but said, "I see."

"Such a nice young man. Such nice manners. He bowed to me on his way to work this evening," the landlord said, handing Shimada a spare set of keys. "You just missed him," he added, naming a small sum for the keys.

Shimada paid him and for good measure bowed politely before he left. Up in his now very clean room, he found the refrigerator full of food, and a stack of school books by the right side of the bed.

"Hmmm, how long do you plan to be here, Yoshi?" Shimada asked the empty room and, predictably, didn't get an answer. He helped himself to an apple from the bowl on the counter and settled down with the paper.

He'd had dinner with Ikoma, who'd roared through his story of rescuing Yoshi as if it were the greatest comedy he'd ever heard. "You're a romantic at heart, Ryuu," he'd said. "Oh, where will it all end?"

In retrospect, and listening to Ikoma laugh, Shimada found it funny himself. He was still smiling about it as he skimmed over the slick ads and ads thinly disguised as "news" stories in a new Tokyo magazine Ikoma gave him at dinner. Advertising made him sick, but that evening nothing could ruin his good mood.

He wasn't sleepy, so he decided to head for the café to walk Yoshi home and met him on the stairs. "You're early."

"I didn't have to close tonight," Yoshi said, handing him a bag. "I brought some noodles for dinner."

Shimada didn't tell him he'd already had dinner. But he really liked the café's noodles, so he dished up a smaller portion for himself and sat opposite Yoshi and waited for the kid to finish his prayer before eating. "Any trouble tonight?" he asked casually.

"How'd you know?"

"Your former neighbor seems like the kind of guy who doesn't get the message the first time." Shimada omitted that he'd been on his way to make sure Yoshi got back ho– back to the room safely.

"He did show up, but the cook chased him off with a butcher knife," Yoshi said cheerfully. He went on to recount that he'd explained being attacked after his work shift, but not why he was attacked, and so the whole café staff was on the alert for trouble. Sure enough, his ex-neighbor was loitering behind the café and an alert cook scared some sense into him. The same heroic cook had walked Yoshi ho– walked Yoshi back to the apartment building that night.

"That cook sounds like a nice guy," Shimada remarked. "He makes good noodles, too." He listened to Yoshi make a yummy noise. "Does he have room for you at his place?"

"I doubt it," Yoshi said, slurping broth. "He's got a wife, two kids and a new baby in a place not much bigger than this."

"Did you have a chance to look for a place today?"

"Well, no, I went right from school to work today."

"And when did you have time to wrap the landlord around your little finger?" Shimada asked.

"Eh?" Yoshi looked up, surprised.

"You heard me."

"I had to come back here to change clothes and drop off my books," Yoshi said with the barest hint of a pout. "I happened to meet the landlord, he seems like a nice old guy..."

"He's usually a cranky bastard, but he was positively cuddly about you," Shimada said thoughtfully. "Play your cards right and you could end up owning this place."

"What? What do you mean? Are you throwing me out?" Yoshi said, alarmed.

"Not yet, but this place is too small for two, and it was never a permanent arrangement."

Yoshi stared at him for a moment and then looked around the room. "You're right," he finally said. "This place is too small. And it's kind of dark and depressing."

"I've been very happy here," Shimada almost snapped. It was a lie; he'd suffered greatly there and survived. "Where do you go to school anyway? The Polytechnic?"

"No, I'm a senior in high school."

"How old are you anyway?" Shimada envisioned how much or how little Ikoma would laugh if he got arrested for harboring an underage–

"I'm eighteen. I missed a year, so I'm finishing now," Yoshi said defensively. "And excuse me, but I have to do some homework before bed."

Shimada didn't ask to see his identification card to verify his age; he merely cleared the table, took a bath and read in bed while Yoshi diligently did his homework. Eventually the kid tidied up his books and stacked them neatly by his side of the bed. He disappeared into the bathroom, splashed around in there, and came out in his own pajamas: sweat pants and an oversized t-shirt. Shimada was wearing his version of that ensemble when Yoshi joined him in bed. "What did you mean if I played my cards right?" the kid asked.

"Nothing." Shimada kept innocently reading.

"Something."

Putting the newspaper down, he gave the kid an appraising look. "I think the landlord likes really young guys."

"Ew!"

"Ew?"

"Yeah, ew! What makes you think I like creepy old guys?"

"You jacked off your neighbor," Shimada said blandly.

"That was just busi–" Yoshi turned red as a beet when Shimada laughed at him. "It's not funny, I was scared to death when I did that."

He shuddered honestly. "I don't know if I like guys. I didn't like my neighbor and I don't think I like the landlord, but I like you."

"Wait until you get to know me better," Shimada deadpanned and turned off the light. "Go. To. Sleep," he said firmly when he felt Yoshi shifting toward him. The kid shifted away and he fell into a deep sleep.

He dreamed of Seiji, of waking up next to Seiji. He woke in the dawn light to find Yoshi watching him.

"Who's Seiji?"

"No one." Shimada rolled over.

Yoshi leaned over him. "Someone. Nobody moans someone's name like that if they're, um, no one."

"He was a guy I used to know." Shimada burrowed into his pillow.

Unfazed by these evasive maneuvers, Yoshi asked, "How well did you know him?"

"Really well." Shimada pulled the covers over his head.

"Like a boyfriend?" Yoshi asked, burrowing under the duvet. "Hey, Shimada-san, do you like guys?"

Shimada flung the covers off and faced his tormentor. "And what if I do?" he snarled. Yoshi leaned forward and pressed his lips against Shimada's. "Oh, don't do that..."

"Why not?"

"I might like it too much," Shimada said, pulling him close and kissing him back. "Ah, saved by the bell," he said disengaging with difficulty when the alarm went off.

"Hey!"

"Sorry, kid, gotta follow a politician around today," Shimada said, running into the bathroom and locking the door behind him. "You!" he yelled at his half erect penis and also at Yoshi banging on the door. "Settle down now! Both of you!"

Without hurting the kid's feelings or starting World War III, Shimada managed to ward off Yoshi and his sweet, wonderful, too wonderful kisses, that morning. The politician was an idiot, but an interesting one and Shimada convinced Ikoma to let him follow him up to Osaka. "Just to see if he says the same stupid things," was Shimada's pitch.

Ikoma was amused and handed over some travel money. "I hope Osaka isn't too close to Tokyo for you," he said to Shimada's back.

Dashing home to grab a suitcase and catch the train, Shimada ran into the landlord on his way out. "Oh, hello, I'll be gone for a few days, but Yoshi will–"

"Such a nice young man," the landlord said dreamily. "You know there's a larger place on the third floor you two could move into."

"Ah, well, I–"

"I'll renegotiate the lease and only charge you a little more."

"...How much more?" Shimada could never resist the right kind of deal and he knew the views from the third floor were nicer than his current room. The landlord named a sum, they haggled pleasantly, and a deal was struck. "But I won't be back until the weekend–"

"Oh, I'm sure Yoshi-kun can handle the move," the landlord said smugly. "This was his idea anyway. Happy traveling."

In the cab to the station, Shimada refused to think about coming hom-about coming back to the ro– oh fuck it, coming home to Yoshi in their new place. "Damn that kiss," he thought to himself. "One moment of weakness and we're moving in together."

Following the politician up to Osaka was as boring as Shimada suspected it would be, but he ended up staying on it longer than he thought he would because there were several stops in small towns on the way to Osaka Shimada hadn't planned on. Nevertheless, at every stop, in every speech, the guy said the same dumb things, was surrounded by the same thuggish bodyguards, and gave the same non-answers to variations on the same questions Shimada had asked him in Nagasaki. By the sixth or seventh speech—Shimada had lost count—he was bored enough to stand at the back and watch the crowd.

"This guy's about the same as the one we have in the Diet now," a voice murmured in Tokyo dialect beside him.

Shimada glanced over at a sharp dressed young man, not flashy, but his posture and hair were perfect. "You think?" he asked quietly in Tokyo-ese.

The young man raised his eyebrows and smiled. "I do," he said as if they were standing in Akihabara, not Osaka. "Except for the bodyguards," he went on. "They're a little rougher than the usual." He looked around them and lowered his voice. "I hear there's drug money behind this political run," he added.

"Ah, do you." Shimada began to smell a rat; a big fat smear campaign rat.

The young man offered a business card with a polite bow. "Masa Ishii," he said. "I'm with Shimada Miyagi."

Staring at the card, Shimada could feel Ishii waiting for him to offer his card, when a scuffle between the politician's bodyguards and some teenage boys broke out near the podium. The scuffle escalated into a brawl; Shimada melted into the panicking crowd in one direction, not failing to note that Ishii melted away in another direction. Same technique, different motives. Shimada was getting away, but he felt sure Ishii was heading toward something.

Shimada paused long enough on the edges of the escalating melee to make a few mental notes and get socked on the jaw. But enough was enough, even for him, and he caught the next train heading toward Nagasaki. Ikoma was suitably impressed when he walked into his office after a sleepless night writing up his notes on the train.

"Nice bruise and that suit needs pressing," he quipped.

"I need a computer and some coffee first," Shimada said, as he sat down at a vacant terminal and banged out his impressions of what became a small riot in Osaka. There were already stories circulating that the teenagers were in the pay of the rival candidate, but it still didn't excuse the violence of the politician's bodyguards. Shimada wrote his story with the angle that the riot was planned by the other side and intended to bring out the worst in the politician's overworked bodyguards. The fact that the teens showed up at the end of a grueling campaign when the politician's bodyguards would be at their most frayed suggested a smear campaign in the making. Shimada wrote his story as a human interest feature that bordered on an editorial. He used a pen name in the byline.

"I thought you didn't like this politician guy," Ikoma commented as he toned the writing down on his own computer.

"I don't, but I don't like Shimada Miyagi fixing an election that was fixing itself," Shimada said between bites of the sandwich Ikoma got him. He hadn't realized how hungry he was.

Ikoma looked up from his computer. "See anyone you know?" he asked.

"No, but I made a new friend." Shimada dug Ishii's card out of his pocket. "Heard of him?"

"No," Ikoma admitted. "But your brother would never send a big name to do a dirty job." He finished his editing and sent the file to be shoehorned into the next edition. "That was wonderfully inflammatory writing, thank you. I think I'll keep you on sports and culture until the fuss dies down," he said lighting a cigarette. "Any idea who Shimada Miyagi's client is?"

"Could be anyone," Shimada said wearily. "Anyone who doesn't want the delicate political balance messed up. That politician was a brash idiot, he would have lost just from that. Now he'll lose because my brother will smear him and the voters will think he's something worse. Senseless, stupid, typical overkill."

"I wish your brother's firm would stick to advertising and stay out of politics," Ikoma said. "I like their snack food ads."

"Oh, that's just money," Shimada said, getting up and stretching. "Politics is for fun."

"You could go to the police about what happened in Osaka," Ikoma suggested. "I'd back your suspicions up."

"All the tracks would have been covered by now," Shimada said. "No one could ever prove the teens were paid by Shimada Miyagi to start that brawl. The money would have gone through three or four different hands before it got to them. And don't forget, a member of Shimada Miyagi was observing the event. How could they be implicated if they had a man there?"

"Hey, at least you didn't run into Takashi," Ikoma said a little too casually.

"Yeah, well, he must be too far up the foodchain for my brother to send him out on a mere smear job like this one." Shimada shrugged. "I feel dirty even thinking about it. I'm tired, I'm going ho– home, yeah, I'm going home."

On the way to his apartment, the new one he'd never seen, Shimada could hardly believe he'd forgotten Yoshi had moved them into a new apartment while he was gone. It was early afternoon, so probably Yoshi would still be at school and might go straight to work from there.

Shimada was more relieved to be back in Nagasaki than he'd realized in Ikoma's office. The streets, the shops, the rhythm of daily life crowded around him, relaxed him, welcomed him. The orchestrated blurring of the line between political event and street theater in Osaka had unnerved him. He'd spent so many years in Tokyo trying to tell the difference between art and presentation, truth and spin, love and manipulation that now anything beyond black and white, right and wrong, and good and bad freaked him out. "How spoiled I've become on simplicity," he thought on the bus. "A wimp, almost, but I like it that way." He was glad Ikoma had him covering sports and culture stories for the next few weeks. Much as he liked covering politics, running into a representative of his brother's ad agency engaged in a dirty trick, one where innocent people got hurt, and not being able to do anything about it was more than Shimada could stomach.

To distract himself, he thought back to the kiss Yoshi gave him the morning of his trip, but suddenly all he could remember was that they had used Tokyo speech that morning without even realizing it. Or had they? The kiss and fumble were now secondary in Shimada's mind; had he and Yoshi used Tokyo-ese or not that morning and if they had, why would they? He was so distracted by this he didn't notice his landlord and an older man standing in front of his building.

"There's Mr. Shimada," the landlord said, looking like his usual sour and cranky self. He turned the full charm of this on his tenant. "I

11

didn't know when he'd be back. I suppose you want your new key."

"If you don't mind," Shimada said blandly, and urbanely nodded to the stranger. Shimada never forgot a face, but he was having trouble remembering where he'd seen this one before.

"I'd like to have a few words with you about Yoshi Katayama," the stranger said while the landlord stomped around in his office-cum-residence getting Shimada a key to his new place.

Not wanting to get into a discussion in front of the landlord, Shimada simply said, "Sure," and led the guy to his new apartment. "Oh, this is nice," he murmured once inside.

"Yes, Yoshi said you hadn't seen it before," the man said.

"Is he in trouble?"

"No."

"And you are?" Shimada asked.

"I'm his uncle. Eijiro Ichimonji." He held out a hand and Shimada shook it. "I'm married to Yoshi's mother's sister. I own the café."

"Oh, yes, that's where I've seen you before. Good noodles there," Shimada said, trying to figure out what to say to Yoshi's uncle, without knowing what Yoshi had said already. He figured he'd keep it simple.

"I just wanted to meet you since Yoshi says he's going to live with you," Ichimonji went on.

"Oh."

"Yoshi told me about the trouble he had at the boarding house." Ichimonji looked sad. "The landlady had some hard things to say about Yoshi. Most of them I don't believe–"

"What did she say?"

"She said Yoshi seduced her boarder, Mr. Watanabe."

"I think that's very wishful thinking on Mr. Watanabe's part," Shimada said blandly.

"I think so, too," Ichimonji said, nodding. "Although I don't know what was really going on there...ah...do you?"

Shimada sighed and decided the truth would be the least amount of work. "Mind you, I only have what Yoshi said and what I saw, but it seems Mr. Watanabe was trying, unsuccessfully, to coerce sexual favors out of Yoshi."

"I thought so," Ichimonji said, nodding some more. "That would explain why my oldest son is so protective."

"Is he a cook with a meat cleaver?"

"Yes! How'd you know?"

"Yoshi mentioned it." Figuring there was more to the story, Shimada fell silent and waited. And waited and finally asked, "Was there anything else?"

"Yoshi's a good kid..."

"Yes."

"His parents and older brother died in a car accident in Tokyo last year," Ichimonji said slowly. "Yoshi came to live with us, but I didn't really have room for him with my family. I thought he'd be safe with that landlady, but..."

"A guy like Watanabe isn't your fault, Mr. Ichimonji," Shimada said. He decided to ask a few questions rather than ask Yoshi himself. "Is Yoshi really 18?"

"Oh, yes," Ichimonji assured him. "He couldn't go to school when he first came to Nagasaki, so he just worked in the café and helped take care of his cousins for the first few months he was here. So he missed most of the school year, that's why he's still in High School."

"Why couldn't he go to school?"

"He couldn't stop crying."

It turned out that Ichimonji's main concern was to make sure Shimada wanted Yoshi there and that he, Shimada, would come to him, Ichimonji, if anything, anything at all odd happened.

"Like what?" Shimada had asked.

"Yoshi gets a little absent minded sometimes," Ichimonji said. "He loses things, like, money, identification, books..."

"Did he have a nervous breakdown after...after he came here?" Shimada asked.

"No, no, he just couldn't stop crying," Ichimonji said. "Sometimes he didn't even know he was crying, there'd just be tears on his cheeks. And he slept a lot."

"Oh? How much?"

"Fifteen or sixteen hours a day," Ichimonji said. "But then he got better."

"Oh."

"May I ask you a question, Mr. Shimada?"

"Sure."

"Where did you get that bruise on your chin?"

"In a brawl in Osaka," Shimada said blandly.

"Oh! We heard about that on TV," Ichimonji said. "Some drug dealers working for the politician we had here a week or so ago started the riot. They were trying to force a schoolgirl to take some drugs when some local teens tried to stop them. That politician is a horrible person."

Shimada merely nodded and saw Mr. Ichimonji to the door where he assured him he'd be in touch if anything odd happened with Yoshi and, yes, he'd be happy to have Yoshi with him as long as Yoshi was happy to be there. Mr. Ichimonji either failed to notice or willfully didn't comment on the fact that although it was clean, well-lit, and freshly painted, it was an awfully small apartment for two grown men, or one grown man and a mostly grown man, to be sharing. What Mr. Ichimonji didn't know was that the futon in the bedroom was larger than the one in the previous apartment, but Shimada marveled that he didn't notice that there was only one bed in the whole place. There was a wreck of a couch in the main room, but it was more of an over-sized over-stuffed chair than something even a mostly grown adult could sleep on. Perhaps Yoshi's uncle thought his nephew was going to sleep in the kitchen or the bathtub.

So, later on, after Ichimonji left and Shimada was left with his thoughts as he soaked in the much larger tub that came with the new apartment, Shimada began to wonder exactly what he was dealing with in Yoshi Katayama. He was so engrossed in his musing that he didn't hear the front door open and jumped when a scrawny grey short-haired cat ran in. "What the–?"

"Oh you're back!" Yoshi said happily, looking him over in the tub.

"Get out," Shimada said, covering himself as best he could. "And take that stray with you."

"I have to use the bathro–"

"Get out! I'll be out in a minute!" Shimada yelled and Yoshi and the cat fled. "You'll live for two minutes!" The difficulty now was that he didn't have anything to cover his nakedness and Yoshi was way too interested in his nakedness. He wrapped a towel around his waist and came out. "I suppose if you're going to live here, I'll need to buy a robe," he said as Yoshi strolled past him.

"There's a yukata in the closet," the kid said as he neatly closed the door in Shimada's face.

Shimada finished drying himself off and put the yukata on. It fit him, so he knew it wasn't Yoshi's kimono. "Where did this come from?" he asked when Yoshi stuck his head in the bedroom. He was holding the cat, which was one of the most pathetic looking cats Shimada had ever seen.

"The previous tenants left a bunch of stuff here," Yoshi said, standing in the doorway. "Like this cat and the couch and dresser over there." He gestured to the scratched-up, four drawer bureau in the corner and watched Shimada nod. "And it was a mess in here. My cousin and I cleaned it up, so the landlord gave us a little off the first month's rent."

"How much off?" Shimada asked.

Yoshi named a small figure and Shimada said he'd remind the

landlord when he paid the rent. "I think he took advantage of you, but it's the thought that counts." He went into the main room and took a closer look at the couch. It was still a wreck: a low, saggy affair, with a few neat mends in the cushion covers, but looked clean and didn't smell bad. There was a larger low zataku table than in the previous apartment.

"He bought the paint," Yoshi said. "We just–"

"Supplied all the labor," Shimada finished for him. He glanced at Yoshi, who was standing uncomfortably in the middle of the room. "It looks nice in here."

Yoshi visibly relaxed. "There's a real kitchen," he said, cheerfully. "Want some tea?"

"Sure. Don't you have to go to work?" Shimada asked.

"I have the night off!"

"Great, just great," Shimada muttered as he went into the bedroom to put on some clothes. He'd be having a serious conversation with Yoshi sooner than he thought he would and he felt he better be completely dressed for it. He found his clothes hanging tidily in the closet and what wasn't there was neatly folded in the battered dresser.

The cat sauntered in and settled on the bed while he was dressing. "Hello, Kitty," Shimada said, and was ignored. "Are you the Kitty Welcoming Committee?" he ventured, and got hissed at. "Well, maybe I'll have better luck in the next room," Shimada thought.

He found Yoshi setting mugs on the low table and sat with his back to the couch. "Your cat doesn't like me."

"He's our cat," Yoshi said, settling next to him. "Or this is his apartment and we just live here. He gets friendlier. He didn't like me at first either."

"Does he have a name?"

"I don't know, I've just been calling him Cat."

They drank tea in silence for a while. "Your uncle was here today," Shimada finally said.

"Why!? What did he–"

"Just calm down." Shimada stared at Yoshi until the kid looked ready to listen. "Your uncle seems like a good guy–"

"He is!"

"–and he was just here to make sure I'm not a lunatic. Because only a lunatic would take in some kid off the street."

"But you know me," Yoshi protested.

"Not really," Shimada said, thinking back over the uncle's story. "But your uncle told me a few things, one of them explains why we've been talking like Tokyo people since I got home...yeah, home." He looked around, watched the cat arrogantly cross the room to sit in Yoshi's lap. "Yeah, this is my home," he thought, and didn't find it unpleasant. "Anyway..." he said, distracted by how peaceful he felt.

"How long did you live in Tokyo?" Yoshi asked after some silence.

"I was raised there."

"Me, too."

"You miss it?"

"Sometimes...Sometimes I wake up and can't remember where I am." Yoshi stared into his empty mug. "Did my uncle tell you about...about my family...in Tokyo?" He looked up at Shimada's nod. "It took a while to get used to it, but now I...I kinda like Nagasaki now."

"Me, too." Shimada ignored the hissing, displaced cat and pulled Yoshi into his arms. He planted a neutral kiss on the kid's temple. "Look, Yoshi, you don't have to sleep with me."

"I want to!"

"Well, I want that, too," Shimada admitted. "But you can live here if you want to. You can sleep on the couch or we'll get another futonmmmmmm–"

"I want to be with you, Shimada-san," Yoshi said breathlessly when he took his lips off Shimada's.

"You hardly know me," Shimada murmured, deeply moved by the kiss and the emotion in it.

"But I feel like I do," Yoshi purred, gazing happily into his face. "Ever since you looked at me so strangely in the cafe that time. Like you knew me."

Shimada sighed. "You remind me of someone."

"The Seiji you dreamed about?" Yoshi asked.

"Yeah." Shimada nodded sadly. "You should be more than a reminder to somebody," he said vaguely.

"Then give me a chance to be more."

Shimada looked into those big determined brown eyes. Seiji was never so bold. "Then call me Ryuu," he said, tightening his arms around Yoshi and smiling into his hair. When Yoshi got restless, Shimada easily coaxed him off the couch and into the bedroom.

"How did you get that bruise on your chin?" Yoshi asked as Shimada was carefully removing the kid's clothes.

"I was in a brawl at a political rally in Osaka." Shimada paused to admire Yoshi's slight but so far well proportioned body. His skin was pale and soft, but he could feel good muscle tone underneath. "Like an adolescent tom kitten, just on the verge of being sleek and graceful, but not quite there yet," he thought, and then mentally smacked himself for thinking like a novelist.

"Oh. I heard about that. That yakuza politician was here, wasn't he? You interviewed him, right? I read it in the paper!"

"Yakuza politician?" Shimada thought, but he was distracted by Yoshi's lips on his chin.

"Does this hurt?" he asked, gently kissing along Shimada's jaw and under his ear.

"I'm not sure," Shimada said trying very hard to keep his cool. "You better keep doing it until I know." He snuggled the giggling, half-naked kid against his shoulder. "Now, look, Yoshi, it's been a long day for me. In fact a day that started yesterday, so we're not going to do much tonight—no, no pouting."

"I can do everything!"

Shimada sat back on the futon. "Like what?"

The edges of a frown crept into Yoshi's really adorable pout. "Um..."

"Just how much experience with men do you have?" Shimada asked.

"Um..."

"Mr. Watanabe doesn't count."

"Of course not!" Yoshi yelped.

"But that's not a bad way to start," Shimada said thoughtfully. "I mean without the extortion aspect of it. Hey, get under the covers." He rose to remove his clothes. "Lights on or off?"

"Can we have this little one on?" Yoshi pointed at a tiny goose-neck lamp by the futon.

"Sure." Shimada rose and went into the main room. He turned off the lights, but not before the cat sneered at him from the couch, and headed into the bathroom to grab a towel. Back in the bedroom, he turned off the overhead light and tossed the towel on the futon. He smiled at Yoshi, who was leaning back against the pillows wearing nothing but his wary kitten look. The kid must be completely unaware of how sexy that was; it certainly wasn't lost on Shimada's dick. "Don't you have homework?" he asked, trying to break the spell a little.

"I did it at school," Yoshi yawned, politely covering his mouth. "There were books I needed in the library to write a paper." And then his eyes got big as Shimada took off his shirt. Shimada's body was lithe, if somewhat rangy due to being tall. Nevertheless, the muscles in his chest, arms and shoulders were well defined without being bulgy.

"On what?" Shimada asked, stepping out of his trousers and shorts.

"Um, it was, um." Yoshi stumbled verbally trying to process

Shimada and his long legs and tumescent rosy cock coming toward him, sliding into bed next to him. "A history paper!" He jumped as Shimada drew his entire naked body against him, his own cock leaping to attention.

Shimada chuckled. "What kind of history?" he asked to slow the kid down a little.

"Oh, let's see, Edo," Yoshi sighed, melting into Shimada's arms. "Textiles in the Edo period," he added, pawing softly at his chest.

"How interesting," Shimada said, nudging Yoshi's hand toward his hardening cock.

"It was either that or coal mining in the Meiji period," Yoshi said, distracted by the heat and softness under his hand. "Oh..."

"Oh what?" Shimada asked, kissing his neck.

"It's just...different, y'know...from..." Yoshi fumbled with Shimada's cock as he fumbled with his words.

"I know." Shimada pulled him closer and kissed him softly. "We don't have to rush," he said, wishing he was less tired. He gently pinched one of Yoshi's nipples. Yoshi gasped and clutched at him, pressing his hard, leaking erection against Shimada's hip.

"Sorry," Yoshi said. He was still exploring Shimada's rapidly hardening penis and experimenting with grips. "Is this okay?"

"It's effective," Shimada said dryly.

Yoshi paused. "Do you like it?" He seemed a little startled when his partner's member twitched in his hand.

"I do," Shimada said. He reached for Yoshi's hand and showed him a few strokes he liked, mainly so he could get completely hard. He felt guilty that he was ignoring the kid's erection, but he was afraid to touch it lest it explode before Shimada was ready to come.

Having reached a state of arousal acceptable to him at the moment, Shimada gently shoved Yoshi onto his back and pushed his knees apart. Or tried to, the kid tensed up on him.

"Are you going to fuck me?" Yoshi asked, sounding a little panicky.

"Not tonight," Shimada said, panting a little. "But you'll like this, it's called frottage." He lowered his hips to Yoshi's and slid his cock along the younger guy's cock. "See?" Shimada said, playfully pressing their erections together. "Frrrr-oooo-tttt-aaaa-ggggg." After oral sex, he'd always liked this kind of sex play. He found it relaxing when done right.

Yoshi laughed, involuntarily undulating against Shimada's belly. He added his hand, mimicking the way Shimada caressed them both, mixing their pre-cum so their cocks were hot and slippery against each other. "Oh...Ryuu...oh!"

Shimada held him still and kissed him deeply, calming him enough so he could catch up. When he left off Yoshi's mouth to bury his face in his neck, they were only a few strokes away from climax. "Oh God..oh Yoshi...oh fuck!" Shimada groaned hard against the kid's shoulder as he came hard against his belly. He was dimly aware of Yoshi's muffled shriek and shuddering orgasm beneath him.

The kid was still shaking when Shimada propped himself up on his elbows. "Okay?" he asked, looked down at him in the dim bedside lamplight.

Eyes shining, chest softly heaving, flushed and adorable, Yoshi looked up at him and nodded. "Oh, more than okay," he breathed into Shimada's chest.

Shimada kissed him, but since he didn't have another orgasm in him that night, he didn't get too involved in it. "There was a towel here...ah, here it is." Feeling slightly more energetic, he wiped them both down and tossed the towel to the end of the futon. Yoshi lay floppy and boneless watching him through hooded eyes. "What?" Shimada asked.

"I love you."

"If you say that in six months when we're not in bed, I might believe you," Shimada said, equal parts amused and touched. And then regretted it.

"But I do!" Yoshi sat up violently, ready for a fight.

"Okay, you do, and if you love me, you'll let me sleep now." Shimada tugged Yoshi down into his arms.

"I'm kind of awake now," Yoshi said a few moments later.

"Then stay up," Shimada mumbled. "But quietly. I must sleep...or die..." He felt a soft kiss on his lips before the gentle blackness of sleep rolled softly over him.

Shimada woke up with Yoshi and the cat sleeping on his chest and the sun pouring in the big window across from their bed. He felt crushed and his left arm was numb, but Yoshi was such a pretty sight, Shimada figured he could lie there a little longer. The cat opened one sleepy green eye and glared at him. "I'll fix you, kitty-cat," he thought. "Maybe literally, too, if you're not already nipped. But first, I will think up a stupid name for you and mock you with it." Oblivious to the danger he was in, the cat with no name re-closed its eye and went back to sleep.

But sleep was not on the agenda for that morning. Nor sex. Shimada took a few seconds to mentally prepare evasive maneuvers if Yoshi happened to be feeling amorous. The kid's erection pressing against his leg wasn't much of an indicator that he'd want to get frisky, but it was an undeniable fact nonetheless. "Okay, it's morning," Shimada said, hoping it sounded like leadership and not just lame. He jostled his bedmates and got sleepy feline and human whines. "And I don't know about you, Yoshi, but I have to go to work, sooo..." Shimada wrestled his way out of the futon and looked down at the cat and the boy. The cat was curling into the warm place and Yoshi was trying to focus on the clock.

"Oh, damn, I have to go to school," Yoshi said, flinging himself back on the futon. He looked up smolderingly at Shimada. "Don't I?"

"Yeah, you do." Shimada picked up the towel and the yukata from the floor on his way into the bathroom. He was only mildly startled when Yoshi joined him in the shower.

"This is okay, Shim–, I mean, Ryuu? Isn't it?" he asked shyly, half way in and half way out of the shower.

"Sure. Just come in already, you're letting all the steam out," Shimada said, drawing Yoshi's scrawny, but leggy, form into his arms. He tasted like minty toothpaste, but so did Shimada, and their erections didn't last long under their soapy hands. "Aaah, that was nice," he thought, holding the very floppy, post-climax Yoshi up against him. "That's a nice way to start the day, hm?" he asked, leaning down for a smooch, but not letting it get too serious.

"Yeah." Yoshi beamed up at him. "I guess that'll keep me going until I get home tonight." He used the hand-held shower to rinse off.

"Are you working tonight?" Shimada asked over instant coffee. He hated instant coffee and made a mental note to buy some real coffee. He watched Yoshi open a can and dump the vile looking contents in a bowl for the cat, who stared at it for a moment and then walked away.

"Oh, you stupid cat!" Yoshi glared at the cat's retreating form.

"Maybe he doesn't like to eat in front of an audience," Shimada suggested. Finickiness was one of the things he liked about cats, so he never took it personally.

"Well, maybe...but don't feed him again if it's still there when you get back," Yoshi said sternly, still glaring at the cat. "What?"

"I said, how late are you working?" Shimada repeated.

"Nine or ten, depends on how busy the café is," he said, gathering up his backpack and coat. "It's usually quiet on a Tuesday night, so I might be back earlier than that. See ya!" Yoshi gave him a peck on the cheek and was gone before Shimada could think of anything witty to say.

Washing up gave Shimada a chance to look around the kitchen and determine that some serious food shopping was in order if they didn't want to end up sharing the cat's leftovers. Which would be few since the cat had come back and was plowing into his breakfast. "You swine-kitty, teasing that poor boy by acting like you don't like the food he gives you," Shimada thought sternly at the cat, who was either unaware of or blithely ignoring his mental scolding. "For shame, for shame," he thought, but he was smiling as he tidied up the bedroom and called Ikoma for that day's marching orders. "An art gallery?" he asked.

"Yup, our Style readers want to know what artists they can't afford are showing on Gallery Row, where they never go. And as long as you're in that part of town, have lunch at that new bistro," Ikoma said, rattling off a fashionable address. "Pay attention and keep your receipts so you can write a review of it for tomorrow's edition."

"Just lunch, not dinner?" Shimada asked, thinking that if it was nice enough, he'd take Yoshi there.

"Well, if you like it enough for lunch, maybe you should try it for dinner and write them both up for the Sunday edition," Ikoma said.

"I'll let you know," Shimada said. They said minimal goodbyes and Shimada figured he'd have lunch at the swanky bistro first and look at the gallery afterwards. "How elegant," he thought, putting on his one nice business suit. "I've been wasting my time on hard news, I could have been eating my way through high culture all this time."

He found his lunch overpriced and mediocre, but the gallery was large, well-lit and showing good work by a local artist. Shimada didn't consider himself an art critic, so he confined his observations to the location and ambience of the gallery space and the neighborhood. He did mention that the art was something one could look at for a long time, like a lifetime and never get tired of. It wasn't decorative, but it wasn't combative either. He didn't have words for it, which was why he wasn't an art expert. The gallery owner seemed to him to be a gallerist in the truest sense of the word in that she was protective of the artist she was showing and very interested in what Shimada could do for that artist (as well as the gallery). It was her lucky day because Shimada was genuinely moved by the paintings, enough to consider getting the paper to send an interviewer to the gallery. He might even do it himself, if he was in the right frame of mind. He parted from the gallerista in a high good humor and headed for the newspaper office to write up his reviews: thumbs down on the bistro and thumbs up on the gallery.

"Well, you're in a goddamn good mood," Ikoma growled at Shimada as the reporter was cheerfully typing up his stories.

"Isn't it a fine day to be in a goddamn good mood?" Shimada

lightly teased. "One of those fine Nagasaki days to be in a goddamn good mood?"

Ikoma merely scowled at him. A riposte eluded him; he hadn't seen Shimada in such a good mood since the reporter moved to Nagasaki. "You look like you're in love," Ikoma ventured.

Shimada stopped typing but didn't look up at him. "You ought to send one of your really good art writers to interview this artist," he said, and began typing again.

"Ah ha," Ikoma thought, but didn't say anything. He just went back into his office and waited for Shimada's reviews to hit the copy queue. Then he called one of their art critics to interview the gallery owner and the artist. "Damn you, Shimada, you always come back with some of the best writing, even if you don't know a damn thing about the subject." After reading the lukewarm, but almost poetic, restaurant review, Ikoma was about ready to bet money Shimada was in love. He looked up speculatively when Shimada stuck his head in the door.

"I'm leaving, if you want any re-writes now is the time to ask me for them," Shimada said, trying to read Ikoma's unreadable look.

"No, no...no, seems fine to me," Ikoma drawled. "I think you should review more restaurants."

"If you like," Shimada said, matching Ikoma's cool tone. "Just send me, I'll find something to say."

"Just you?"

"I might take someone with me," Shimada said slowly. "If there's enough in the budget for it."

"Perhaps you should write some sports as well," Ikoma said. "I should get you some ball game comps." He watched Shimada nod. "One or...two seats?"

"I don't know," Shimada said. "I'd have to ask him—"

"AH HA!" Ikoma bounced in his squeaky editor chair. "You are seeing someone!"

Shimada rolled his eyes. "Well, there's no law against it."

Ikoma beamed at him. "Nope. Lemme know what you two lovebirds want to do and I'll have my assistant dig up comps or whatnot to cover it. It will give me a vicarious thrill to sponsor your new romance. Who is the lucky guy anyway?"

"Remember that kid I rescued—"

"The kid in the alley?" Ikoma asked. Shimada nodded. "I hope he's legal." Shimada nodded. "Well, that's good...um..." Shimada laughed, something Ikoma heard very seldom since his friend had moved to Nagasaki to work for his paper.

"Look, Jun, I'm leaving," Shimada said, still smiling. "I'll call tomorrow for leads. If you want to meet him, next time Yoshi has a free night, we'll all have dinner. Good enough? Later, pal."

"Ah, so there IS something to look forward to," Ikoma mumbled, watching Shimada walk out with the spring in his step that could only mean he was in love, or going to be in love very soon. Ikoma had mixed feelings about this: he wanted Shimada to be happy, but Shimada's first love had left a lot of scars on the guy. But people do heal up and love again, at least Ikoma hoped so. He wished his friend and...and...Yoshi! Yeah, that was the kid's name. He wished Shimada and Yoshi the best. But Shimada had loved Seiji Hayashida so deeply, anyone new would have a very tough act to follow, and he wondered if Shimada realized this.

Unaware of Ikoma's gloomy train of thought, Shimada felt happier, lighter and more optimistic than he'd felt since he left Tokyo almost a year ago. He grocery shopped and even bought some fancy cat food for the furry little hellion at home. Yes! Home! He had a home, a lover, a cat, a job he liked, in a city he was used to, and all was right with the world. At home, he stopped by the landlord's office to renegotiate Yoshi's contribution to preparing the apartment. Shimada could be quite persuasive and even guilt-inducing when inspired by affection and protectiveness, and eventually the landlord gladly relented and gave the happy couple even more off the next month's rent than he'd originally offered Yoshi.

"You look different, Mr. Shimada," the landlord observed as Shimada was leaving.

"Oh? How so?"

"I dunno, younger somehow, cleaner, too," the landlord mused. "And taller."

"Younger, cleaner, taller, eh?" Shimada grinned at him. The landlord looked alarmed and took a step back. "I'm surprised you recognized me at all." He bowed politely and took his groceries upstairs where he immediately sought out the long mirror in the bedroom. "Taller?" he muttered. "Well, maybe I'm standing up straighter."

The cat made a show of ignoring him from its excellent vantage point on the couch as Shimada put the groceries away. Shimada glanced at it from time to time, idly wondering if it was a male or female. On very slim scientific evidence, but sound-ish observation, Shimada deduced from the cat's big head and bull neck that it was a tom cat. He further deduced that he was a neutered tom, because the place didn't smell of cat spray and the cat was far too mellow to have nads, at least far too mellow in Shimada's rather limited experience with cats, neutered or no. He liked cats, but his gender precluded him from being able to see expressions on their faces. They all looked horribly bored to him except for the occasional flashes of interest in food or prey. But he still liked them.

There were no signs that Yoshi had been home. Shimada figured that the kid must go from school to work. He further wondered how much Yoshi worked at the café and it began to dawn on him how very little he really knew about the boy he was living and rapidly falling in love with. "Ah," he thought bravely. "There, I've thought it. I'm falling in love with the kid and I know almost nothing about him. I know he's legal, goes to high school, works in his uncle's café, and makes noise in bed. Oh, and he likes cats." Shimada made himself a good cup of coffee and realized he was looking forward to finding out more about Yoshi Katayama.

Around nine thirty, when his evening started to drag, Shimada wondered if he shouldn't go to the café and walk Yoshi home. He used to spend his evenings writing at the newspaper, drinking with Ikoma, or drinking alone. If he was going to sit at home waiting for Yoshi, he might as well take Ikoma up on his offer to lend him a laptop and do some writing while he was waiting for the kid. Or surf the web for news stories and porn while he was waiting. As he was mulling this over, Yoshi let himself in and flung himself into Shimada's arms.

"Mmmmm...hi," Shimada said after a fierce kiss. "How was work?"

"Mmmm...fine, my uncle wants to know why I'm so happy."

"Oh my God, please tell me you didn't tell him," Shimada rasped out.

"Nah, he's smart, I think he knows." Yoshi rubbed noses with him. "I'm dead. I just want to take a bath and go to bed...with you." He backed out of Shimada's arms and went into the bedroom. He emerged a few minutes later in the yukata Shimada had worn before.

"That's too big on you," Shimada observed.

"I know," Yoshi said, gathering up the excess material. "But I won't be wearing it long." And he went into the bathroom.

Shimada wondered if that was an innocent remark or a sexy remark. He settled on it being an innocently sexy remark. Having had his bath earlier, Shimada settled into bed with a mug of green tea and a magazine Ikoma's cousin edited in Tokyo. It was new and low budget, almost a zine, but the writing and somewhat limited production values were first-rate. Shimada thought it had promise if it could get enough funding to survive and print on better paper. The news and culture writing had a nice edgy almost-fuck-you quality to it. Just the sort of thing Shimada liked to read and, even better, write. But not lately; his life was mundane news stories and whatever was going to happen with Yoshi.

Right on cue, Yoshi strolled into the bedroom, flung off the yukata and pounced on Shimada. Whatever else, the kid was direct.

"I liked what we did last night," he panted between kisses.

"We could do it again," Shimada suggested.

"I want more," Yoshi said, sitting up. "I...I want you to be inside me."

The kid was very direct. Shimada pulled him back into his arms. "I have to do a little shopping first."

"For what?" Yoshi dodged a kiss.

"Condoms and lube."

"...Oh..."

"And we don't have to rush into anything." Shimada nuzzled his neck.

"But I want to have real sex!"

"Yoshi, it's all real sex," Shimada said, rolling the kid on top of him. "It's all in how you do it."

"Huh?"

"Okay," Shimada said, stroking Yoshi's nipples. "You want me to be in you, let's start with oral sex." He watched Yoshi's big eyes get bigger and laughed as he rolled the astonished kid onto his back. "I'll go first," Shimada said softly into Yoshi's ear, and mentally added, "Because this is as much of you as will ever be inside of me." He chuckled softly against Yoshi's thigh, but Yoshi was too distracted to notice, let alone ask what was so funny.

Shimada liked oral sex and thought he was pretty good at it. He liked discovering Yoshi's taste, texture, sensitive spots, their responsiveness, and the response he could elicit. Yoshi's enthusiastic response merely confirmed that Shimada was doing it right. In truth, Shimada was simply taking the time to learn his partner. Unlike Shimada's adolescent sexual rush, this was a more studied approach for him. Although he realized he had a lot to learn about Yoshi, when running his tongue under the head of Yoshi's cock caused the kid to ejaculate immediately, Shimada, as he swallowed and ran his tongue over his teeth, felt they were off to a good start. He nipped softly at Yoshi's inner thigh before sliding beside him, hugging him and soothing his post-climax shudders. When the kid was calmer, Shimada drank a little more of his green tea, now cold, and asked, a little too casually, what Yoshi thought. He got a big, wet kiss for an answer.

"Hmmm, is that how I taste?" Yoshi asked, licking his lips.

"Like green tea?"

"No...you know." Yoshi hesitantly slid his hand down to stroke Shimada's rapidly hardening cock. "I could..."

"Could what?"

"You know." Yoshi snuggled closer, stroked a little harder.

"If you want," Shimada said. He was breathing a little harder. "I like what you're doing."

Yoshi thought about this for a moment and then eased himself between Shimada's legs. Being very new at this, Yoshi spent some time just licking the head and sides, which nearly drove Shimada wild with pleasure. After such an auspicious start, Yoshi moved on to what he thought was the next level of taking it in his mouth. He could get much of Shimada's member into his mouth, but none of it into his throat. It was a blessing, to Shimada, that Yoshi's gag reflex didn't including snapping his jaws shut.

"That's pretty advanced stuff, Yoshi," Shimada said, gently massaging the gagging kid's head. "How about you wrap your hand around the base...yeah, like that...and then kind of pulse your hand...oh, yes...and suck or lick or both the parts above...yeah...oh my God, uhmmmmmmmm..." He moved his hands to Yoshi's shoulders to resist the urge to press his head onto his cock. "Yoshi...I'm about to–"

In response, Yoshi sucked in as much as he could and tried to do the same thing with his tongue as Shimada had done to him. Appreciatively, Shimada came, and came hard. He barely registered Yoshi's muted squeak of surprise and convulsive swallow. "Let it rest for a minute," Shimada panted when Yoshi grasped his limp cock. "It's too sensitive right after."

"Sorry." Yoshi snuggled beside him, licking his lips. "Can I have some of your tea?"

Shimada nodded. "You didn't have to swallow."

"It was okay," he said vaguely.

"Just okay? I liked it a lot." He couldn't see Yoshi against his chest, but he could feel him smile.

"I liked it, too," Yoshi said softly, and a little more softly. "I liked making you squirm."

"Yoshi, honey, you can make me squirm anytime," Shimada said, and then had to restrain him when he started to move. "But not tonight."

"Was I too rough?"

"No, no, you were perfect," Shimada said, soothing him. "But it's oversensitized now and, um, hard to explain...especially when you're ready to go again," he added, as Yoshi's hard-on nudged his thigh.

"Oh, I can wait," Yoshi said, understandingly. "Another half hour or so."

Shimada managed to wait about twenty minutes before he moved them into a sixty-nine. They slept very well afterwards. His last sleepy thought was that the next day he'd go shopping for condoms and lube.

Shimada woke up for the second morning with Yoshi cuddled up on his right and the cat sitting on his chest. The cat was staring at him; Shimada stared back. "Flounder," he said. "Your name is Flounder."

"Hmmmm?" Yoshi snuggled closer.

"I just named the cat."

The kid opened a sleepy, but loving eye. "Yeah? What did you name him?"

"Flounder."

"Flounder? Like the fish?"

"Yeah," Shimada said with more confidence than necessary that early in the morning. "I woke up with it. It was inspired."

"Then Flounder it is," Yoshi said solemnly. "What time is it? Oh damn, I have to go to school." He almost made it up, but flopped back down. "If you kiss me, I'll get up."

"That's dangerous thinking, Yoshi," Shimada said, dislodging Flounder from his chest and hauling himself and the kid up. "Neither of us has that much willpower."

"Oh, you're no fun," Yoshi pouted.

"I plan to be a great deal of fun later on tonight," Shimada said to Yoshi's cute back as he pulled on the yukata. He put water on for coffee and then gave in and joined Yoshi in the shower. "We can do this because we're standing up and can't fall asleep," he murmured into Yoishi's steamy neck as the kid undulated against him.

"Yeah...whatever you sahhh-oh!"

As turned on as they both were it didn't take them long to get off and shower, even including washing each other's backs. "See how efficient that was?" Shimada asked as they were drying off. "Sex and hygiene all in one."

The tea kettle's whistle cut through Yoshi's laugh and Shimada made his exit on it. Yoshi skipped the coffee in favor of orange juice and toast while Shimada read the morning paper. "What's your schedule like this week, Yoshi?"

"Me? School and then the café, but I have Sunday and Monday nights off this week," he said. "Why?"

"I might have tickets to ball games and plays and concerts and stuff like that," Shimada said. He was feeling slightly guilty that he'd skipped the dating-Yoshi part of their relationship and gone right into the living-with-Yoshi part, but it wasn't like he could go backwards, only forwards. "But I'll try to get them for nights you're free."

"The café is really busy Thursday through Saturday," Yoshi said, opening a can of cat food for Flounder. "But I can ask my uncle for time off."

"If it's something great, okay, but otherwise, don't let him down." Shimada took a sip of coffee. "I don't want your cousin to kill me."

"I won't let him." Yoshi frowned as the cat walked away from his breakfast. "Flounder, you jerk."

"He eats it after you leave," Shimada said, feeling he should defend the cat now that he had a name. Yoshi just sighed and started gathering up his books. "What, no kiss good-bye?" Shimada asked.

It was a nice kiss that gave them something to look forward to.

After Yoshi left for school, Shimada tidied the apartment up. As he was making the futon up, a call from Ikoma interrupted his musing on how he'd ended up with all the housework.

"I got a call about that editorial on your politician," Ikoma said with no preamble.

"My brother moves fast," Shimada said bitterly.

"And surreptitiously, too," Ikoma said. "The call was from a reporter at one of the big Tokyo papers."

"How do you know it's not legit?" Shimada asked. Ikoma had always wanted his local paper to get more attention.

"No one in their right mind runs down a wild-eyed editorial in a local paper like that," Ikoma said, with some bitterness. "It wasn't a threat either—we're not big enough to be a threat—but it wasn't praise either. It was fishing. The guy called to see if I'd let something slip."

"Who was it?" Shimada asked. He didn't know the name Ikoma gave him.

"He's just a mid-level editor," Ikoma said. "I know this because I called the paper back to make sure he worked there."

"How thorough," Shimada said, calmly. "What have you got for me this week?"

Ikoma rattled off a number of assignments, half a dozen of which Shimada accepted, including a high school kendo match on Sunday afternoon and a movie screening on Monday night.

"Since when do you like–?" Ikoma began to ask.

"I asked for two passes, didn't I?" Shimada asked back.

"Oh..." Some silence and Shimada could hear Ikoma's chair squeak in the background. "When do I get to meet him?" Ikoma finally asked.

"How about dinner after the kendo match on Sunday?"

They set a time and place. "Look, Ryuu, what's your brother up to?" Ikoma asked, real concern in his voice.

"Probably nothing," Shimada said lightly. "Or he's just trying to rattle us."

"He's only half succeeded then," Ikoma admitted.

"You'll get over it, Jun," Shimada said. "As long as I don't give him a chance, there's nothing my brother can do to me anymore."

"Then it's all good!" Ikoma said, his chair squeaking in agreement in the background. "I'll need your story on the dog that saved the little girl from drowning this afternoon for tomorrow's paper."

Shimada left off housekeeping, put out some fresh water for Flounder and headed into the city to get his story. He completely forgot about shopping for condoms and lube, but he made it up to Yoshi orally that night.

"I really want to–" Yoshi began, still panting from his recent climax.

"I know, we will," Shimada assured him, slightly more recovered because Yoshi had gotten him off first. The kid was definitely getting the hang of oral sex. "It would be better if we did it on a night when we didn't have to get up the next morning. Like this Saturday."

"That's too–"

"Two days away, yes, you'll live." Shimada hugged him close. Flounder jumped on the futon and made himself comfortable between Shimada's legs. "Look, Yoshi, I don't want to rush into sex. I did that once. I kind of feel bad about it, but–"

"With Seiji?" Yoshi asked.

"Ah, yes, as a matter of fact, it was with Seiji," Shimada said, slightly flustered by Yoshi's directness. "But, as I started to say, I rushed it because I didn't know any better. And neither did he, but, um..."

"What?" Yoshi asked, sitting up.

"Well...I don't think Seiji ever really enjoyed it with me..."

"Fucking?"

"Yoshi, please." Shimada was torn between admiration and embarrassment.

"That's what it is." He licked his lips. "Hey, I want some juice. Want some juice?" He scrambled out of bed, but didn't beat Shimada to the yukata. "We have to get another one of those," he said, putting on an old pair of Shimada's pajamas.

Shimada looked him over as he knotted the sash on the yukata. "I don't know why; you look very cute in pajamas."

Yoshi poured them both some orange juice and they settled on the couch close together for warmth and because the couch was small. "Okay, why didn't he like it?" Yoshi prompted. "Seiji, I mean."

"We got off to a bad start, I didn't really know what I was doing. I think I could have been gentler, prepared him more, just taken more time," Shimada said, ticking off the reasons he'd decided were the cause of Seiji's stiffness while they were doing it. Not that Seiji would ever tell him what was wrong; Shimada had to figure these things out on his own. Shimada had already figured out, with some relief, that this could not be a problem with Yoshi. The kid had no problem telling his lover what was on his mind.

"But if he loved you, it should have been okay, right?"

"I was kind of an asshole then, Yoshi," Shimada said, mentally inventorying his guilt and filing it away. "I wanted him to be mine, I was impatient, demanding, clumsy. I only figured out how much better it could be later on." And their sex life had gotten better, or as much better as their stressful closeted life together allowed it to. "He did love me, just not enough," he added almost to himself.

Yoshi was very still. "What happened to him?" he finally asked.

"We broke up."

"Because of sex?"

Shimada laughed. "Ah, no, no, because, oh God, it's a long story..." He looked down at the boy in his arms. "But I guess you want to hear it. My mom got sick, and she asked me to break up with Seiji. I did, but it was only supposed to be until she got well, and then I'd leave my family for Seiji and we'd live happily ever after. Unfortunately..."

"Unfortunately?"

"While I was making my mother happy, Seiji fell in love with someone else and..."

"And?"

"And I moved to Nagasaki about a year ago." Shimada sipped his juice. "I had a huge fight with my brother, too. He never liked it that I was gay. He told my mother Seiji and I were lovers. He made it sound like a crime. And then the guy Seiji left me for went to university with us and works for my brother. We all worked at the same place, knew the same people. It was a huge mess." He sighed and tightened his arm around Yoshi. "There was just no way I could stay in Tokyo."

"I'm glad you came here, Ryuu," Yoshi said, snuggling. "We don't have to rush. We'll do what you say. I just..."

"Just what?"

"I just want to be yours."

Shimada held him close and said, simply, "You are, Yoshi, you are."

"Did you get them?" was the first thing out of Yoshi's mouth when he bounced in that night. "The condoms and lube," he added when Shimada, sitting on the couch with a book, the cat and a cup of tea, just stared at him.

"As a matter of fact I did. They're by the futon," Shimada said, dryly. "Hey, no kiss hello? What is this?" he yelled at Yoshi disappearing into the bedroom.

He got a big kiss when Yoshi came back and flung himself into his lap. "Mind the tea, kid," Shimada growled against his neck as Yoshi examined the packages.

"So these are condoms," he said, fiddling with the seam.

"Don't open them," Shimada said firmly.

"Why not?"

"I don't know, the air makes them brittle," Shimada improvised. "Or something. I just know you can't use them if they've been open."

"Oh...I've never seen one before, so..."

Shimada gave in. "Open it." He watched the fascinated kid on his lap unroll the condom and stretch it for tactile strength and then get bored. "See, not that exciting, is it? There's only one thing we can do with it now." He took the floppy latex from him and blew it into a balloon. Yoshi nearly fell off his lap laughing. Flounder looked horrified when Shimada batted the balloon-dom at him. He left the room in feline high dudgeon. "There are more interesting things to do with condoms," Shimada added when his boyfriend was less hysterical.

"Oh, I know, I mean, I suppose, but I'd never seen one before," Yoshi got out between giggles. "So, what about this stuff?" he asked, holding up the tube of lube.

"Well," Shimada sighed, opening the tube. He was half admiring Yoshi's natural curiosity and half alarmed by it. What if the theory and explanation were different from the reality of sex for Yoshi? What if Yoshi wanted to try these things...on Shimada. "It's very slippery stuff." He squeezed a pearl onto Yoshi's fingertips and watched the kid work the viscosity with his thumb. "It has to be slippery so I don't hurt you."

"You could never hurt me," Yoshi said, as if he could order such things to be so.

"The muscles in your ass might say different," Shimada said coolly and then smiled evilly at Yoshi's blush.

Yoshi made a "humph" noise and went into the bathroom to wash his hand. "We could do it tonight," he said when he came back.

"Don't you have school tomorrow?" Shimada asked.

"So?"

Shimada smiled at his determined face and said they'd have to see how things went that night.

As far as Shimada was concerned, events later in bed went quite well, but Yoshi thought differently. "Why are you stopping?" he asked as Shimada was wiping lube off his fingers.

"You're too tight to keep going." Yoshi's groan of frustration was almost heart-rending. "Look, Yoshi, if you thought one finger was uncomfortable–"

"I didn't!"

"Uh, well, you weren't exactly relaxed, kid, and I'm in charge of fucking you," Shimada said, too tired to argue nicely. "Why are you in such a big damn hurry?" he asked.

"I just...I worry that it won't happen," Yoshi mumbled. "You'll slip away from me somehow..."

Shimada remembered how Yoshi had lost his family and felt like a huge jerk. He gently pulled the kid into his arms and held him close. "I'm not slipping away from you," he said softly. "We'll do it tomorrow night, when we can stay up late and sleep in in the morning. Okay?" He felt Yoshi nod against his shoulder. Shimada slid his hand down the boy's back to cup his cheek and felt him tense. And then relax. "I guess that's progress," Shimada thought. Feeling Yoshi dozing off, Shimada mulled over the possibility that once they'd actually had sex, and the unknown aspect was behind them, Yoshi would be more confident and relaxed. This had been the case for Shimada; once he'd made love to Seiji, he'd felt a tremendous sense of accomplishment. It was only later that he realized what a lousy, self-centered lay he'd been. This was hammered home by Seiji's angry recital of his flaws versus his new lover's graces.

Shimada smiled against Yoshi's hair. He must be happy because recalling that horrible scene, which had oddly enough ended in one last episode in bed with Seiji before he left Tokyo, Shimada didn't feel especially horrible. "Maybe I've grown up a little over this year," he thought as he fell asleep. "Or maybe I just don't give a damn about moody, thin-skinned, passive-aggressive Seiji anymore. He's Takashi's problem now, and he's more than welcome to him."

Saturday dragged for both of them; Yoshi in school and at the café, Shimada interviewing a woman whose cat led the neighborhood to a little girl stuck in a tree.

"Slow news day, eh, Ryuu?" Ikoma asked as the furious reporter was flailing away at the keyboard.

"Fuck you, Jun."

This made Ikoma laugh. "Hey, at least we pay you badly to write this weirdness up," he said and didn't even try to interpret the guttural noise that came from his friend.

Shimada flung his chair back from the computer desk. "Here, do you want to fix this or just run it the way it is?" he asked, tilting his chair back.

Ikoma rolled another chair over and sat down. He read for a while, fixed a few typos, and sent it down to production. "Only you could make a silly neighborhood story read like a spy thriller and not make fun of those silly people," he said.

"Everyone's life is important to them," Shimada said. "It doesn't take much to see that if you look for it."

"I knew you were the right man for the job," Ikoma said, and nodded at Shimada's thanks. "We still meeting for dinner tomorrow? For me to meet the boyfriend?"

"Yup," Shimada said, and reconfirmed the time and restaurant. "I'll have to write up the kendo match after dinner to make the morning paper."

"It's the area finals or I wouldn't be sending a reporter at all," Ikoma said. "I could send someone else."

"Nah, Yoshi likes kendo, he wants to go," Shimada said. "Tell you what, lend me a laptop and I'll give it back at dinner."

"Sounds like a plan." Ikoma went off to find one of their lightest weight machines.

As much as Shimada liked his job, and he was liking it more and more lately, he was glad to leave the cares of the office behind. With the mundanities of making of a living out of the way, Shimada could relax until Yoshi got home. He had a sleek laptop in his shoulder bag and a pleasant evening ahead of him.

At home, he was pleasantly surprised to discover a wireless connection strong enough to do a little internet research on the next day's kendo tournament. Depending on which site he read, there was a fierce or lukewarm rivalry between the schools, who had either great or pathetic teams. After digging up the schedule and some reliable-looking statistics, Shimada read some news and checked his email. He didn't get much email anymore, unless it was junk or a news alert. The email on his business card went to Ikoma's mailbox, which was what Shimada had requested.

"I'm home!"

Shimada was washing up his dinner dishes when Yoshi bounced in and flung himself on him. "Welcome home," he said after a big wet kiss. "How was school? How was work?"

"Boring and busy in that order," Yoshi said disgustedly. "What reporter thing did you do today?" Shimada told him. "You're kidding?" Shimada said he was not kidding. "But that's, so, um, so..."

"Stupid?"

"Um, no, not exactly, it's kind of, of..."

"Stupid?" Shimada was enjoying this.

"No, no, it's just, uh–"

"Stu–"

"Wait, it's weird! That's it, it's weird and odd that the paper would–"

"Waste time and money on a stupid story like this?"

Yoshi frowned so hard, Shimada could almost see the shockwave. "No! I mean that they'd send a great writer like you on such a story," he said firmly. "I've read your stories. They're great."

Shimada leaned forward until their lips were touching. "Thank you for liking my writing," he said against Yoshi's lips, and deepened the kiss.

Later in the dim bedside lamp light, Shimada spooned up behind Yoshi and eased the head of his latex sheathed, heavily lubed erection into the kid. There was a little resistance, but Shimada was gently persistent until the head slipped in. He stopped at Yoshi's gasp. As they were laying on their left sides, he took Yoshi's right hand and placed it on his right hip. "Push my hip when you're ready for more," he murmured against the kid's ear. "And relax, okay?"

He felt Yoshi relax fractionally, urge Shimada a little deeper and then tense. Shimada was enjoying holding him and not being in charge while still being in charge. When he was all the way in, he reached down to stroke Yoshi back to full hardness before he started gently fucking him. He hit Yoshi's sweet spot and pumped harder into the undulating young man in his arms. If this wasn't Yoshi's first time, Shimada would have rolled him onto his stomach and fucked the living daylights out of him. But, as it was Yoshi's first time, Shimada controlled himself and stayed in the less gravity-intense spoons position they were in.

Yoshi could hardly resist the overwhelming combination of Shimada inside and outside him and howled into his climax, back arched, shaking and clinging to Shimada's arm around him, which tightened as Shimada thrust into him a few times and came with a guttural moan. "Oh wow..." Yoshi sighed when he was a little more composed.

Shimada chuckled against his neck. "Yeah, wow."

"Um, what now?" Yoshi asked tentatively.

"Well, we live happily ever after and eventually your ass will let go of my dick and I can get rid of this condom," Shimada recited blandly. Yoshi shifted a little next to him. "Relax, take your time...ah, yeah..." Carefully disengaging, Shimada went into the bathroom and got rid of the condom. He brought a warm, damp towel back to bed. "How do you feel?" he asked, gently wiping Yoshi's chest, soft dick, and, after a minor struggle, ass.

"I feel great! Hey, what are you doing?" he asked when Shimada turned on a brighter light.

"Checking for damage."

"Oh," Yoshi said, squirming a little under Shimada's fingers. "You don't have to."

"Oh, but I do," Shimada said huskily because Yoshi's squirming turned him on. "I want to do this again, but need to know if you tore a little. You did, but we can go again–"

"Now?"

"Tomorrow night, if you feel like it," Shimada said. "I'm ready to sleep, are you, baby? You should be very ready to sleep."

"Yeah, I guess," Yoshi said and yawned.

Shimada put out the lights and took Yoshi in his arms. He cradled his lover and felt him fall asleep. A few seconds later, he felt the cat curling up next to him. Happier than he'd been in years, Shimada slipped into a sweet, dreamless sleep.

The rain woke him. "Ah, nothing like listening to the rain, being warm and cozy in bed with your boyfriend," Shimada thought as he lay wrapped around Yoshi with Flounder sprawled across them. "Yes, your boyfriend and your cat. Mmmm, maybe they'll cancel the kendo finals and we can stay in bed all day long." Then he remembered the event was being held indoors, so there went that. But if it was far too comfortable for humans to be stirring, this was not true of the feline population.

"'N'kay, Flounder, I'm awake," Yoshi mumbled and dug deeper under the covers by Shimada's side to get away from the cat batting at his head. "Mmm, morning," he cooed as he came up for a kiss, trying to ignore Flounder meowing at them.

"He wants breakfast," Shimada said, sitting up.

"It's too early." Yoshi's voice was muffled by the covers.

"He's on Flounder-time." Shimada was improvising. His bladder wanted relief almost as much as the cat wanted food. "How do you feel?" he asked when both pressing issues were taken care of (he'd left Flounder mulling over whether he was going to eat his half-can or not) and slid back into bed next to Yoshi.

"I feel okay," Yoshi said softly. "I feel different..."

"Sore?"

"A little," he admitted. "But that's not what I mean. I don't know what I feel, I just like being here with you."

"I like being with you, too, Yoshi," Shimada said, feeling more but not wanting to spook the kid with the words. Dare he say it? Love? Adore? Cherish? Delight in? Not delight in, that was too creepy, but the others were the feelings he thought he could never feel again. He put gratitude on the list as well. "And we get to watch kendo today," he said dryly.

"I love kendo," Yoshi said snoozily. "And dinner with your friend, too."

"Ah, yes, I'd nearly forgotten," Shimada said, drifting in to a peaceful doze.

As he'd half predicted, Shimada wrote up half the kendo during the match, including some mini-profiles of the teenage kendoka. He found them an intense, but cheerful, bunch and got some good quotes on sportsmanship and what they planned to do in the future, all responses included plans to continue to practice kendo at university. As usual, Shimada hid his boredom because the paper's readers would eat this stuff up with a shovel. And Yoshi was enjoying it so much, Shimada was almost having a good time just from that. On the other hand, Yoshi was getting some appreciative looks from the kendo studs, and that pleased and bothered Shimada in equal measures.

The restaurant was fairly crowded, but Ikoma had a booth in the back. After introductions and drink orders, Shimada finished up his story while Ikoma charmed the events of the kendo match out of Yoshi. Having never seen him in a social situation, Shimada hadn't realized how shy Yoshi was. Luckily, Ikoma could talk to anyone and very soon Yoshi was telling him all about the important moments in the matches. None of these moments were in Shimada's story, but as a cultural reporter, Shimada had a different perspective (and couldn't care less about, let alone even see, the heroic moments of high school kendo). By the time the first course arrived, Shimada was ready to hand the laptop over to Ikoma.

"I see you and Yoshi went to different events," Ikoma said dryly after skimming through the story. He gently pushed Yoshi away from the screen. "Not to worry, Yoshi-kun, I'll put some of your observations in. They're all fresh in my mind," he said, eating with one hand and typing with the other.

Yoshi looked a question at Shimada. "We're trying to make a deadline, Yoshi," Shimada said. "Eat your dinner."

It appeared that Yoshi'd worked up an appetite by the way he plowed into his meal. Shimada was hungry, too, and, thinking back over it, they'd pretty much stayed in bed all morning and only had snacks and blow jobs that day. This was the first real meal they'd had since yesterday. "I'll have to take better care of feeding him," Shimada thought, suppressing a smile.

"Hey, they have wireless here," Ikoma said, setting the laptop aside, but still where he could see the screen. "I sent it to the paper, so I won't have to rush off after dinner and you can take the laptop home with you," he added, finally eating his less-than-hot meal. "You're about the age of those kendokas today, Yoshi, are you going to university, too?"

"No, I don't have the grades or the money," Yoshi said. "I'm going to vocational school, though."

"For what?" Shimada asked, and got a wry look from Ikoma.

"Haven't talked about this, have you?" Ikoma asked.

Shimada ignored him and asked Yoshi, "For what?" again.

"Graphic design," Yoshi said. "If that's okay with you," he added somewhat defensively.

"It's fine, fine," Shimada said, feeling kind of stupid. "Better than, um, auto repair."

"Probably more money in auto repair, but tough on the hands," Ikoma observed with a smile. "But graphic design's a good field. You'll be able to get a job easily, I'm always hearing about places that need good designers."

Shimada was relieved when Ikoma and Yoshi started talking about layouts and computers and magazines they liked, it let his stupid reaction fade into the background. So, Yoshi wasn't going to university like he and Seiji did, so what? As long as they were happy, what difference did it make? Especially in Nagasaki where Shimada didn't have to live in his brother's shadow. And he thanked all the gods for that.

Two drinks past dessert, Yoshi asked what time it was. "Oh, Flounder will be hungry," he said.

"You're probably right," Shimada agreed, giving the waitress the high sign for the check. He had a different kind of hunger, and planned on going to bed with Yoshi immediately after feeding the cat.

"Flounder?" Ikoma asked.

"He's our cat," Yoshi said happily.

"You named your cat Flounder?" Ikoma looked from Yoshi to Shimada and got nods. "After the fish or verb?"

"Um, the fish, but the verb suits him, too," Shimada said, laughing.

"Does not," Yoshi said, defending their cat.

Ikoma smiled at their happiness as he hijacked the check and gave the waitress his credit card. "No, no, it's on the paper," he said over Shimada's protests. "You worked through the first part of dinner, it was the least I could do," he added, acknowledging Yoshi's polite bow and warm smile.

Shimada and Yoshi went home to an angry, but easily mollified with food, cat and a warm bed full of love.

The next afternoon Shimada dropped by the paper to pick up his assignments for the rest of the week. He also wanted to ask Ikoma what he'd thought of Yoshi.

"He's adorable," was Ikoma's answer.

"Doesn't he remind you of Seiji?" Shimada asked.

"No."

"No? Not slightly?" Shimada asked. "He's like Seiji in High School."

"I only knew Seiji at university," Ikoma said. "He was repressed where Yoshi is just a little shy. Seiji was fearful, where Yoshi is just young and unsure. You made Seiji crazy nervous, but Yoshi loves you like crazy."

"Jun, I'm stunned..."

"That I noticed?" Ikoma asked. "I wanted to be a novelist once, budding novelists notice all kinds of things. It's a hard habit to break." It was obvious Shimada didn't have a come-back for that, so Ikoma went on with a grim smile, "You and I have never talked about Seiji. I never liked him much, could never figure out why he stuck with you when he was so freaked out by you. It was weird."

"Because he loved me?" Shimada said, inwardly cursing himself for making it a question.

"Then he had a strange idea of love," Ikoma said bluntly. "And you're different now, tougher and nicer somehow. I guess interviewing housewives and shopkeepers has done that to you."

"Yeah, I was pretty high-strung back in Tokyo. Don't make me remember. Writing ad copy for my brother was killing me," Shimada admitted. "Thanks for helping me get set up here."

"Like I had a choice the way you just showed up here," Ikoma laughed. "But you've been good for the paper, so it's all good. Speaking of Tokyo," he said, peering at his computer. "I got an email from my cousin who has a little magazine there. He'd like to republish your article on that artist and gallery and is willing to pay Tokyo money for articles on Nagasaki culture. You game?"

"Money is money, forward the email and I'll think it over,"

Shimada said. He got his story assignments and they parted in good spirits. It was only when he got outside that Shimada realized that everything Ikoma said about Seiji and Yoshi was dead on the money. "Damn," he thought. "What was I thinking with Seiji? Was I just so scared of losing him, I crushed him and pushed him away? I'd never have the guts to ask him either." But he managed to drive the past away again when he got home to Yoshi.

Much to his surprise, Shimada found Yoshi and his uncle, at the apartment. At least the futon was made and the place was tidy. They weren't clean freaks, but they both did like order and clean surfaces, which pleased Shimada a lot.

"Oh...Mr., um, Mr. not Katayama," Shimada fumbled. "C'mon, Yoshi, help me out."

"Eijiro Ichimonji," Yoshi said, or actually spat.

"Mr. Ichimonji," Shimada said, hoping whatever it was, Yoshi wasn't going to make it more difficult. "How nice to see you again. And a surprise, at that. I'll make some tea—"

"I can't stay, but I came to invite you and Yoshi to dinner at the café tonight," Mr. Ichimonji said.

"Oh?" Shimada said politely.

"We have a table in the back for family," Ichimonji went on. "Yoshi knows the way—"

"I—" Yoshi began.

"We'll be there!" Shimada cut him off. He saw Ichionji downstairs to the street. "What time should we be there?"

"Five-thirty," Ichimonji said, his face unreadable. "Yoshi knows the way."

"Well, so do I," Shimada thought as he bowed politely to his lover's maternal uncle. "So, okay, what happened?" he asked Yoshi back in the apartment.

"He cornered me after school—"

"'Cornered you'?"

"Well, he walked me home," Yoshi said, scowling at the coffeetable. "And asked me all kinds of questions about you and me and why I'm so happy. It was embarrassing." He looked up when Shimada didn't say anything.

"And?" Shimada said when he had eye-contact.

"He asked if you were sexually abusing me."

"Huh," Shimada said after a while. "Well, if your hotheaded cousin kills me, make sure Ikoma gives me a good funeral."

"Ryuu!" Yoshi flung himself into Shimada arms.

"Just kidding, kidding," Shimada soothed him. "Sort of." He

hugged him tighter. "You really are eighteen, right?" He felt a nod against his chest. "Of course if your family thinks I'm no good, none of that is going to matter."

"We don't have to go tonight, we–"

"Yes, we do." Shimada brushed the hair out of Yoshi's tense brown eyes and rubbed the crease between his brows. "This is your family."

"I'd pick you instead of them!"

"Hopefully you won't have to," Shimada said, wishing he'd been so brave for Seiji. But he wouldn't be here consoling Yoshi if he had. Or maybe he would; Seiji wasn't the type to endure hardship and near-poverty for love. Of course, they never had the chance to find out: Shimada had caved into his mother's request and lost everything he'd ever cared about.

But now he cared very much for Yoshi and this was worth fighting for. "Hey, it's just dinner, and we better get with it," he said, glancing at the clock.

Yoshi reluctantly rose to change out of his school uniform. "I wanted to spend the evening with you," he said from the bedroom.

"Dinner's at five-thirty. How much of the evening can this take up?" Shimada asked him.

"I have homework."

"Good thing we still have the laptop!" Shimada said, locking the door behind them. "Cheer up, Yoshi, this is the easy part of the evening."

Apparently the family was evenly split between the pro-Shimada and the not-sure-about-Shimada camps. The butcher-knife-wielding cousin was a fan of Shimada's sports writing, his waitress-wife liked his culture stories, but Yoshi's aunt and uncle were less interested in his newspaper career. The conversation at the family table tucked away in a corner of the kitchen ranged from local and national news to Shimada's past in Tokyo and his present in Nagasaki. They even lightly touched on his religious beliefs, or at least ascertained that he was vaguely Shinto and Buddhist, as they were. This seemed to be a great relief to Yoshi's aunt and uncle, but only elicited smiles and shrugs from the rest of the family. Overall, it was a nice evening. Shimada thought he got off lightly on the interrogation side of things and the dinner, which was even better than the café's delicious noodles, was excellent. The café's dinner rush started around seven and was intense for a Monday.

"You've brought us business, Shimada-san," Mr. Ichimonji said as he cheerfully headed for the dining area.

"Thank you for dinner." Shimada bowed to Mrs. Ichimonji.

"I'm so glad to meet Yoshi's, um, Yoshi's friend," she said and went into the food preparation part of the kitchen. Yoshi's cousin and his wife were already hard at work, so Shimada and Yoshi cleared and cleaned the family table and put the dishes in the dishwasher. They said a quick good-night to whoever had time in the bustling café to hear it and left by the back door, which opened into the alleyway in which Shimada had rescued Yoshi from Mr. Watanabe not so long ago.

"Ah, where we met," Shimada said. "How romantic." Yoshi sighed with obvious relief. Shimada hadn't realized he'd been holding his breath. "That went well, didn't it?"

"Yeah, I guess," Yoshi said, bumping his shoulder against him. He was startled, but didn't resist, when Shimada put his arm around him.

"They're nice people," Shimada said. "They just want you to be okay and maybe even happy."

"How can you tell?" Yoshi asked.

"They wanted to know who I am to you," Shimada said, thoughtfully, remembering how isolated he and Seiji had been after university. Besieged almost, always careful not to appear as the couple they so very much were. They'd never had a dinner even remotely resembling this one. "If I were some crazy person, they'd be right to object to me. I'd even object to me."

"Why don't they just trust me?" Yoshi asked.

"I think they do, Yoshi," Shimada said, getting bored with the subject. "You're still living with me, right?"

"Oh...well, yeah..."

They were passing a convenience story. "Want some ice cream?" Shimada asked.

"Yeah!"

They ate it in bed later that night.

Their life together settled into a nice rhythm of school and work for Yoshi, writing and reporting for Shimada and as much time together as they could manage. Now that Yoshi had more financial support, his uncle only asked him to work three days in the café. There were regular family dinners there that included Shimada, who continued to endear himself to them. Yoshi's family could not fail to be impressed that Yoshi had fallen in love with a fine person and they were deeply relieved that their cousin and nephew was able to be happy again.

Ikoma was happy, too. The paper was flourishing and readership was up partly due to Shimada's writing. It was also partly due to the competition Shimada's writing sparked in the paper's other writers and the new writers who came on board to learn from them. Ikoma even had to clean up his writing to keep up with his flourishing reporter staff. He was also pleased that Shimada was writing for his cousin's edgy magazine in Tokyo, Perspectocity, even though Shimada insisted on writing under an alias. The magazine was small, but had a loyal readership who devoured the in-depth reporting and analyses Ikoma's cousin, Masao Naganuma, published. Over the months that Shimada wrote for it, the subscription- and advertising-base grew, and so did Shimada's compensation. This was not strictly due to Shimada's contribution, many fine writers were published in Perspectocity, but he was still an important part of it, even if it was under an assumed name.

And Shimada welcomed the extra money. He loved Yoshi very much, but keeping a High Schooler was more expensive than Shimada had realized. In addition to pocket money, he'd agreed to pay half Yoshi's school fees so he didn't have to work at the café so much. Then there were school supplies, transit passes, and Yoshi's final school trip, which Shimada insisted he take.

"After all, Yoshi, I won't even be here while you're in Bali," Shimada said, clinching the argument. "I have to go out to the suburbs to cover that arson story."

The story took him to the suburbs for several weeks interviewing people whose homes had been set on fire. Following a lead, Shimada realized that all the victims had sons that went to an elite high school. Furthermore, all the sons were on the soccer team. After interviewing the coach and chatting with several team members whose homes hadn't been arson sites, Shimada went to the police with his suspicions. He now believed the fires were being set by a girl from a not-so-elite school who'd been raped by certain members of the soccer team. Sadly, it turned out that it was she and her boyfriend, and the police found them dead in her bedroom. The boyfriend had strangled her and then hung himself.

Shimada's story caused quite a stir. He offered no prescriptives, he merely recounted the hopelessness of the lovers' suicide pact and the arrogance of the elite rapists. There was much editorial hand-wringing in other papers, and some soul-searching in a few news magazines, and, of course, congratulations when Ryuu Shimada won a very prestigious national newspaper award. And being newspaper people writing about one of their own, and because they were a thorough lot, many stories mentioned Ryuu's illustrious advertising mogul brother, Daitaro Shimada of Shimada Miyagi, one of the most prosperous ad agencies in the country.

"Shit," Shimada said, slumped in a chair in Ikoma's office.

"Maybe he won't notice," Ikoma offered in a reasonable voice.

"Are you kidding, Jun? He has full time staffers who do nothing but look for references to him in the press," Shimada said, scowling. "If I'd parachuted onto his terrace, I couldn't be in his face anymore than I am with this award."

"Congratulations again, by the way," Ikoma said. As miserable as Shimada was, Ikoma was ecstatic to have this kind of honor showered on his little local paper. "When are you going to the award ceremony?"

"I'm not, I asked Masao to accept it for me," Shimada said blankly.

"That's good for Perspectocity," Ikoma said approvingly. "He'll out you as one of his writers."

"I know, he's already said he wants me to write under my own name from now on. It was in the PS of his letter of congratulations." Shimada looked up at Ikoma's chuckle. "I guess I'll have to stop hiding from the past."

"Why not?" Ikoma asked. "You have a beautiful present and a bright future. You have Yoshi, why not just enjoy it and forget all the bullshit that happened in Tokyo?"

"Yeah, okay." Shimada dragged himself out of the armchair.

"Where're you off to?" Ikoma asked. They'd just gone over Shimada's leads for that week and he knew he didn't have anything until the next day.

"Home, to finish a story for your slave-driver cousin in Tokyo," Shimada said over his shoulder.

Ikoma had a good laugh about that, knowing his cousin would get as much mileage out of Shimada and his award as he could before what fuss there was about it died down completely.

Yoshi had been very pleased when he read the notice in the paper that Shimada had won some kind of important newspaper award. "Of course you won, that was an incredible story about those kids," he'd said. "It made me cry."

"It was supposed to make you angry at the injustice and elitism of our class system," Shimada had said.

"Really? It all seemed so sad to me."

"Because it was sad," Shimada had said, giving in and changing the subject. The story had made him sad and angry in equal measures, but now only the sadness lingered. The soccer players would never be punished now that there was no one to press charges. The parents of the dead girl and boy would never understand why their children chose death instead of asking for help. The schools and community would go on as before, the haves would have, and the have-nots would be their victims. It was an old story, one that never changed, and, in the end, that was what made Shimada sad. "I'm no crusader," he told himself. "I'm a coward at heart. I can't fight these battles, only write about them. I have to leave it to others to fight for what's right and good and they never do. Nothing's going to change because of my story, but at least those two dead kids have the truth as a memorial, for all the good it does them."

Shimada was sad for a few days, but he let Yoshi cheer him up. Then he was nervous for a few days after he won the award, but let Yoshi cheer him up again.

They were in the midst of enjoying Yoshi's summer vacation—sleeping late, taking day trips, making love in the middle of the afternoon—when Daitaro Shimada showed up.

Yoshi answered the door, Shimada being occupied in the bathroom.

"You must be Yoshi Katayama," Daitaro said with a leer, in what he thought was an easy-going friendly voice.

All it did was make Yoshi suspicious. "How do you know that?"

"I'm Ryuu's older brother," Daitaro said, edging closer to the half-open door Yoshi was blocking with his body. "It's an older brother's business to know with whom his brother is living."

"You're his older brother?" Yoshi asked, not moving an inch.

"Yes, Daitaro Shimada, that's me." Daitaro tried a smile, but it only got as far as a smirk. "Do you think I could come in?"

"Maybe." Yoshi merely turned his head to yell over his shoulder, "Ryuu! Your dad's here!"

"I'm his brother, brat!"

"You look like his dad!" Yoshi nearly shouted. "And don't call me a brat!"

"Then don't call me his dad!"

"Then don't-!" The bathroom door opening cut off whatever Yoshi was about to shout at Daitaro.

Shimada sauntered up to the squabbling pair at the door and pulled Yoshi behind him. He let Daitaro come in, but left the door open. "What are you doing here, brother?" he asked in a cold voice.

"Now, now, bro, I've just come to congratulate you on your award," Daitaro said, strolling around their modest living room. "Nice place, oh, and you have a cat. How nice, how homey."

Shimada felt Yoshi stiffen behind him as Flounder, the traitor, rubbed around Daitaro's expensive pant legs. "Thank you. Now get out."

"Brother, how unkind," Daitaro said, not moving. "After all this time, and I see you've found some consolation-"

"Hey! Does he mean me?" Yoshi broke in.

"Well I don't mean the cat, kid!" Daitaro snapped.

"Why you-!"

"Daitaro, leave!" Shimada was holding Yoshi back with some difficulty.

"Well, at least this one has some spirit," Daitaro drawled as he headed for the door.

"You jerk," Shimada snarled, and gave him a good shove into the hallway before slamming the door in his face. He wrapped his arms around Yoshi to calm them both down. And then he started to laugh softly.

"What?" Yoshi, still angry, asked.

"You found his weakness right away, didn't you? My brother hates anyone to think he's old," Shimada said, leaning down for a kiss.

After kissing him back, Yoshi asked, "Why did he come here?"

"To let me know he knows everything about me," Shimada said, sadly.

"He knew my name," Yoshi told him.

Shimada frowned and then shrugged. "Then it was to let me know he knows everything about us," he said. "But it doesn't matter. He's in Tokyo and we're here. It doesn't matter," he repeated, as if to convince himself.

"Your brother dropped by yesterday to congratulate me on your award," Ikoma said before Shimada sat down. "He said you threw him out."

"I did. What's it to ya?"

Ikoma didn't pursue it; this was the old Tokyo Shimada in front of him again: mean, cold, and angry. The editor in Ikoma rose up and decided Shimada was in exactly the right mood for some crime reporting. "Try not to get arrested," he said by way of farewell. He got a grunt as a response. Ikoma hoped Shimada was not taking his mood out on Yoshi. The poor kid probably wouldn't understand a bit of it. Ikoma wasn't sure he really understood how Shimada let Daitaro and Takashi ruin his life with Seiji. Seemed to him like Shimada did most of the damage himself.

Shimada's mood was in direct proportion to how much he wasn't taking it out on, or confiding in, Yoshi. He was half annoyed and half admiring that Yoshi had provoked Daitaro so quickly before Shimada got there and the only thing left for him to do was to throw his brother out. He felt Yoshi had limited his options, even though throwing Daitaro out was at the top of things Shimada wanted to do before one of them died.

He was proud of Yoshi for not being intimidated by this brother as most people were. But Yoshi had lost so much: he was fearless and sometimes reckless, and would fight to keep Shimada any way he had to. As much as Shimada welcomed this kind of love, and was damn glad he could feel this way again, Yoshi's love weighed heavily on him. At least Yoshi wasn't going to be charmed into caving in to Daitaro like Seiji had been. That wasn't exactly fair to Seiji; Takashi was Daitaro's rising star in the agency. Seiji would have to be at least polite to his lover's boss.

After several hours of interviewing policemen, witnesses, victims of the burglaries, and chasing a few leads to dead-ends, Shimada fell by the paper to write up what story he had and be more civil to Ikoma. The crime beat was not Shimada's forte, but since he'd just won a big award for it, he thought he ought to make some kind of effort to please his new-found fans. They'd get sick of his cynicism and angular prose soon enough. But being hard-headed with hard-headed people had gotten most of the bitterness over Daitaro out of his system.

"So what did Daitaro say?" he asked without preamble.

"You won't like it," Ikoma said, watching Shimada curl his lip. "He said he was glad you were succeeding at something."

"That fucking jerk." But Shimada didn't get much oomph into it. Daitaro's put-down was to be expected. Shimada was no longer under his thumb, so all Daitaro could do was jab ineffectually at him.

"I think he's jealous." Ikoma broke into his meditations when they'd gone on too long.

"Huh?"

"You won a real award for real world serious reporting on a contemporary problem that no one else has had the guts to face, let alone splay out for everyone to see," Ikoma said slowly. "You took a risk in standing up for those dead kids; you took the side of all the victims of bullying. It could have gone very wrong, but you made heroes out of what society considers losers, and villains out of the usual heroes."

"Please, Jun, you're making me blush," Shimada said. That got a laugh, so he figured it was good to leave 'em laughing. "So—"

"How swamped are you with Perspectocity stories?" Jun asked, rising to his feet with Shimada.

"Very, can't take anymore work from you this week, sorry," Shimada said. "And I'm negotiating articles with Moda Weekly and Journal Nouveau."

"My poor cousin," Ikoma said with mock sadness. "His discovery is being stolen away. I'll miss you if you dump the paper. Ah, such is the tragedy of the clan Ikoma."

"Oh relax," Shimada said, laughing a little. "I'm not doing anything that takes me out of Nagasaki for more than a day or two. Preferably somewhere I can take Yoshi."

"Hooray for Yoshi," Ikoma said, seeing him out. "My cousin and I salute him."

"Yeah." Shimada headed home feeling better than he'd felt that day.

At home he found Yoshi making dinner. "Are you packed for tomorrow?"

"No, but it's only two days," he said after a warm, but not too warm kiss, because he still had to pack. "I can just toss a few things in the backpack later."

Shimada grunted and got a beer from the fridge. He sat down at the laptop to write his minimal story. Another reporter would have to finish up when there were new leads or the cops actually caught the burglar or burglars. Based on what he'd pieced together, it sounded like more than one perpetrator, but he really didn't have enough to go on so his story was going to be very short.

Opening the laptop he saw that Yoshi was in the middle of an email. "Okay, who's Hiro?" he asked.

"Friend from school." Yoshi looked in from the kitchen. "Oh, the email..."

"And why are you telling him about my brother's visit?"

"Hiro knows about us," Yoshi said, slightly defensively. "He reads your stories in he paper. He wants to be a reporter, like you. He knows who your brother is, too, somehow."

"'Wow! Your bf's brother is THAT Shimada of Shimada Miyagi!!!1!!'" Shimada read from the previous email. "I can see that he knows, or thinks he knows."

Wiping his hands on a towel, Yoshi sat down next to him and saved his email in the Drafts folder. "Is your brother a big deal?" he asked.

"In certain circles, yes, I guess," Shimada said, sulkily. "He fancies himself a political/cultural influence peddler when he's not selling soap and tampons to bored teens with too much money." He looked at Yoshi's confused face, which confirmed his suspicion that he wasn't making much sense. "My brother is in advertising. He took over my uncle's interest in Shimada Miyagi when my uncle died five years ago. SM was a good, solid agency with boring accounts in groceries, hardware, insurance, stuff like that. My brother has moved it into more exciting things like high fashion, perfume, cosmetics, cars, and lately, into finance and politics. Those intimidating bank ads on billboards are his kind of advertising. 'Buy this or your life means N O T H I N G.' Daitaro occasionally gets mentioned in the gossip pages— he and his wife like to swan around with pop stars and actors—that's probably why your pal Hiro knows his name. I met Hiro once, didn't I?"

"Uh huh. He brought me his notes when I had a cold and couldn't go to school," Yoshi said.

"Ah, now that's a friend," Shimada said, remembering a bulky nervous youth. "I didn't realize he was my fan."

"Sort of," Yoshi laughed. "He's more impressed about your brother, though."

"Great, just great," Shimada sighed. "That's my whole life right there, you know."

Yoshi hugged him. "I wasn't impressed with your brother," he said. "He's like those pushy jerks at the café that drive me crazy when I have to wait on them." Shimada hugged him back, but they were interrupted by the kitchen timer. "Hey, write your story so we can have dinner," Yoshi said disentangling himself and going into the kitchen.

As Yoshi rattled plates, Shimada skimmed though his notes and cranked out a draft of his story before dinner was on the zataku. "Was I a jerk at the café?" he asked, settling in front of white rice and steamed fish and vegetables. Yoshi didn't have a huge range to his cooking, but it was always fresh and he leaned toward simple, clean foods that were not noodles.

They were silent for a few moments giving thanks for the food, before Yoshi answered. "I only saw you there once or twice, and you ran away the first time." He smiled warmly at his lover digging into his cooking. "Why are you so nice and your brother's such a jerk?"

"I don't know, Yoshi," Shimada said, between bites of surprisingly spicy fish with cabbage and carrots, cooling it off with rice. "He's the guy who's always right about everything and no one has ever told him he's wrong. And he's wrong about a lot of things."

"But you did, didn't you? Told him he's wrong, I mean."

"Kind of, mostly I just ran away from the situation," Shimada said, impressed that it really didn't hurt much to talk about it...nearly two years later. "It's like this: my brother was right that I shouldn't be with Seiji because he was able to break us up."

"That's stupid!" Shimada laughed, but Yoshi went on, "And you were just being a good son and bowing to your mother's wishes that you break up with Seiji."

"That's true, I was going to get back together with him when she was well again," Shimada said, dishing up more fish, vegetables and rice. "But good old Takashi grabbed him while I was being a good son."

"That sucks."

"Not for Takashi, he'd had his eye on Seiji since he met him at Tokyo U," Shimada said. He smiled at Yoshi's honest, open, fearless face and big brown eyes, and remembered that as much as Seiji loved him, he'd never seen as much confidence in Seiji's face as he was seeing in Yoshi's. But his future with Seiji in Tokyo had been a minefield compared to the simple joys of Nagasaki. Which reminded him... "We're leaving for the hotel very early–"

"I'll pack, I'll pack," Yoshi chanted as he cleared the table. He brought Shimada a fresh beer and settled down beside him with a cup of tea while the reporter edited his story and sent it off. "Can I finish my email?" he asked and Shimada handed him the laptop.

"Say good stuff about me," Shimada said, and went off to pack for himself.

There were a few more trips before the summer ended, but end it did and Yoshi went back to school. Shimada had been busy over the summer, but with Yoshi busy with school and work, he took even more writing jobs. Especially from Perspectocity, which was asking him for more and more editorial direction, which was something he was reluctant to give.

Ikoma even asked him about it. "My cousin–"

"Your cousin needs to hire an editor that thinks like me," Shimada growled.

Undaunted, Ikoma tried again. "Know anyone?"

Shimada sat heavily in one of the side chairs. "No, alas."

"You know Perspectocity is becoming one of the hottest monthlies in the region," Ikoma said slowly. "It's probably not your fault you're lucky and talented and that rubs off on the places you work." He paused to acknowledge Shimada's sneer. "Maybe it has nothing to do with you, but this paper's circulation is higher than it's ever been and we've doubled our ad revenue."

"Jun, I'm not the only good reporter here," Shimada said, defending his fellow journalists.

"Don't tell them I said this, but they got better when they had to compete with you," Ikoma said. "Hell, Ryuu, you got better when you started competing with yourself."

"That only sort of makes sense, Jun."

"I know, I know." Ikoma waved it away. "Look, I'm a desperate man, I'm about to screw my own paper, but here goes: my cousin and his magazine need you."

"They need me?"

"They've got a syndicate of investors now," Ikoma continued. "This is a once in a lifetime shot for my cousin to make it as a big time publisher. He says your articles set the standard for each issue. He thinks you can work editorial magic for him. He's willing to pay real money for it, too." Ikoma named a figure that would keep Shimada and Yoshi in comfort, if not style in Tokyo.

"How much editorial control?"

"Masao says complete control."

"Can I do it from here?" Shimada asked.

"Would you want to try?" Ikoma asked back.

Shimada sighed; a Tokyo magazine had to be edited from Tokyo for the feel of the city. He knew this; it was inescapable. Though he didn't want to go back there, this was incredibly tempting. Neither he nor Yoshi had deep roots in Nagasaki, and though they both had painful pasts in Tokyo, deep down they missed the city they grew up in. "Let me talk to Yoshi," he finally said. "I'm not going anywhere without him."

Ikoma merely nodded, and they discussed more local issues. But he rose and bowed to Shimada when they parted.

"Move back to Tokyo?" Yoshi lifted his head from Shimada's chest to look at him in the dim bedside light. "I thought...you didn't want to go back there," he said quietly.

"Nothing is settled, Yoshi, but this is one helluva opportunity," Shimada said, brushing the hair out of his lover's eyes and stroking his cheek. "I'd like to try for it, and I think I could face anything with you beside me."

"That's how I feel, Ryuu." Yoshi nuzzled the hand on his cheek. "I love my aunt and uncle and cousins, but, I, you know, I never really felt like this was home until I met you. So, I guess, um, that where you are is home for me and that can be in Tokyo."

Shimada held him close and kissed him for a long time. The next day he made arrangements to go to Tokyo to discuss editing Perspectocity with its owner, Masao Naganuma.

Thereafter Shimada spent more and more time in Tokyo and eventually decided he and Yoshi should live there. It would be socially complicated for Shimada, who'd have to at least visit his parents, but less complicated than trying to live in two places at the same time. Yoshi could study graphic design in Tokyo as well as Nagasaki and probably be happier in Tokyo, too. He was already frowning over the amount of time Shimada was away from home. But as autumn turned into winter, Shimada was still shuttling back and forth, staying with Masao or friends from university and avoiding his family, Seiji and Takashi. It was easy, too easy; Shimada began to believe they were avoiding him. This caused him to have mixed emotions, part relief and part disappointment. He decided that it must be that Seiji and the others were as over him as he was over them, and all this elicited in him was an emotional shrug. More focused on finding an apartment and the future than he was on the past, Shimada simply didn't see Seiji in the lobby of the Perspectocity office that afternoon. "Oh..."

"'Oh'? That's it after two years?" Seiji asked, smiling uncertainly, just like he always did.

"Oh, hi, I, ah, almost didn't recognize you." Shimada fumbled around, looking at his watch. "I have a plane to catch, so..."

"I know, I'll go to the airport with you," Seiji said, sounding more composed and confident as he opened the door for them. He had a taxi waiting for them.

"How'd you know I'd be here, Seiji?" Shimada asked when they were underway.

"Subterfuge," he said. "I called to make an appointment to interview you and then cancelled it. But not before I knew your entire schedule."

"Clever, but unnecessary."

"Would you have seen me if I'd just called you up?" Seiji asked, the old endearing uncertainty creeping into his voice.

"No, I wouldn't, but you could have spared us both this surprise attack." Shimada said, surprised at how annoyed he suddenly was.

"Ryuu! I thought you were over it, I–"

"Me!? Over it?" Shimada stared hard at him and almost felt bad at how miserable Seiji looked. Adorable, yes, but also very miserable.

"Please don't kill me, but Daitaro said you'd found someone new," Seiji said, cowering a little. "He said Yoshi looked like me in High School, even showed me a picture of–" He broke off with a small squeak when Shimada's hand landed gently on his shoulder.

"Daitaro has a picture of Yoshi," Shimada said, mostly to himself, but did notice Seiji, wide-eyed and trembling slightly, nodding. "So, what did you think? Of Yoshi's picture, I mean."

"He...he's cute," Seiji said hesitantly. "I don't think I was that cute in High School."

"No, you weren't," Shimada said, trying to remember what it was in Seiji that attracted him.

"Gee, thanks," Seiji said, pouting.

Shimada patted his shoulder. It couldn't have been easy for Seiji to face him after everything that happened, and, if he was honest, Shimada's own gutlessness had caused Seiji a lot of suffering that should have been avoided. But the past was past and nothing could be done. "Are you still with Takashi?" he asked.

"Of course!"

"Well, how would I know?" Shimada asked, sourly. "Why track me down then?"

Seiji made a disgusted sound and looked out the window. If they hadn't been on the highway, Shimada thought Seiji would have asked the driver to stop and let him out. But Seiji had a brave streak, Shimada couldn't deny him that. "We meant a lot to each other once," Seiji said slowly. "It's not like you died, so I don't see any reason I can't come to say hi to you and congratulate you on your award. Congratulations on your award, okay? I would say that even if you hated me....Do you hate me, Ryuu?"

Shimada relaxed a little. "No, I don't hate you, Seiji," he said, omitting that it would be too much effort to hate him at this point. "My life is very different now, though. No all night parties, no big spending, no exotic travel."

"You never liked that much anyway," Seiji said warmly.

"Neither did you," Shimada said dryly. "We only did it to please Daitaro and I 'spose you and Takashi are on the same treadmill."

"Oh, sort of," Seiji said with a shrug. "I quit SM after you left and got a data entry job at the National Archives. It's rather dull and I'm part of a huge department, but it really does suit me better than advertising."

"How'd Daitaro and Takashi take that development?" Shimada asked, marveling at Seiji's nerve in quitting his brother's company. He'd always thought Seiji had the soul of a clerk, but would never admit it to either of them.

"They don't care," he said. "I nearly had a nervous breakdown after you left Tokyo, so the less stressful job was necessary and also means I can take better care of Takashi."

"Does he need care?" Shimada asked, half kidding. The Takashi he remembered was cool, confident and ready for anything.

"A little," Seiji said calmly. "He took care of me when you left–"

"You. Dumped. Me."

"I know, but it was still painful." Seiji looked at him with such honesty, Shimada had to look away. "And then Daitaro dumps a lot of work and personal stuff on him."

"That's my bro," Shimada said bitterly. "No friends, just husks of people he sucked dry and cast aside."

"Well, it's not that bad," Seiji said.

"Yet."

"Ever," Seiji said firmly. "Takashi isn't you or me; he's getting as much out of Daitaro as Daitaro is getting out of him. It's a little scary sometimes how much alike they are."

"More like terrifying, alarming and disgusting, if you ask me," Shimada said. "Oh, we're here." He'd almost begun to enjoy their chat.

Seiji thrust a business card at him. "Ryuu, please call me or email me," he said, a grace note of desperation in his voice. "I miss being your friend and I don't have many of my own friends. Hasn't enough time gone by that we can be friends now? Please?" he asked, glancing at the restless taxi driver. "I'll take care of the cab, I have to take it back anyway. Don't miss your plane."

There were tears in Seiji's voice, if not his eyes. Shimada knew the sound of this raw honesty and was moved by it. He could not trust his own voice, so only nodded and got out of the cab. He watched it pull away, taking Seiji back to Takashi, and this bothered him not at all. "Maybe we can be friends," he thought as he hurried to the gate to catch his plane back to Yoshi.

Takashi was pacing their apartment when Seiji got home.

"You're late, Seiji." Takashi looked at his Rolex for the nth time.

"I saw Ryuu."

Momentarily poleaxed by visions of his hard-fought and hard-won lover in a love hotel with his former rival, Takashi fought for cool and control. "Oh my God, please don't leave me, Seiji!" he cried, falling to his knees and wrapping his arms around Seiji's waist.

"Ta-kashi," Seiji said wearily. "I'm not leaving you. Please get up. Or stay there, and I'll sit down."

Takashi leapt to his feet and apologized. Seiji indicated that he wanted a drink by glancing at the drink cart and graciously accepted a Seven and Seven. Flopping down next to him on the couch, Takashi asked, "Where did you see him?"

"In a cab," Seiji said with a sigh. "I ambushed him at Perspectocity and he allowed me to share a cab ride to the airport with him."

He worked hard to drum up visions of Seiji and Ryuu having sex in a cab, something so out of character for both of them, that Takashi finally gave up on that scenario. Seiji was more loyal and comfort-loving than that. Takashi felt momentarily ashamed for doubting him. If Seiji were going to cheat on him, he'd leave him, and that would be infinitely worse and, technically, wouldn't be cheating. "How was he?" Takashi finally asked to distract himself from his own train of thought.

"Barely civil, but he didn't throw me out onto the highway."

"Ah, that's good," Takashi said, steeling himself to ask, "Why did you–?"

"See him? Because we meant everything to each other once, and I can't act like that's nothing," Seiji said firmly. "We were friends and lovers, Takashi, I hope enough time's gone by that we can be friends again. And you know there's someone new in his life, so maybe he can finally forgive me for chickening out on him." He glanced at his lover, who had his completely neutral listening-to-client-bullshit face on. This annoyed Seiji enough to continue. "Besides, Daitaro broke us up, it really wasn't Ryuu's fault!"

Smiling, Takashi snaked his arm around Seiji. "And I just profited from your former lover's inability to stand up to his family." He kissed the frown off Seiji's brow.

"It was Daitaro mainly, you know that," Seiji said, leaning up and briefly returning a kiss. "You know what a monster he is, how ruthless and relentless he is when he wants something. It's unnatural."

"I still think Ryuu was a fool for letting Daitaro and his mother–" he raised a hand to still Seiji's objection, "–his mother was undeniably in it, Seiji, you can't blame it all on Daitaro–"

"That's like blaming the gun for the bullet," Seiji snapped.

"Now, now, where was I?" Takashi hugged him closer. "For letting anyone break you two up for any reason. I would have fought them to the end for you."

"That's easy to say now," Seiji said, leaning his head on Takashi's Armani-clad shoulder. "But what if Daitaro opposes us? You work for him, your future is with him."

"My future is with you, Seiji," Takashi said, reassuringly. "And you've hit the nail on the head. I only work for Daitaro, he's not my elder brother. Not to worry, though, if I got canned from SM for being your lover, I'd dig ditches or write poetry or just live on your salary."

"You'd hate it," Seiji said softly. "You'd be miserable every second."

"Not if you still loved me." In his deepest heart, Takashi hoped he'd never have to choose between his family and Seiji. In his private honest moments, he saluted Ryuu's attempt to dodge that bullet even when he failed and a grieving Seiji threw himself into Takashi's waiting arms. Occasionally Takashi wondered if he'd played a part— other than being the one person Seiji would bring his broken heart to and the one person who wouldn't let him go and the one person Ryuu would never take Seiji back from—in Daitaro's dreadful scheme. But the one thing no one had foreseen was that Ryuu would tell them all to go to hell and vanish from their lives. Yes, they all knew he was with some dinky little local paper in Nagasaki, but as far as being reachable, Ryuu might as well have been on the moon these past two years. And soon he'd be back in Tokyo with a new love, and...ah, damn, it was too much to think about just then, it was enough just to hold Seiji, the love of his li–

"Takashi?" the love of his life said softly.

"Yes, darling?"

"What's for dinner?"

At home in Nagasaki, Shimada found Yoshi reading in bed and wearing the cute silk pajamas Shimada brought home from the last trip to Tokyo. Shimada was not a mushy boyfriend, but he could not resist seeing Yoshi in these particular white silk pajamas he'd seen in a department store. They looked cute on Yoshi for as long as he got to wear them, which was usually not long at all. That he was wearing them for Shimada's homecoming, made it all that much sweeter. "Hey," he said. "No, don't get up, I'm taking a shower and joining you." Cute pajamas notwithstanding, Shimada realized he needed a little more time to figure out how to tell Yoshi he'd seen Seiji. He also needed a shower to give him enough energy to make it into bed with Yoshi.

Refreshed and rosy, Shimada decided to take the offensive. "What are you reading, hon?" he asked, toweling his hair dry.

"'The Red Pony'."

Shimada, who occasionally read *The Economist* magazine, looked more closely at the book; it was in English. "I'm impressed," he said. "I didn't realize your English was that good."

"Don't be too impressed, it's a simplified version." Yoshi smiled at him and stuck a Perspectocity subscription card in the book to mark his place. "Or maybe not," he added, looking at the cover before tossing it aside. "This book is so simple, it's like for idiots."

"But you're reading it," Shimada teased, pulling him close.

"I like English class, so I guess I'm good at it," he said, twisting a little in Shimada's arms to give his lover better access to his neck. "I like reading and listening, but I don't like speaking very much."

"'Let's speak English!'" Shimada said in that language.

"Maybe later," Yoshi said, not in English, and pulled Shimada down for a kiss.

The pajamas didn't stay on very long, which was a relief to both men. Deftly moving them into a sixty-nine that would have been enough for the fatigued Shimada, he could not help but smile when Yoshi tapped him on the shoulder with the tube of lubricant.

"I want to," Yoshi said simply, and then turned his oral attentions to Shimada's burgeoning cock.

"I want to, too." Shimada said, and playfully devoured Yoshi's rock-hard erection, teasing out his teenage lover's orgasm as he gently stretched and lubed him.

It had almost become a game with them: usually Yoshi came first due to his youth and Shimada's brilliant fellatio technique, but as

Yoshi's technique improved, he could sometimes get Shimada off before Shimada had him ready for sex. But that night Yoshi wanted to get laid, so he only got Shimada really hard, and then came hard himself when he'd gone just a little past his limit. Yoshi was trying to build up some stamina and control, but a good orgasm after Shimada was away for a few days was not to be missed.

Shimada spent a little more time applying lube and stretching before taking Yoshi's renewed erection in his mouth again. He sucked him to half-hardness and shifted them until they were face to face, Yoshi spread out beneath him and Shimada lifted the kid's knees and began gently easing his condom-clad, lubed-up shaft into Yoshi's body. The kid seemed a little tense, so Shimada leaned down to kiss him. This did the trick and Shimada was able to slip the head into him. "Okay?" he asked, and got a nod from Yoshi, who was breathing heavily beneath him.

Moving slowly and gently, Shimada worked his cock all the way into Yoshi's body and then began to fuck him in short pulses, gradually lengthening his thrusts. At one point he hit Yoshi's sweet spot and had to hold the thrashing, sex-crazed teen down so he didn't tear his delicate tissues. Nevertheless, with a writhing, moaning young man in his arms, Shimada didn't delay either of their orgasms much longer. Reaching between them, he put his hand with Yoshi's to stroke the kid to climax, just an instant before Shimada drove his cock in to the hilt and came with a heartfelt, grateful moan against Yoshi's neck. "Thanks," he panted. "Oh God, thank you so much."

Yoshi, panting and barely recovered from his own orgasm, kissed Shimada's temple and hugged his shoulders. They lay like that, breathing each other in, wordlessly loving, until Yoshi's muscles relaxed enough for Shimada to pull out. Shimada rolled onto his back and sighed; the trip to the bathroom was always the toughest part of sex.

Although Yoshi could tell Shimada was extra tired that night, he felt no remorse about the sex they just had. "Hey, I'll do that," he said pushing Shimada down and carefully removing the condom. He disposed of it in the bathroom, where he took a moment to clean himself up, and came back with a warm towel and wiped his ejaculate off Shimada's chest, and took a few gentle swipes at Shimada's limp cock. As gentle as Yoshi was, this caused Shimada to twitch a little. "Sorry."

"It's okay," Shimada said, sleepily. "Just sensitive from your hot sexy lovemaking."

Yoshi leaned down and kissed him softly. "That sounded really stupid," he said.

"But my heart is true," Shimada mumbled, half asleep.

Not disturbing his tired lover with a snappy come-back, even if he had one, Yoshi got up and put the towel to dry in the bathroom. He came back to a completely conked-out Shimada. Curling around his sleeping lover, he began to doze off himself. Musing on their lovemaking, which had been sweet and carefree and, yes, even hot and sexy, Yoshi thought back to Shimada's homecoming that night and sensed that something was bothering his lover. But, since Shimada preferred to make love rather than talk about his problems, Yoshi figured it was something that could wait until the morning.

The last thing Yoshi felt as he drifted off to sleep was Flounder making himself comfortable in the narrow space between their bodies. His last waking thought was that Flounder would never learn from all the times he'd had to scramble out from between them on amorous mornings, which was what Yoshi hoped for tomorrow. Luckily, they'd never crushed their cat, but they had annoyed the cranky feline more than once and more than a little.

Yoshi woke up late with Flounder meowing for his breakfast. He fed the cat and rushed through bathing and breakfast. Shimada kept pace with him, suggesting that they'd save time if the showered together. This didn't save any time, but it was a lot of fun.

"Hey, what was bugging you last night?" Yoshi asked as they hurried into the streets of Nagasaki.

"Oh, nothing."

"Oh, something. I could tell when you came in," Yoshi persisted. He watched one of the buses he usually took take off.

Shimada sighed, figuring he'd better get it over with. "I saw Seiji yesterday."

"What?!"

"Calm down." Shimada raised his hands, but didn't touch him. "He tracked me down at the magazine and we shared a cab ride to the airport."

"What did he want?" Yoshi asked.

"To say hello," Shimada said calmly. "We were close once–"

"Close?"

"Very close, and now he wants to be friends," Shimada said blandly.

"Friends? Just friends?" Yoshi asked intensely. "That's all he wants to be with you?"

"Well, baby, that's all he's going to get no matter what he wants," Shimada said, watching a bus come and go with Yoshi rooted on the spot, not even noticing it. "He's not in love with me any more than I'm in love with him. He belonged to Takashi even before I left Tokyo. So, honey, don't worry."

"I'm not worried. You loved him once–"

"I love you more," Shimada insisted.

"I love you, too. Tell me again why you broke up with him?" Yoshi asked.

"My mom was sick, she asked me to break up with him before she had surgery," Shimada said by rote. He'd said it to himself enough times to have it down pat. "I was going to get back with him when she got well enough to withstand the shock of me leaving the family–"

"You would have left your family for him?" Yoshi said; it was obviously the first time this fact had registered.

"Yes, and I did, sort of anyway, when I left Tokyo," Shimada said patiently. "That visit from my brother was the first contact I've had with any of my family since I left. And, you know, Yoshi," he continued, watching another bus go by. "I might have to take formal leave of my family over you, so don't be so shocked that I was willing to do it over Seiji."

"But–"

"But, what? I love you, I want to spend the rest of my life with you," Shimada cut him off. "And, by the way, I'm not on a tight schedule today. Like, I'm not the one who's going to be late for school!" He stared hard at Yoshi.

Yoshi stared back equally hard, and then slumped. "Tsk, okay, you win," he mumbled, pouting.

"I love you, Yoshi," Shimada said, smiling at his profile. "More than anyone, okay?"

Yoshi blushed. "Okay, I love you more– Oh! There's my bus! See you later!" he said, and darted off.

"Yeah, later, darlin'," Shimada thought, watching him go. He caught the next bus for Ikoma's office.

"How's Perspectocity?" Ikoma said by way of greeting.

"Flourishing," Shimada said, looking through his mail. Two readers loved and hated the same story; now, there's some diversity. "Don't you ever talk to your cousin?"

"Often, but he brags constantly," Ikoma said, leaning back in his squeaky chair. "I need to ask a newspaper man to get the straight scoop."

"It's flourishing and we need more writers," Shimada said, not sitting down. "It's got more ad revenue than you can shake a stick at, but I'm keeping the ad page to text page ratio low and driving the ad rates up."

"My cousin is right. You're a genius," Ikoma said.

"And a vicious one at that." He walked out on Ikoma's laugh.

It was too early to call Takashi at Shimada Miyagi, so he drank coffee and worked on a culture feature he'd thought up in Tokyo: Tokyo artists in Nagasaki. Now if only he could find some. He made a note to call the gallerist he'd interviewed earlier in the year. She seemed like the kind of person who'd know who and where they were. It would also be nice to chat with her over a good lunch. Lunch! Something he'd forgotten how to do in Nagasaki, but was rediscovering in Tokyo.

At eleven o'clock he called Shimada Miyagi and asked for Takashi Okamoto. When asked, he gave his name as Junichiro Tanizaki.

"Mr. Tanizaki, how interesting that you have the same name as Ryuu Shimada's favorite author," Takashi said when he got on the line.

"And your receptionist isn't very well read," Shimada shot back.

"Yeah, well, the office manager doesn't hire them for their reading habits," Takashi said, relieved and grateful that Ryuu's literary code had prepared him for whatever his old rival had to say. He could never understand what Ryuu saw in "The Makioka Sisters." Takashi was more of a Yukio Mishima man himself. "To what do I owe the honor–?"

"Cut the crap, Takashi, you know why I'm calling," Shimada snarled, remembering how much this slick bastard annoyed him. "So why is your boyfriend ambushing me at my office?"

"Fuck if I know, Ryuu," Takashi snapped back, cursing himself for letting Ryuu rile him so quickly. "Something about being friends with you. What did he tell you?"

"Same thing. He wants to be friends, I don't mind being friends, but not if you and he are on the rocks."

"We are very very very happy," Takashi said firmly. "I'm sure I have nothing to worry about if you and Seiji are friends."

"Well, that's very very very good, Takashi" Shimada drawled. "Very big of you, too. As you must know, there's someone new in my life."

"Yoshi, isn't it?"

"Of course you know that from my brother's stalking us," Shimada said coldly. "Don't you think he looked like Seiji? I was struck by the resemblance."

Takashi stared at the phone in horror. "Uh...no, not at all, but I only saw a photograph."

"He looks just like Seiji in High School."

"I only knew Seiji at university, Ryuu, and this is a weird conversation," Takashi said.

"Really? I was just warming up to it, but if you must go..."

"I must, I must, but congratulations on your award, and I do have a question," Takashi said, almost laughing. This was the old Ryuu, slightly odd in that he could find amusement or beauty in off-kilter or even ugly things most people passed by. This made him a good ad man, but a better journalist.

"Thank you, and what's your question?"

"You know how thorough your brother is, so I got a pretty good picture of your life in Nagasaki, your job, what a fine young person Yoshi is, his nice family, how happy you are, but there was one thing Daitaro's operatives couldn't suss out," Takashi said.

"Which was?"

"Your cat's name." There was silence on the Nagasaki end of the line. "Ryuu?"

"Our cat's name is being suppressed to protect it from the glare of publicity. I'm hanging up now." And he did.

Takashi leaned forward on his desk smiling, then he frowned, then he smiled again. Then he went off to a meeting with executives from a perfume company who were not nearly as witty as Ryuu Shimada. And this was a tremendous relief for Takashi.

Eventually, and with Seiji's gracious assistance, Shimada found an apartment cheap enough to support him and Yoshi in while the kid devoted himself to graphic design school. Yoshi had found the school on the internet and Shimada had visited and approved of it. Although Perspectocity paid well for a small-but-growing magazine, it still wasn't enough to live in Seiji and Takashi's neighborhood even if Shimada wanted to. Takashi had even pitched in with the apartment hunt, but all he knew were high-rollers who'd never set foot in the district Shimada and Yoshi would be living in. Seiji, on the other hand, worked with many borderline-impoverished clerks who knew all the cheap but reputable neighborhoods. As a thank you, Shimada sent a huge box of candy to Seiji at his office and took him and Takashi out for lunch.

"When do you move in?" Takashi asked over miso soup.

"Next month," Shimada said. The couple seemed to be waiting for him to go on, so he did. "Then Yoshi comes up here after New Year. I'll spend Christmas with him in Nagasaki and get whatever there is left finalized. He's been very organized, even talked the landlord into letting us out of our lease without too much agony."

"Is Yoshi a Christian?" Seiji asked.

"Nah, but everyone does something special on Christmas," Shimada said. "Don't they? What do you two do?"

"We went skiing last year," Takashi said, with a smile at a happy memory Shimada couldn't work up enough bad humor to begrudge him. "And the year before–"

"We went to some ostentatious party for your work that year," Seiji said, frowning. "And it was a drunken, disgusting nightmare."

"Which is why we went skiing last year," Takashi said wryly.

Successfully suppressing a laugh, Shimada nodded sympathetically. "Yeah, those ad client parties can get rough," he observed. "What will you do this year?"

"Go skiing again," Takashi said and then brightened. "Why don't you and Yoshi join us?" Seiji's eyebrows shot up in surprise, but he smiled so Takashi went on. "You'll be our guests, I can easily get another ro–"

"Thank you, Takashi, but Yoshi and I really will have to tie up loose ends in Nagasaki over Christmas," Shimada said firmly, but not unkindly. "But we'll invite you over when we get settled in January."

Takashi and Seiji graciously said they'd look forward to it and thanked Shimada for lunch. And peace reigned over Tokyo that week.

Shimada moved into the little furnished apartment in an unfashionable neighborhood and went about settling in as much as he could without Yoshi there. The fact that Yoshi would be there in less than a month gave him something to look forward to. Otherwise, Shimada worked long hours at the flourishing Perspectocity, shopped for housewares not included in the rental and cat supplies for Flounder. He made plane reservations to fly down to Nagasaki on Christmas Day and fly back with Yoshi and the cat on New Year's Eve. Seiji and Takashi decided to be back in Tokyo for New Year's Eve to spend it with Ryuu and Yoshi.

Grudgingly, but graciously, Shimada accepted a ride for himself, Yoshi and Flounder from the airport to their new place from Seiji and Takashi.

"Are you sure you won't regret it?" Shimada asked.

They said no, they were disinclined to go to any of the parties they were invited to, especially the Shimada Miyagi debauch, and they wanted to welcome Yoshi to his new home in Tokyo.

"Why are you being so nice? Guilt?" Shimada asked them over a quick lunch near the Archives. Seiji's schedule was a little more rigid so Shimada and Takashi met him in a shopping district near his office on weekdays.

"We're friends again, and this is fun?" Takashi suggested.

"Of course!" Seiji was less tentative. "It's great having you back in Tokyo. I can't wait to meet Yoshi and your cat, what's the cat's name?"

"Oh, look at the time!" Shimada managed to derail the conversation, grab the check and make a gracious exit before he had to refuse to disclose Flounder's name.

Things were going so well, Shimada didn't want to jinx it by visiting his parents. But it was his opinion that when things were going well it was the best time to do difficult chores. And seeing his parents might be tough. He hadn't really had any direct contact with them in two years, they probably knew he was back in Tokyo and were annoyed that he hadn't visited them yet. Well, he would schedule his visit close to Christmas Day when he would have Yoshi to cheer him up after it.

A weekday late morning seemed safe enough: Daitaro would be at work, Daitaro's horrible wife and two sons would be occupied elsewhere, so no chance of running into them. Shimada's parents liked peaceful mornings so they scheduled appointments for the afternoon and early evening hours. Having thus carefully laid his plans, Shimada felt great confidence as he rang the doorbell of his childhood home on Christmas Eve morning.

His father opened the door, looked stern but ushered him into the living room. His mother was less composed: she cried out his name and flung herself into his arms. This softened his old man up and he exchanged smiles with his younger son. "So, you're back, I see," the elder Shimada said.

"Yeah," Shimada said, prying his mother off him. They talked about their health for a while; his mother assured him that she was completely recovered from her hysterectomy, his father was still walking several miles a day, but Shimada had long ago figured out that that was to get a break from his mother. It was a relaxed, almost normal conversation after a period of familial stress. As far as Shimada was concerned it was a complete success. Shimada even had the patience to hear what elite private school his horrible nephews had gotten themselves tossed out of lately.

"So, how's Daitaro's magazine working out for you, Ryuu?" his father asked pleasantly.

"Daitaro's magazine...?" Shimada was nonplussed.

"You know, dear, Perspectocity," his mother said, she looked so happy. "We've read every issue since you started writing for it. We're so proud of you!"

Shimada turned his full attention on his father. "What do you mean by 'Daitaro's magazine'?" he asked in a flat voice. "Masao Naganuma owns it."

"Yes, yes, Daitaro doesn't own it, but since you won your award, he's been pouring money into it," his father said, slowly and carefully because all the color had drained from his son's face. "Didn't you know?"

Shimada's knees buckled and he fell heavily on them. "Oh my God, why is he doing this?" he appeared to be asking God directly because he had his eyes screwed shut.

"Dear, he said he wanted you to move back to Tokyo," his mother said, leaning forward in her chair, but unable to reach him.

"Why?" Shimada asked, eyes still closed, but he was aware that his father had knelt down and was supporting him on one side.

"Um, I–" his father began.

"So you'd leave all that silliness in Nagasaki behind and get married," his mother said, as if this were a great idea.

Shimada opened his eyes. "Silliness?" He frowned into the middle distance and then sighed. More composed, he looked from his smug mother's face into his concerned father's face. "What have you got against gay people?" he asked.

"Nothing really," his father admitted. "I kind of liked Seiji."

Unasked, his mother yelped, "I want more grandchildren!"

"You do know you just canceled each other out, don't you?" he asked, continuing to address his father.

"That's marriage for you, son," his father grunted as he helped him to his feet. "What are you going to do now?"

"I'm not sure, but, dad, I am sure of one thing." Shimada clapped his father on the shoulder. "If you liked Seiji, you'll like Yoshi, too. And hopefully someday mom will get over it." Ignoring his mother's outraged squeak, Shimada bowed deeply to his parents and left their home.

Once in the street, he found his way to a park he'd played in as a child. He called Takashi's cell phone. "Did you know?" he demanded when Takashi picked up the call.

"Know what?" Takashi said neutrally.

"That Daitaro's been funding Perspectocity to lure me back to Tokyo?!" There was silence. "Takashi?"

"Hold on, Ryuu," Takashi said. Ryuu could hear him moving and then, "'Have you been funding Perspectocity to lure your brother back to Tokyo?'" There was a brief muffled answer, then Takashi said, "This is the meanest or second meanest thing I've ever seen you do, Daitaro. Excuse me.'" More silence and then a door closing. "Ryuu?"

"Still here," Shimada said, sitting on a bench by the deserted sandbox. "He didn't deny it, did he?"

"He's fucking proud of it!" Takashi yelled, furious. "I'm sorry he's your brother, but I'm glad he's not mine."

Shimada thought that didn't make much sense, but was essentially positive and supportive. He drew a long breath and sighed. "Oh fuck."

"What are you going to do?" Takashi asked, sounding calmer.

"I don't know, but I can't keep working for that bastard now that I know what's going on," Shimada said in a hollow voice. "In a few days, the apartment in Nagasaki is gone, I've got a year lease on the one here, Yoshi's enrolled in school here...oh God, what a huge fucking mess."

"Ryuu, if there's anything I can do—"

"I'll need a job when I get back," Shimada said, his voice firming up. "Writing, editing, but not in advertising. Say hi to Seiji for me. I'll see you on New Year's Eve at the airport."

The next call Ryuu made was to Masao Naganuma to quit his job. After that, he turned his cell phone off. If Yoshi called, he'd call him back, but Yoshi knew he'd be home in the next day, so Yoshi, who hated talking on phones, likely wouldn't call. Everyone else could go to hell.

When Takashi came out of the broom closet, Daitaro was waiting for him. "He's hysterical, right?" the elder Shimada brother asked.

"Not really," Takashi said coldly.

"You're hysterical."

"No, but I'm upset about this," Takashi admitted. "I was hoping we could live in peace now, but you're not past trying to run your brother's life."

"He's not doing such a great job, Takashi," Daitaro said, coolly examining his fingernails. "I did him and that stupid rag, Perspectocity, a favor. And is it appreciated? No, hell no. It's not easy being a nice guy around here."

Takashi slumped against the broom closet door and briefly considered just going back into it. But their new designer dress account clients were just getting off the elevator, so that option was out. "What?" He'd not heard Daitaro's question.

"I said, did Ryuu say what he was going to do?"

"Uh, no, no, he didn't," Takashi said, hoping he sounded convincing. "Hey, boss man, we're on." He smiled charmingly in the direction of the reception area.

But Daitaro was fumbling with his cell phone. "I'll be right there," he said.

Not that he was listening, but before he was out of earshot, Takashi heard Daitaro say in a deeply shocked and hollow voice, "He quit his job on Christmas eve?" And this almost made Takashi laugh. Nonetheless, it did make it easier for him to smile through the meeting with Daitaro, who seemed slightly dazed.

Shimada's trip to Nagasaki was uneventful. He continued to ignore his voice mails and text messages. There were several from Seiji and Ikoma, but none from Yoshi, so he didn't bother to look any further. Yoshi's welcome home kiss was as warm and sweet as ever. "I have no future, but my present is unbeatable," Shimada said sadly to himself. Over Yoshi's shoulder, he made eye contact with Flounder, who almost seemed glad to see him. "I hope you still feel that way on New Years Eve after a plane ride to Tokyo, buddy."

"Mr. Ikoma came by this afternoon," Yoshi said, taking Shimada's coat and bag.

"What'd he want?" Shimada sat next to Flounder on the couch.

"To talk to you." The kid sat next to him and started petting Flounder in a distracted way. "He said he'd try to get in touch with you in a day or two." He looked up from an annoyed cat that he was petting too hard. "Did something happen?"

"Yeah." Shimada sighed and figured there was no point in avoiding the inevitable. "I quit Perspectocity yesterday–"

"You–?"

"–because Daitaro was financing it," Shimada continued. "It was a trap to get me back in Tokyo. I guess everyone thought I'd leave you here in Nagasaki." He looked up, expecting to find emotional devastation before him, but there was the usual loving smile, maybe more so.

"I never thought that," Yoshi murmured, snuggling into his arms.

"Neither did I, but there are certain parties in Tok–"

"Who? Seiji?" Yoshi sat up and demanded. He was a charming combination of fierce and cute like that.

"Ah, no," Shimada said. "This is something Daitaro cooked up for my parents."

"How do you–?"

"I went to see them yesterday and they thought I knew Daitaro was financing the magazine's rise to fame or whatever," Shimada said. "I think my father might be okay with me being gay and happy instead of miserable and more miserable. My mother remains firmly entrenched in the pro-heterosexuality camp."

Yoshi sighed and leaned back into Shimada's arms. "I guess we'll work it all out in Tokyo."

"Yosh, it's not going to be easy," Shimada said. "I don't have a job, a few contacts, but it's still going to be rough. It might be better–"

"What might be better?" Yoshi was frowning again.

"If you stayed here."

"Then they win," Yoshi spat and tried to get up, but Shimada restrained him. "Let me go."

"Yoshi, just give me a little time—"

"Like you said to Seiji?" Yoshi stopped struggling, but Shimada had already let go of him.

"I..."

"I'm not going to let you go, Ryuu," Yoshi said, almost coldly. "I'll do whatever I have to do to stay with you. I can work, I don't have to go to school, I even got a little money from my uncle for graduation." He named a sum that would cover a little over a month's rent in Tokyo or a few months of groceries if Shimada would take his money, which he wouldn't. "I can't go back to being the way I was before I met you. I won't go back to that." He leaned his head against Shimada's shoulder; he was shaking but not crying.

Shimada put his arms around him, but inside he was very still and felt like crying. "I can't go back to the way I was before you, Yoshi," he said when he thought he could control his voice. "You brought me back to life."

"You brought me back to life, too," Yoshi said, smiling only with his eyes. "I was so lonely, so empty before you loved me."

"It'll be rough in Tokyo," Shimada said. "But we'll work it out."

"As long as you're with me, Ryuu, I can do anything," Yoshi said, hugging him.

"Sorry about your school."

"Oh, it's okay," Yoshi said, looking around for Flounder, who'd made a hasty exit when the yelling started. "Maybe there are scholarships or grants or something to help pay for it next year. Don't worry." Locating the cat sitting by the kitchen, he patted his leg for Flounder to come to him. "Oh, but don't tell my family what happened when we visit them this week, they'll freak out."

"I wasn't planning to tell anyone on our round of good-bye visits," Shimada said, staring at the unmoving cat. "Ikoma must know, but everyone else can find out someday in the distant future when we've hit the big time."

"Hell, yeah!" Yoshi gave him a big wet kiss and then looked at Flounder again. "What's wrong with that cat?"

"It's dinner time, isn't it?"

"Daitaro, Daitaro, Daitaro," Seiji chanted as he paced their suite in Niseko. "He's like a curse Ryuu can't shake off." Takashi hadn't told him what had had happened with Ryuu until they were in the air on their way to Sapporo. Seiji had been wondering why Ryuu wasn't returning his calls, but hadn't a clue what a disaster Daitaro had orchestrated for him. They'd been traveling most of the day, this was the first time they'd been alone in a quiet enough place for Seiji to vent about it.

"Yeah, this is pretty bad," Takashi said neutrally. He was surprised at how well Seiji was taking it all.

"They are still coming to Tokyo, aren't they?" There was some agitation behind this question, but Seiji was still very calm.

"It sounded like it," Takashi said, tired, bored and starting to get hungry. "He said he'd need a writing or editing or both job, but not in advertising."

"Do you–?"

"I might, I put out a few feelers before we left." Takashi looked at his watch. "But quitting all of a sudden like that isn't going to look very good. People will want to know why and few people will understand the situation. Most of Tokyo would love to have and would do anything to have Daitaro as a sugar daddy. It's just going to look odd, Ryuu quitting a flourishing magazine like that."

"Yeah, well, I–" Seiji looked up helplessly at Takashi. "We won't let them starve!"

Takashi put his arms around his lover. "Nah, we won't let them starve," he said. "Or live in the streets or–"

"Don't joke," Seiji pouted.

Takashi kissed him. "But speaking of starving..."

"Eh?" Seiji opened his eyes.

"It's dinner time, isn't it?"

Tokyo

On the afternoon of their flight to Tokyo, Yoshi did something that impressed Shimada very much. He mixed Flounder's tranquilizer with a little caviar left over from their pre-New Year's Eve celebration. This was the celebration they knew they couldn't have on the thirty-first. It had involved having sex all over their soon-to-be-former apartment and, at one point, Yoshi licking caviar off Shimada's nipples. It was, in fact, rather amazing there was any caviar left at all. So Flounder was down for the count when Yoshi gently laid the grey kitty on the blankets from their bed comfortably arranged in the crate.

Unfortunately, the Kitty Quaaludes had worn off by the time their luggage was unloaded in Tokyo and a howling, yowling cat carrier came rattling down the luggage carousel.

"Oh, there they are," Seiji said, indicating with his chin because he was too polite to point.

"That must be the cat with no name," Takashi observed dryly.

Introductions were made, cat and luggage collected, Yoshi and Seiji looked each other over pretty carefully, but with Flounder carrying on like his world was ending—and maybe it was—there wasn't much conversation on the ride into town.

"Poor kitty," Seiji said, once they were in the new, small one room-plus-kitchenette-plus-bath apartment. "What's your cat's name anyway?"

"Don't tell them," Shimada said intensely. "Privacy concerns," he added vaguely when Yoshi wanted to know why not.

More worried about Flounder's mental state than his identity, Yoshi had bigger things on his mind. "Oh, boy, he's gonna freak," he said to Shimada. "Did you get a catbox? I don't see one."

"I got one," Shimada said, taking Seiji and Takashi's coats.

"And litter?"

"Yes, dear."

"And cat food?"

"Yes, dear," Shimada said. "Seiji made sure the cat would be well taken care of."

Takashi laughed and put his arm around Seiji. "It became a mission with him."

"It did, I even did some research," Seiji said, gracefully disengaging from Takashi and opening the closet door. "I put the cat box in here, so your cat can hide in a safe and comfortable place until he gets used to the new smells. That's what the webpage said cats go on, um, smells to acclimate."

"Huh," Yoshi said, setting the cat box in the closet. "Let me get some water and dry food for him." After provisions were placed within easy reach, Yoshi opened the cat carrier door. Flounder wouldn't be coaxed out, so Yoshi left the carrier door open, left the closet door slightly ajar for air, and bowed deeply to Seiji and Takashi. "Thank you very much for all your help and support," he said politely.

"Yes, thank you both," Shimada murmured, also bowing.

"You're very welcome," Takashi said equally politely and everyone bowed again.

"But, Ryuu," Yoshi said, looking innocently into his face. "Why can't these nice people know Flounder's name?"

"Flounder? Like the fish?" Seiji asked, delighted. "That's perfect!"

"Or like the verb?" Takashi asked, trying to see what was so perfect about it.

"I think there's a journalist trapped in your ad man body, Takashi," Shimada said blandly. "Only Ikoma has ever asked that question."

"It's like the fish," Yoshi said to Seiji, ignoring their boyfriends. "Speaking of fish, I'm starving. Can we get some food?"

Takashi insisted on paying for the Chinese food take-out order but Yoshi won his bid to pay the delivery person's tip. Shimada had put a couple of bottles of champagne in the refrigerator before he left, so they were able to toast the new year like civilized people.

"To Ryuu and Yoshi." Takashi proposed a toast. "Welcome back to Tokyo!"

And although their future in Tokyo was uncertain, Shimada and Yoshi felt it was a little brighter for having at least two friends to make a happy start of it.

It took about a week for Flounder to come out of the closet, but Yoshi and Shimada were too busy to do more than make sure he had food, water and a clean catbox.

Following up on several journal and newspaper leads from Ikoma took up most of Shimada's time. As Ikoma, blameless and deeply shocked by the Perspectocity mess, had warned him, the word was out that Shimada had abruptly quit what was considered one of the hottest jobs in Tokyo publishing with an up-and-coming magazine and everyone in publishing who cared about such things were looking at him for signs of insanity. Perspectocity had been a mediocre magazine before Shimada's brief editorial tenure; many editors were wondering if it would maintain its excellence or fade back to what it was. This especially was on everyone's mind since there was also a rumor that

Perspectocity's funding had dried up with Shimada's departure. This made Shimada a figure of much speculation and a certain amount of suspicion. Still, he managed to cobble together enough free-lance work to cover the survival basics for his little household.

For Yoshi, things were a little simpler. He went to the vocational school he'd hoped to enroll in first thing after the holiday and, apologizing profusely, de-enrolled. But then came the argument over his deposit, which was small, but every yen counted in those lean days. The argument at the cashier's office became quite heated and drew a small crowd, more than three-fourths supporting Yoshi's right to have his deposit back. The other quarter just wanted to make a payment or be reimbursed and had no opinion. Eventually, the cashier gave up fighting with Yoshi and referred him to the Business Manager one floor up. Yoshi bowed in what he hoped was a very arrogant manner and turned to flounce out, but ran smack into a little man wearing a large camera. "Sorry," he murmured hoping he didn't look too stupid.

"Oh, not to worry, I wanted to speak to you."

Yoshi looked up warily and the man snapped a picture. "Hey..."

"Sorry, sorry, my turn to apologize. My name is Shinobu Kurogane, I teach photography here part-time." The man offered Yoshi a sweaty nicotine stained hand that the kid didn't shake too long or too hard. Kurogane had a short frame, bad posture and a pot belly. But he had a nice smile that Yoshi automatically returned with his own shy one. "I think I might have a job for you," Kurogane said, passing a hand over his thinning grey hair and smiling.

Some strange and muted warning bell went off in Yoshi's gut. He considered walking away, but, in fact, as Kurogane had probably heard, he needed a job and badly. "What kind of a job?"

"Let's step out in the hallway, too many bodies in here," Kurogane suggested. "Or perhaps a cup of tea?"

"Sorry, no time, I'm on a tight schedule," Yoshi said as briskly and politely as he could. "And I–"

"Ah! I understand, then let me tell you where the job is," Kurogane said pleasantly with a touch of amusement. He went on to give Yoshi the address of a cheap clothes store in a shopping district not far from the school. Many of the school's students bought their clothes and accessories there, and Kurogane took the shop's advertisement pictures. "The owner's a cheap bastard, but tell him I sent you." Kurogane gave Yoshi a business card. "His name is Norboru Fugiwara and don't let him pay you less than." Kurogane named a sum that seemed high to Yoshi, but according to Shimada, everything was higher in Tokyo." And good luck." Kurogane gave him a fatherly pat on the shoulder and went off down the hall. Bells were ringing and there was a general migration in the same direction as Kurogane had gone. Yoshi felt a pang that he wouldn't be roaming around this school, sitting in classrooms and learning graphic design. But he had other pressing things to do, so he shrugged off his pang and went up one flight to reason, beg, or battle with the Business Manager to get his deposit back. He, Yoshi Katayama, was a special case and he would be victorious.

As it turned out the Business Manager had better things to do than argue with a determined teenager, so he wrote a voucher for Yoshi's deposit and the cashier grudgingly paid it. Yoshi took it as a good omen and went to the cheap clothing store where he was promptly hired, mainly for being cute and because they were horribly shorthanded just then. He began working that very afternoon.

Around nine that night, he got a call on his cell, but he was so busy, he had to let it go to voicemail. He wasn't able to check it until there was a lull half an hour later. It was Shimada wondering where the hell he was. "I got a job! The store closes at ten, so–"

"Where is this job?" Shimada asked. "Hold on, I'm writing it down. I'll be there to walk you home, you're too short to be roaming around at night by yourself."

"Heh, sez you," Yoshi laughed. "Wow, more customers! See you later!"

Shimada got to the cheap clothes shop a little before ten and was brusquely told they were closed. "I'm not here to buy," he snarled back. "I'm here to walk Yoshi Katayama home."

"Hey, dingleberry! Close the shutter! It's closing time! Let's go!"

From where he was standing, Shimada couldn't see who was yelling, but the clerk could and yelled, "Yes, Mr. Fugiwara!"

"And who's that? We're closed! Get out!" A scrawny old man came out on the mezzanine and stared down at Shimada, who stared back at him.

"He's the new guy's bodyguard," the clerk said, running off into the cavernous store.

"Bodyguard, eh?" Fugiwara snorted. "I guess he's cute enough to need one." He looked around the vast floor of his establishment. "Hey, Yoshi! Your bodyguard's here! Go home! You can learn to close tomorrow!"

Yoshi came out of the maze of shelves and smiled brilliantly at Shimada. He had his coat, so they headed for the door. Shimada put his arm around the kid's shoulder as they went out. Behind him he very faintly heard Fugiwara say, "Bodyguard, huh?" and punctuate it with a snort.

"What kind of place is that?" Shimada asked when they were on the street. After the overheated maze of the store it felt good to be in the open air again.

Yoshi shrugged. "Just a shop, I guess. I've never done retail before."

"That guy seemed nuts–"

"Which guy?" Yoshi asked.

"The one yelling from the balcony," Shimada said.

Again, Yoshi shrugged. "I only talked to him for five minutes and he hired me. That was lucky, right?"

"I hope he doesn't get the wrong idea," Shimada grumbled.

"About what?"

"About you. And stop shrugging."

Yoshi stopped mid-shrug and laughed. "He seems okay," he said. "And if not, you can beat him up. He's only more than twice your age." He smiled up at the noncommittal noise Shimada made. "But isn't this lucky I got a job so quick? Aren't you glad?"

Shimada pulled him closer. "Very." Listening to Yoshi's day, Shimada was by turns pleased that he got his deposit back from the school, somewhat alarmed by the photographer Kurogane's forwardness, and intrigued by the chaos of the cheap clothes store. "Sounds like a madhouse."

"It was and there was a huge delivery, so I spent part of the day stocking shelves," Yoshi said.

"What are they paying you for all this?" Shimada asked.

"Oh...I forgot to ask."

The next day, Yoshi was soundly teased about his "bodyguard" and told what his hourly wage was. It was the minimum sum Kurogane had advised him to negotiate. Shimada said that sounded all right, and when he showed up to walk Yoshi home, he got a warmer welcome than the night before. Cries of "The bodyguard! The bodyguard!" rang through the store, and Mr. Fugiwara didn't bother to make an appearance. Shimada was relieved that this part of their life was settled. Yoshi wouldn't bring in a lot of money, but he would be busy and not have time to brood over how much Shimada was working.

On nights when Shimada was working, he sent Takashi to walk Yoshi home. The building that housed the SM offices was two train stops away from the shopping center; many of the clerks from the building went over for the cheap restaurants and shopping, so it was not inconvenient for Takashi to work late and then walk Yoshi home. Seiji often joined him on these jaunts, which were pleasant. Takashi didn't get as warm a welcome at the shop as Shimada usually did, but he was impressed by the camaraderie of the place. Yoshi had merely smiled at his naiveté since it was obvious Takashi had never had a job anywhere near a cheap clothes store in his life.

Although he liked being walked home by Shimada, Yoshi really thought it was stupid that Shimada asked Takashi to walk him home. Yoshi was too polite to complain to Takashi, he informed Shimada that nothing ever happened and that he, Shimada, was just being a mother hen. Then one night Takashi couldn't make it so he asked Seiji to walk Yoshi home. The whistles, kissy noises and calls of "Kitty!" "Baby!" "Cutie!" were almost deafening. Yoshi and Seiji exchanged nervous looks.

"I guess because it's Friday..." Yoshi said.

"Ah," Seiji answered looking around nervously.

"Here kitty kitty kitty!" Their path was blocked by a middle aged drunk.

On the verge of flight, Seiji and Yoshi were startled by a voice behind them.

"Oh, there you are, Yoshi-kun!" An elderly man stepped between them and the drunk, who lost interest and wandered off.

"Oh, Mr. um, I forgot your name," Yoshi fumbled, shaking from the adrenaline rush.

"Kurogane," he said and bowed to Seiji, who nervously bowed back. "You know, there's a bus not far from the shop."

"This has never happened before," Yoshi said.

"Thank you for the rescue, Kurogane-san," Seiji said, and Yoshi chimed in with his belated thanks.

"You're very welcome, but you could have easily gotten away from him," Kurogane said with a smile. "I'm glad I was here, let me walk you to the bus." When they were in a better lit part of the shopping district, Kurogane asked how the job was going.

"Really well," Yoshi said.

"Fugiwara thanked me for sending you," Kurogane said. "Ask him for a raise next week. He should be in a good mood by then."

"Oh, why more then than now?" Yoshi asked.

"I'm working on some ads for him," Kurogane said. "That's why I'm down here, we're meeting to discuss the photos for the project. He's always in a better mood when ads are running and business is flooding in."

"It's pretty crazy now," Yoshi said.

"Well, in a shop like that, survival depends on volume," Kurogane said sagely. "Fugiwara's been in business a long time, he knows what sells, but the volume can never let up. Ah, here we are."

"Thank you very much," Seiji and Yoshi said with cute bows.

"Now, next time it's just you two, turn left out of the front door of the shop and there's a bus stop two blocks down," Kurogane said. "That bus will take you to where you can get this bus. It's a little out of your way, but much less annoying than walking by those dark bars and shops."

Yoshi assured him that they could get the bus by themselves, but Kurogane waited until they were on the bus before he left. This bus required Yoshi and Seiji to take a circuitous route and change to another bus to get within three blocks of Yoshi's building. "We were closer at the bus stop but I didn't know how to tell Mr. Kurogane that and I didn't want him to walk us all the way here."

"He was a nice old bird," Seiji said with a smile. "Thank goodness he was there."

"I guess we're really that cute," Yoshi said, and, now that the danger, real or imagined, was over, they had a good laugh about it.

Seiji declined a cup of tea and Yoshi waited with him until his taxi came. Back upstairs, with Flounder purring in his lap, Yoshi decided that he and Seiji could have handled the situation, but it was nice that Mr. Kurogane had been there to rescue them. And after explaining the alternate bus stop situation, Shimada agreed that Yoshi could get home on his own when Shimada wasn't there to walk him home, and it was worth the price of the bus fare.

Although this new arrangement relieved Takashi of his escort duties on nights when Shimada couldn't get there, it didn't stop him from showing up occasionally to take Yoshi to lunch, which was nice of him and nice for both of them. They had very little in common, but Yoshi was a good listener and Takashi liked to talk, so Yoshi got to hear more about Daitaro and the Shimada-and-Seiji break up than Shimada ever told him. This wasn't why Yoshi never mentioned these lunches to his lover; his lover was far too busy for idle conversation and when Shimada was home and not completely exhausted, Yoshi preferred making love to talking.

The days eventually got warmer and Mr. Fugiwara bought several pallets of cheap ugly nylon pajamas in garish colors. The clerks got used to them, but customers coming upon the pyramid display shied away from them in alarm. Fugiwara then deployed them all around the store in hopes that if they looked unusual or unique, they might sell. They didn't sell, and they didn't sell, and they didn't sell, and the store became minutely quieter, something Fugiwara blamed on the pajamas. There were too many to dump, no one to dump them on, and this was probably why he'd gotten so many for a song. But refusing to admit it was a bad buy, Fugiwara went on the offensive. He photocopied some home-made flyers and sent out his cutest clerks to hand them out in the shopping district. Unfortunately there was a picture of the pajamas on the flyer and, cute as they were, the clerks were hard pressed to get anyone to even take a flyer, let alone come to the store and buy anything. The next day there were ten percent off stickers to put on the flyers, but still no takers. On the third day, Mr. Fugiwara was out of the store, but left strict orders that the flyers were to be handed out as usual. Yoshi decided a little marketing was in order; possibly some of Takashi's advertising talk had worn off on him. He put on a pair of the least ugly pajamas in a size too large and marched bravely into the mid-day lunch crowds with his flyers.

The effect was positive: Yoshi handed out a lot of flyers and got a lot of compliments. He even ran into Takashi, who was on his way to offer Yoshi lunch.

"Why are you wearing pajamas?" Takashi asked, nonplussed.

"The store has to sell them." Yoshi handed him a flyer. "Come buy some."

Tentatively reaching out to feel the sleeve material, Takashi frowned. "What's this made of?"

"Plastic," Yoshi said, handing flyers out around the ad man. "You don't have to wear them, just buy them and throw them away or give them away. We're desperate people, Takashi, the boss will have us out here forever if some the these PJs don't sell soon."

Takashi began to laugh helplessly. The thought of Yoshi roaming around in pajamas forever handing out flyers was absurdly funny. "All right, all right," he said when he could control himself. "I'll buy some pajamas, but have lunch with me first."

"In these pajamas?" Yoshi asked. "Forget it!" He had to raise his voice because a crowd had formed and unfortunately he was out of flyers. The sudden interest in pajamas was acute and had a slightly dangerous feeling to it. Yoshi edged closer to Takashi for whatever protection that might afford him.

Luckily a familiar voice rang out from the middle of the crowd. "Now, now, folks, there's some nice young men over yonder you can get flyers for these very pajamas from. Not, however, the ones Yoshi-kun is wearing." Mr. Kurogane and his camera edged into the center of the crowd and the onlookers began to disperse.

They dispersed even more when Mr. Fugiwara caught sight of Yoshi in pajamas and started yelling. "What the hell are you wearing those pajamas for?"

"Hey," Takashi said, sounding pissed off.

"Now, Norboru, this is brilliant," Kurogane said to the enraged shopkeeper. "Didn't you see that crowd?"

"I'm going to see those pajamas taken out of your next paycheck, Katayama!" Fugiwara yelled. "Believe it!"

"I'll buy the goddam pajamas he's wearing," Takashi said, furious. "How much are they?"

"Oh, I don't have a flyer," Yoshi said, somewhat dazed by all the emotion around him. "They're ten percent off with the flyer."

"I'll pay retail," Takashi said, and handed Yoshi enough cash to cover the purchase and walked briskly away.

"I–" Yoshi began, but Takashi didn't turn back so he just put the money in the pajama chest pocket.

Another clerk came up and gave Yoshi more flyers and Kurogane winked at him as he led the still fuming Fugiwara away.

"Don't worry," the clerk said. "He blows up like that when he doesn't know what to think."

"Oh yeah?" Yoshi handed a flyer to a couple of kids.

"Yeah, he'll be fine when he cools off," the clerk said, handing out a few more flyers. Yoshi was attracting another crowd, so there really was no better place to be handing out flyers at the moment. "But you'll still have to buy those you're wearing."

"Oh, I guess," Yoshi sighed. "I have gotten them kind of sweaty."

When they ran out of flyers they went back to the shop where there was a smallish pajama-buying riot in progress. Yoshi didn't even have time to change back into his street clothes.

Things had subsided to the normal shop chaos by the time Shimada showed up to walk Yoshi home. "And why are you dressed like that?" he asked.

"Only to sell a lot of pajamas," Mr. Kurogane said behind them. He waved a stack of photographs at Mr. Fugiwara, who came down from his aerie to join them. "This is the best one," Kurogane went on, handing a photo to Yoshi. "But these three will be in tomorrow's throw-away paper."

"What?" Yoshi asked.

"May I see those?" Shimada asked and Kurogane graciously spread the dozen prints out on the counter for his perusal.

"When we got back, there was a reporter here looking for Norboru to ask about Yoshi," Kurogane said proudly. "So I rushed to my studio and printed up the best of the lot."

"Isn't this Takashi?" Shimada asked, tapping a glossy print. Yoshi nodded.

Mr. Kuragane went on. "Was his name Takashi? He seemed like a nice young man. That one and the two next to it will be in the paper and these others will be in ads and posters and–"

"And did you sign a release and get paid for all this, Yoshi?" Shimada asked bluntly. When Yoshi said, "No," Shimada turned to stare hard at the photographer and shop owner.

"He owes me for those pajamas he's wearing," Fugiwara said sourly. "That can be his fee."

"Oh, come now," Shimada said. "You both know you can't do any ads without his agreement. I suggest–"

"I suggest we talk about this in my office," Fugiwara said. Ushering Shimada and Kurogane up to the mezzanine, he yelled at the clerks to close up and go home and for Yoshi to put some damn clothes on.

It wasn't a long wait for Yoshi, but a nervous one. However, Kurogane and Shimada came down stairs smiling, so he relaxed a little. He tucked his sweaty pajamas under his arm and walked out with Shimada and Kurogane.

"You drive a hard bargain, Shimada-kun," Kurogane said when they were in the street.

"I think Fugiwara-san was tired and willing to negotiate, Kurogane-san," Shimada said with a polite bow.

"And you had us over a barrel," Kurogane laughed. "Thank you for being so kind to two careless old men."

"They're good pictures," Shimada said, sounding tired. "I hope they bring lots of business to the store. And you," he said, turning to Yoshi, "are to stay out of pajamas during business hours."

"Yes sir," Yoshi said sheepishly.

"Fugiwara sold a lot of pajamas today," Kurogane said, smiling. "So I'm pretty sure the flyer promotion is over. He'll let the press and the ads do the rest."

They said good evening and Kurogane left them at the first big intersection.

"He's a funny old guy," Shimada said when Kurogane was out of sight.

"He's nice, he sent me to apply for a job there," Yoshi said.

"He got some nice shots of you," Shimada said, drawing the one of Yoshi and Takashi out of his pocket. "Even Takashi looks nice. What was he doing there anyway?"

"Getting lunch I guess," Yoshi said innocently. "His office isn't that far, sometimes he comes down and has lunch with me."

"Well, that's interesting," Shimada said. "And how often does that happen?"

"It's only happened three times."

"And why didn't you tell me?" Shimada asked.

Yoshi shrugged. "I never thought of it when I saw you," he said simply. "But I'll try to remember next time." He looked up at Shimada, who narrowed his eyes but didn't say anything. "Did you make a deal with Mr. Fugiwara and Mr. Kurogane?" Yoshi asked when the conversation didn't pick up again.

"Oh, yes, actually I did." Shimada handed him some bills and explained that the ads could only run for a week for that amount and he'd get the same if they ran again. "No more promotional pictures without a deal, Yoshi, just say no. Oh, and by the way, you get to keep those pajamas."

"Ah," Yoshi said, as he put the new cash in his pocket next to Takashi's cash. And then thought better of it. "Takashi gave me some money for the pajamas."

"What?" Shimada asked, and listened patiently to the scene in the shopping district. "Um..."

"I can give it back," Yoshi offered. "Or you can give it back."

"Oh, keep it, Yoshi, or give it back," Shimada said wearily. "Or you can buy him lunch next time. Be sure to tell him about tonight. Being in advertising, he'll enjoy it."

As it turned out, the Pajama Boy story was picked up by the larger Tokyo papers and ran for three days instead of the one Kurogane had predicted. Fugiwara and the photographer were euphoric, and remained euphoric even when Shimada twisted a little more money for Yoshi out of them. At least Fugiwara had good reason to be happy: between the press and some judicious advertising, the pajamas were selling like hotcakes. It was not lost on anyone that some customers came to the store to get a look at the famous Pajama Boy, but few recognized Yoshi in street clothes. He became the Mysterious Pajama Boy, and this brought even more people to the store. There was no consensus among the overworked clerks on whether Yoshi was a hero for helping sell the damn pajamas or a villain for bringing so many more people to the shop to buy the damn pajamas. But whatever the case, Fugiwara was easier to work for when stock was moving and the store was busy, so at least the cute clerks didn't have to hand out flyers anymore. It was agreed that the cute clerks were lucky the pajamas were selling because it was not impossible that Fugiwara would have forced them into pajamas to hand out flyers, and this was fortunately avoided.

The press and ads had a different effect on Daitaro. An avid headline skimmer and caption reader, he saw the photo of the Pajama Boy and some unnamed guy in a nice suit in his newspaper of choice

the second day of its run. He clipped the photo with its lurid caption—
"Locus of the Pajama Boy riots earlier this week"—and called Takashi
into his office. "If you're going to get your picture in the paper, you
might as well get your name there as well," he drawled at the
thunderstruck ad man sinking into an expensive desk chair before him.
"And, Takashi, if you're going to sneak around with my brother's
boyfriend–"

"Sneak around? What paper was this in?" Takashi asked in a
hollow voice.

"–I think you should do so when there are no photographers to
document it," Daitaro finished sourly because Takashi ruined his punch
line. "It was in the paper."

"Oh." Takashi fingered the clipping. "Can I have this?" he asked.

"No, I'm starting a scrap book," Daitaro said, taking the clipping
back. "It's today's paper, I'm sure–" he broke off to see if Takashi was
going to take the call on his cell phone; he didn't, so it probably wasn't
a client. "I'm sure you can get one downstairs at the newsstand. In
fact, I'll get you one." And he promptly sent his secretary to get three
copies of the paper. "How could you not know you were being
photographed?"

"You had to be there, Daitaro, but that line about the riot isn't far
wrong," Takashi said in a firmer voice. "It didn't get ugly, but it could
have."

"Ryuu's boyfriend–"

"His name is Yoshi."

"Yeah, Ryuu's boyfriend Yoshi is so cute people riot over him?
Excuse me, Takashi, but what the fuck is that about?" Daitaro asked.

Takashi laughed and then suppressed a yawn; Seiji had been
amorous the night before and Takashi made the most of it far into the
night. "Oh, I don't know, Daitaro, you had to be there. There was
something in the air, it was exciting and outrageous for a cute young
guy to be roaming around in public in the middle of the day in pajamas.
It was like a...a spontaneous flash mob or something. I'm glad it was
documented; it's an ad man's dream," he said. "Yes," he continued to
himself. "I'm glad and will be glad until I have to explain to Seiji and
Ryuu why I'm standing there looking like a hare in the headlights with
Yoshi looking incredibly cute...in pajamas."

"Just a dream or just a wet dream?" Daitaro asked, puncturing
Takashi's reverie.

"Just an ad man's dream, Daitaro," Takashi said, warming to the
subject. "Think about it for a moment: a loosely related group of
consumers spontaneously becomes focused on one thing—cheap

pajamas—they become obsessed with it, not because it's a desirable item—the fabric is vile—but because they feel they are part of a mob surge. Our clients spend millions trying to manufacture that kind of natural event. Yoshi-kun triggered one just being in public in pajamas."

"A riot?" Daitaro asked dryly.

"A consumer riot," Takashi shot back pleasantly.

"You do realize that this is why I pay you so much to think these things up?" Daitaro waited until Takashi finished laughing. "I wonder if he could do it twice."

"I couldn't say," Takashi said blandly. "He didn't know what he was doing, the circumstances were not optimal, and the mob build never quite got legs under it."

"Huh." Daitaro suddenly seemed bored by the subject. "Who called?"

"Seiji." Takashi rose, nodded pleasantly and left the room. He picked up a copy of the paper from Daitaro's secretary and called Seiji back. Seiji had not seen the paper, but was calling to remind Takashi that they were going out to dinner that night. "I'd rather stay home with you and turn in early," Takashi said in a sultry undertone.

"Okay, let's do that instead," Seiji said cheerfully. "I can't stand those people anyway."

Takashi spent the next part of his morning tactfully extricating himself and Seiji from the dinner party at his second cousin's home. They'd only been invited as a courtesy, so no hearts were broken because they couldn't attend. Takashi used the usual excuse to wriggle out of it: Seiji wasn't feeling up to it. If anyone ever added up all of Takashi's excuses, Seiji would appear as glamorous an invalid as Elizabeth Barrett.

The pajama ads were slightly less successful, mainly due to the candid shot nature of the photos. Consumers were accustomed to slicker, cooler photography for their fashion products. Because only a little over half of the massive pajama stock was sold, Mr. Fugiwara decided to part with a little more money and have Kurogane do some real pictures for a new set of ads. This was a sensible decision because if people came in for pajamas, they might also buy other things. Fugiwara was also big and generous in letting Yoshi do the photography session on company time. Shimada was extremely annoyed that Yoshi was not only being taken advantage of like this, but was allowing himself to be taken advantage of like this, and that there was nothing Shimada could do about it at that time.

"I don't know what pajama models make, Yoshi, but I'm very sure it's more than what Fugiwara pays you an hour," Shimada said when Yoshi and Kurogane got to the store as it was closing. "And no more pictures until I get you a better deal." Yoshi nodded but remained silent; he and Kurogane seemed subdued. "What the hell is wrong with you, two?" Shimada demanded when the wordless brooding became too much.

Kurogane cleared his throat. "We didn't get any good pictures tonight," he said. "And Yoshi did his best, but he's not a model."

"I could have told you that," Shimada said bluntly, but put a protective arm around his not-a-model boyfriend. "How bad was the shoot?"

"Bad, but it's too dark here to show you prints," Kurogane said.

"Well, I just got paid, so let's go in this bar and have a drink," Shimada suggested. "If you'll be my guest, Kurogane-san."

Kurogane-san said he would be delighted, and soon they were huddled around a fairly well lit table looking at the pictures. Shimada's inner ad man surfaced to note that there were better set and lighting arrangements for shooting this particular product—the pajamas—but that the problem really was Yoshi, who had no idea how to project through his eyes. Yes, he was cute, but his gaze bounced off the lens instead of penetrating and seducing the viewer. This was something most models worked hard to learn and a few were freakishly blessed with, seemingly from birth, and so not something a sweet normal kid like Yoshi would know how to do. At least the non-ad man part of Shimada was glad Yoshi wasn't a natural model. That would have creeped him out. The natural models he'd worked with in his horrible ad agency days were narcissistic to the point of sociopathy. It would have been a bad shock to find that in the man he loved. Shoving his inner ad man back into a dark crevice in his psyche, Shimada, the normal guy journalist, said. "You're cute, Yoshi, but you're not a model."

"I know, I just feel like I let everyone down," Yoshi said, or rather, slurred, as he knocked back some more sake.

Shimada and Kurogane exchanged looks, and mentally took stock of how long they'd been talking to each other about the photos relative to the diminished level in the sake bottle of which they'd only had two drinks each.

"Yoshi, are you smashed?" Shimada asked, dividing the rest of the sake between himself and Kurogane.

"No-oo," Yoshi said, swaying a little, but staying upright.

Kurogane chuckled. "Ah, but it is late," he said. "Thank you very kindly for the sake and pleasant company. And Yoshi-kun, you're not letting anyone down. Fugiwara and I asked you to try something new and we appreciate that you tried your best for us."

As he paid the bill, Shimada thought that was a very nice thing to say, much better than that Yoshi had tried and failed. He would remind Yoshi of Kurogane's tact and kindness when the kid sobered up. As it was, Yoshi was too smashed to walk properly, so Shimada had to carry him piggy-back. "Good thing he's skinny," Shimada observed to Kurogane as they ambled down the street.

The night was mild, like a spring night should be. Kurogane had hoped to capture the softness of spring and youth in the pajama pictures, but whatever spontaneous magic Yoshi had possessed the day before was stunted in the studio. It was a shame, really, the shots of Yoshi looking away from the camera were almost useable, but didn't quite hit the mark. Kurogane was mulling over what he was going to do about the ads when he glanced over at Shimada carrying the sleeping Yoshi and was thunderstruck.

"What?" Shimada asked, looking around.

"What do people do in pajamas?" Kurogane asked, unable to hear his voice over the roaring in his ears.

"Lots of things," Shimada said, adjusting Yoshi, who mewed, but didn't wake, on his back. "Is this a trick question?"

"They sleep in them!" Kurogane cried. "Shimada-san! Please let me take more pictures of Yoshi, in pajamas, just like you and he are now, please!"

"Now? He's hardly in any shape—"

"He doesn't have to do anything but wear the pajamas and pretend to be asleep!"

"Who can sleep with all this noise," Yoshi grumbled. "Put me down. Please." Adorably mussed and rumpled, Yoshi stood slouching but upright and steady. His eyes were closed and there as a shadow of a weary smile on his lips.

Shimada looked away from this vision to find Kurogane equally enraptured with it. "Where's your studio?" he asked, looking at his watch.

"Not far," Kurogane sighed and led them there.

The shoot finished just shy of dawn. Shimada's back protested from carrying pajama-clad, relatively-sober Yoshi around the studio and then through a pocket park near the train and on certain well-lit streets around it. Kurogane was a one-man-show and didn't have a very elaborate or portable lighting set up, so they had to rely on flash, available light, and one spotlight on a tripod. Shimada's back got a break when Kurogane had Yoshi lay on park benches, or stand on subway platforms. Many of the photos had Shimada standing or seated nearby reading a paper or, in one shot, holding an umbrella over the sleeping Pajama Boy. As dawn was starting to break and the trio was too tired and elated to think straight, Yoshi leaned wearily into the shelter of Shimada's arm. And this was the shot on which Fugiwara spent money buying the back cover of a weekly give-away magazine. It and the half a dozen other ads brought so much business into the store, the pajama stock was gone very quickly. Fugiwara was so pleased, he thanked Yoshi for all his hard work. He didn't give him any more money than Shimada had originally negotiated, but he did thank him most sincerely.

"I should not have agreed to that late night shoot without getting an agreement in place first," Shimada said when Yoshi handed over the pittance from Fugiwara. "I'm sorry."

"Oh, it's okay," Yoshi said, snuggling into his arm. "Kurogane-san was so happy, that made it worth it."

"Yeah, but are we stupid or what?" Shimada laughed. "We kill ourselves so that old burnout can be happy. He did get some great shots, though."

"Yeah," Yoshi agreed. "And he was all lit up and happy during the shoot. I've never seen him like that."

"He was being an artist."

"What?"

"I've only seen it a few times because most artists work alone or in small groups away from the public eye," Shimada said thoughtfully. "But that night, I could see that old Kurogane-san still has a little of the artist spark or magic or blessing or whatever. That's why I couldn't really be a bastard and say no." He looked into Yoshi's smiling face that was shining with love.

"That's because you're a nice guy, Ryuu," he said.

"Shhh, that information is supposed to be heavily suppressed," Shimada said, and spent a long time thereafter pressing his mouth on Yoshi's.

The Pajama Boy ads caused Kurogane's photography business to pick up. In addition to being quite busy with product and fashion shoots that spring, he was approached for ads by a mid-sized manufacturer of casual wear, including pajamas, and they were adamant that they must have the same model as the other pajama ads. Kurogane had been a photographer for a long time, although he'd never really mastered the business end of it. But he felt Shimada was on his side and asked Yoshi if his boyfriend would help him.

"Ohhh, Kurogane-san, he's on a story in Vietnam for a week,"

Yoshi said sadly, but then brightened. "But I know someone else who could help us!" He whipped out his cell phone and called Takashi, who said he'd be delighted to work on the deal. His fee was that Yoshi be his and Seiji's guest for a celebratory dinner even if the deal fell through.

On his way out to lunch, Takashi mentioned to Daitaro that he'd be leaving early the next day.

"Really? Why? Meeting your mistress?" Daitaro asked.

"I haven't the time or inclination, Daitaro," Takashi said, waiting for the inevitable next question.

"Well, if not that, what pure and boring thing will you be doing?" Takashi told him. "Really? This Pajama Boy thing is really catching on. Who's the company?"

"Nagato Fashions."

"Never heard of them," Daitaro said, losing interest.

"They're pretty far down the food chain," Takashi admitted. "But your brother's out of town, so I'm pinch hitting for him."

"What an interesting choice of words," Daitaro said, getting interested again. "Want me to come with you and help out?"

"No."

"I could cut this deal with my eyes closed," Daitaro went on, warming to the subject. "My secretary could cut this deal over the phone."

"Daitaro—"

"And I could art direct!" He clasped Takashi's arm. "It would be the pajama campaign of the century!"

"No."

"Oh, please let me come with you tomorrow!"

"No."

"Please?"

"No."

Shimada came home from his journalist travels to an empty apartment, after being kidnapped at the airport by his editor's minion and held hostage at the newspaper until he'd finished his story. And that was okay because the paper moved the deadline up and needed it an hour ago. Then he was dropped at his apartment, the humble apartment he shared with the adorable Yoshi, who was not home. But this was also okay because Shimada needed a shower and wanted a nap. He found the yukata in the closet and felt glad to be home, and that even if Yoshi wasn't there now, he would be eventually, and that was a nice feeling, too.

Flounder seemed glad to see him and not even hungry as Shimada noted he had dry food and plenty of water on a placemat in the corner of their tiny kitchen. The mat was a glossy plastic oval with a non-skid backing with a cartoony fish on it that Seiji had given them a few days after he learned the cat's name was Flounder. Yoshi had been very pleased, but Shimada had felt a small pang that it somehow locked Flounder into a noun at the expense of the verb. He hadn't felt this pang was worth extensive examination, but he had silently acknowledged Flounder's lost ambiguity nevertheless. Although Flounder's weight on his chest wasn't lost on Shimada, it didn't affect his ability to fall into a deep sleep.

The door didn't wake him, but Yoshi's soft kiss did. Shimada was dimly aware of Flounder's annoyed meow as he was driven off the bed by Yoshi, who was crawling into bed with his lover, and gently sighing, "Welcome home."

"Yeah, I wish I wasn't so tired," Shimada sighed, laying on his back, stroking Yoshi's hair, feeling Yoshi's erection against his thigh, and wondering if he was up to a sixty-nine. It wasn't that Shimada thought he couldn't get it up, or at least get Yoshi off, but that it wouldn't be much good for either of them. But any sex is better than no sex, so-

"Oh, just lay there," Yoshi said cheerfully. "I'll do everything."

Shimada momentarily wondered what he meant, but was reassured when, after a preliminary blowjob, Yoshi slid a condom on Shimada's erection and lubed it. "Oh, let me do that at least," Shimada said, putting a little lube on his fingers and sliding them inside Yoshi and gently stretching him. "Ready?" he asked.

"Yeah..." Yoshi positioned himself over Shimada's hips and eased himself slowly onto his lover's cock. He arched prettily as he hit his sweet spot and then shivered with pleasure when he hit bottom. Even more so when Shimada began to gently pinch Yoshi's nipples. And even more when Shimada began to stroke him in the rhythm of his own movement up and down on Shimada.

"We're not going to last very long like this," Shimada panted before he lost the ability to speak.

"Good!" Yoshi practically wailed this as he flung himself down the length of Shimada's manhood one last time and came with a pent up kittenish roar.

Deeply impressed and nearly as crazed, Shimada held tight to Yoshi's hips and came himself, arching off the futon. He flopped back down and pulled Yoshi into his arms, stroking the shaking kid's back and kissing his neck.

Somewhat awkwardly, because they seldom did it in this position, Yoshi removed himself from Shimada, then he removed the condom and went into the bathroom to dispose of it. He came back with a warm damp towel and cleaned his come off Shimada's chest. "Thanks," he said, curling into Shimada's arm.

"Oh, no, Yoshi," Shimada said over a yawn. "Thank you! That was most impressive."

"I had a week of missing you," Yoshi said, and cuddled closer.

"And I you, baby," Shimada smiled into his soft brown hair and sniffed. "Is this a new shampoo?" he asked.

"No, the stylist used some gloop on my hair for the shoot," Yoshi said sleepily. "I'm doing more ads with Kurogane-san."

"That's good," Shimada said, feeling his second wind, and rolling on top of Yoshi for a nice long kiss that segued into other things.

"A stylist?" Shimada asked over breakfast. "Fugiwara sprang for a stylist?"

"It's a different company," Yoshi said. He was hurrying through dressing and breakfast because, although his libido loved it, sex that morning had thrown his schedule off.

"Which one?" Shimada was still in his yukata and very mellow from sex that morning.

"Nagato Fashions," Yoshi said, collecting his keys and rifling through his shoulder bag.

"Never heard of them," Shimada said, frowning slightly that Yoshi got a new modeling job while he was away. He wasn't sure why it bothered him, but it did. "Who are–?"

"Here's a copy of the contract," Yoshi said, fishing it out of his bag and kissing him firmly. "I'll be home by six!" And ran out the door.

Shimada ran after him. "Who negotiated this!?" he yelled down the stairwell.

"Takashi!" Yoshi yelled back.

"Well, this gets more interesting by the second," Shimada thought as he poured another cup of coffee and settled down the read the Takashi-negotiated contract with Nagato Fashions.

It was, unsurprisingly, a simple and well-written contract and brief enough to read while waiting for the train to his next assignment. Yoshi would be available for five hours over three consecutive days of shooting in Tokyo. He would be paid what Shimada thought was a modest, but reasonable amount. Nagato would be allowed to choose ten to fifteen shots for advertising and catalogue purposes. Yoshi would receive a flat sum for the catalogue photos and a small recurring sum for each advertisement use of his images for one year, which was fair because it was unusual for companies to reuse fashion adverts from last year's styles.

In spite of himself, Shimada was impressed with the contract and that Yoshi was smart enough to ask Takashi to negotiate it. He was further impressed that Takashi, who negotiated deals for gigantic national advertising campaigns, had been kind enough to take the time to help Yoshi. This bothered him slightly, in the same way Takashi taking Yoshi out to lunch behind his back, bothered him. "Well, not behind my back," Shimada admitted to himself while taking notes at a boring press conference. "I just wasn't around enough for Yoshi to run out of enough conversation or sex to be bothered to tell me. Yeah." He listened to a PR flak try to make a new building project sound more exciting than it was. "And I wasn't around when he needed help with the modeling contract, was I?" he asked himself. "I really shouldn't be suspicious of Takashi," Shimada went on, bored with the press conference but taking notes on autopilot. "He's already stolen one boyfriend from me, what would he do with another one?" The press conference broke up and Shimada found a quiet wireless spot to write up and send his story into his editor. Since he had a little time to kill before his next assignment, Shimada put on a happy face and called Takashi's cell phone. "I just wanted to thank you for helping Yoshi out," he said.

"Hey, you're welcome, but Yoshi already thanked me," Takashi said cheerfully.

"How did he thank you?" Shimada snarled into the phone in spite of his best intentions.

"Oh, relax, Ryuu," Takashi said pleasantly. "He thanked me and Seiji by inviting us over for dinner one night."

"Why is he thanking Seiji?" Shimada asked, surprised.

"Because there's no way he'd just ask me to dinner alone in your apartment and there's no way I'd have dinner with him alone in your apartment."

Takashi sounded a little too blasé to Shimada, who could not resist asking, "And why is that?"

There was a long sigh at the other end of the line. "Because I don't want to be your enemy anymore, Ryuu," Takashi said. "I know you're jea– protective of Yoshi and I really want to help if I can and not piss you off." There was a small pause in which Shimada allowed himself to feel guilty for thinking negative thoughts. "And you know there's only one thing I wanted more than to be friends with you at university."

"And what was that?" Shimada asked.

"Seiji." Takashi had to repeat the next bit because Shimada was laughing so hard. "And now that I've got him, and you're happy with Yoshi, can't we all just get along?"

"Yeah, I guess," Shimada was still chuckling. "But seriously, thanks for making my boyfriend a good deal with...with..."

"Nagato Fashions."

"Yeah, them," Shimada said, looking at his watch. If he hurried he could grab some lunch. "He could have gotten really scr– a bad deal."

It was Takashi's turn to laugh. "Yeah, well, I'm glad he called me for that very reason. Furthermore, I'm glad he had the smarts to call me. He's bright, Ryuu, too bright for what he's doing."

"I know, I know, as soon as I'm on my feet, he's going to school," Shimada said, following his nose to a food vendor. "That was Plan A, move here, Yoshi goes to school, I work for Perspectocity, and you know how that ended up."

"I know," Takashi said. "He loves you very much, Ryuu."

"I know, I'm doing the best I can," Ryuu said, paying for a sandwich. "So is he, and that extra money for the modeling is gravy, so just accept my thanks for the deal! Okay?"

"Okay! You're welcome!"

They hung up on a laugh and Shimada ate his sandwich on his way to interview an actress who was the new spokesmodel for a mid-priced line of perfume and cosmetics. This was an easy interview, one he could do in his sleep. It wasn't that Shimada was uniquely qualified to interview this woman about perfume and cosmetics, it was just that shallow people seemed to like to pour their hearts out to him and this got his employers some astonishingly good copy to sell ads on.

Yoshi's Nagato Fashions ads of the Pajama Boy in their pajama line ran in mid-size fashion and leisure magazines aimed at middle-class women. Takashi took pains to remind Yoshi to get tear sheets from Nagato's art department. Even so, Takashi and Seiji collected two copies of each publication they could find and tore the ad pages out for Yoshi. It wasn't that Yoshi was lazy or stupid; he was simply clueless and way too busy. He also had no reason to be building a portfolio since he didn't think modeling was going to be much of a career for him.

At that time Yoshi was still working for Mr. Fugiwara and taking little modeling jobs here and there. A quick study, he'd learned enough from Takashi to haggle on a small scale, which was the kind of thing he and Kurogane were able to get. Mostly it was pajamas, but occasionally it was kimonos, casual wear or overcoats once. He took part of his fee as new overcoats for himself and Shimada.

"Well, no matter how threadbare we get," Shimada said, knotting the belt on his London Fog knock-off. "At least we'll look spiffy when it rains."

This remark made Yoshi smile, but Shimada could not fail to notice that it was an awfully tired smile. "Honey, why don't you cut back your hours at Fugiwara's shop when you have modeling jobs?" Shimada asked. "I mean, you made almost as much in a few days modeling as you did in a week at the shop."

"I would, but I'm scared he'd fire me," Yoshi said. "Or just not give me many hours so I have to get another job. We need the money and, well, I don't know if there'll be much more modeling. I'm not very good at it and the pajama thing was a fad and it's over. I think."

"Eh, maybe it was a fad," Shimada agreed. "But you were getting better at it."

"Really?" Yoshi brightened a little.

"Really." Not that he wanted to say it out loud, but Shimada was glad Yoshi's modeling career was winding down. His sweet, adorable Yoshi was becoming a better model: somehow he had learned or discovered in himself the ability to seduce the camera. Although most of the pajama ads had Yoshi feigning sleep so his eyes were closed, Shimada had begun to notice something highly disturbing to him: whether Yoshi's big brown eyes set in his pointed little face were gazing at the camera or closed with his jet eyelashes brushing his cheek, hit the viewer in the gut and made them want to buy whatever was for sale. Yoshi was vibrant and luminous even with, or in spite of Kurogane's mediocre photography. As much as Shimada loved and trusted him, he really didn't want Yoshi to become an object of some anonymous consumer audience's voyeuristic desire. Shimada had worked for too long with too many empty shells who took great pictures onto which equally empty shells could project their psyches and buy shit. This was the great horror of advertising as practiced by modern media and popular culture. The art of the sell had very little art or heart in it. And this was the last thing Shimada wanted to happen to Yoshi. "You'll get more rest if you don't model so much," he said vaguely.

"Yeah, I didn't know it takes a lot of energy to model. The money's good though," Yoshi said and then yawned. "And I was feeling more confident in front of the camera."

"Yeah..." Shimada's agreement was tepid, but he heated up when Yoshi suggested they go to bed early.

Daitaro had no friends, but he did have people who were useful to him and to whom he was, when he was so inclined, useful as well. That day he was having lunch with Iori Shirane, the president of a smaller ad agency, Shirane Normura, to whom Daitaro had jettisoned Shimada Miyagi's less desirable clients—soap peddlers, feminine hygiene purveyors, bottom-end upscale casual wear, suchlike—on SM's rise to being the premiere influence-peddling mind-fucker in the advertising jungle. Daitaro believed in watching his back, so he made a point of having lunch with old Iori now and then, just to see who was competing with SN and might be coming up on SM's ass. After all, SM was once as pathetic as SN, and had taken out the former premier influence-peddling mind-fucking ad agency just above them to get where they were now. And should some young hotshot ad man or woman end up at SN, Daitaro would want to know such a thing so he could steal him or her for SM. Advertising was a jungle, and Daitaro intended to stay at the top of the food chain. And if this meant a boring lunch with old Iori in a good French restaurant a few times a year, it was a price that must be paid.

According to Iori's droning on and on, there was no new talent at SN worth stealing. Daitaro listened with half his mind on whether he should have dessert after lunch and later tonight demand anal sex from his wife. She hated it, but could be bribed. This led to Daitaro mulling what kind of expensive trinket he could barter with when the words "pajama boy," coming out of Iori's mouth got his full attention.

"This damn client wants those kind of sleepy Pajama Boy ads and I just don't get it," Iori was whining. "I mean, what's the selling point in that?"

"It's the idea of taking those pajamas off the boy, you senile idiot," Daitaro thought, but continued to look like he was listening sympathetically.

"How the hell can you sell clothes someone is sleeping in?" Iori went on. "What the hell are these people thinking?"

"Who are they?" Daitaro asked oh-so-casually and wasn't surprised Iori acted like he hadn't heard him. Never give your client's names away if you want to keep them. He tried a safer question, "Where did they see those ads?" Daitaro had seen them, but he'd sought them and the others out. He'd assigned a secretary to use a fake name and call Kurogane's studio for a list of new ads every week to keep an eye on Yoshi's minuscule and diminishing career. There had only been a few new ads recently and only one was for pajamas. Yoshi was becoming a better model, but he'd be eaten alive in the Tokyo modeling scene if he tried to stay in it. He'd have been thrashed already if Takashi and Ryuu weren't protecting him. The vision of Yoshi, abandoned by his husband and his knight, being sodomized by a tattooed yakuza boss flitted across his inner eye and left a pleasant afterimage. But it gave him an idea of how he could screw Ryuu, Yoshi and, to some extent, Takashi, and get away with it. "Why does it have to be a sleeping pajama boy?" he asked when Iori rattled off the names of the magazines Yoshi's pajama pictures were in. "Why couldn't it be, say, a tennis playing pajama boy, or piano playing pajama boy, or dancing or sprinting...running...yes, hell yes! The Running Pajama Boy! Look, Iori, I don't exactly get the sleeping pajama boy thing myself," he lied. "But see if your people can find a decent model, one who can work with his eyes open so he can see where he's running, then set up some shots of him being chased by hordes of, of, of, whatever! Chased by teenage girls, teenage boys, salarymen, punks, thugs, soccer teams, samurai, whatever, you know, like the Beatles or the Monkees used to be chased in public places. Even today, I bet if Paul McCartney or Micky Dolenz put on a pair of pajamas and started running down the streets of wherever they are, hordes of fans would chase them. Don't you think?"

"That's brilliant, Daitaro," Iori said in a stunned voice. "Why are you giving it to me?"

Daitaro resumed his bored and lofty sneer. "We don't handle pajama ads at Shimada Miyagi." He hailed he waiter. "Check please."

"Well, that's interesting," Takashi said when Seiji shoved the first Pajama Pursuit ad under his nose.

"They're stealing Yoshi's idea!" Seiji was glaring at the glossy two page ad of a cute young man in pajamas being chased by a flock of salarymen with briefcases.

"I think it was Kurogane's idea, actually," Takashi said soothingly, hoping Seiji was going to stay calm about it. "And this pajama boy seems to be awake."

"I hate advertising." Seiji threw himself onto the couch and patted the cushion next to him.

Observing that Seiji's rage had derailed or at least swerved onto some emotional siding, Takashi gratefully sat next to his lover and put his arm around him. "These are nice ads," he said neutrally.

"They should be of Yoshi," Seiji pouted. His anger dispersed and was replaced with sorrow.

"There, there, Seiji. Maybe these ads will get Yoshi more work," Takashi soothed. "If he wants it. Last time I talked to Ryuu, he said Yoshi was tired of modeling."

"When did you talk to Ryuu?" Seiji asked. He hadn't seen Ryuu or Yoshi in weeks.

"He called about a week ago, asking if I could confirm a rumor about that rabble-rousing politician he interviewed last year," Takashi said. "You know, the one that caused the disturbance in Osaka."

"What rumor?" Seiji asked. He'd read about the disturbance in Osaka, but hadn't thought any more about it since.

"That the politician was trampled to death by a flock of sheep in Hokkaido," Takashi said. "I could confirm it, yes, explain it, no."

"I take it that politician wasn't a client of Shimada Miyagi," Seiji ventured.

"No, but his opposition was," Takashi said darkly.

"The sheep?"

Takashi looked down at Seiji in his arms to confirm the intention of his impish tone. Seiji gazed back at him with love, humor and compassion, all the things Takashi had fought so hard for and he felt peaceful and optimistic again. "No, not the sheep," he said with a chuckle. "What's for dinner?"

"Damned if I know."

Although he never said a word about the other pajama boy ads, Yoshi had to have seen at least one of them on the billboard near Fugiwara's shop. Coincidentally, this billboard was near the very spot the original pajama boy had transfixed Takashi with his pajama-clad charms. The original pajama boy went about his life as he always had, deeply in love with his boyfriend and exhausted by his demeaning job. Yoshi had shrugged off so much hurt in his short life, what, really, was so horrible about being passed over for a major ad campaign? After all, he hadn't invented the Pajama Boy, or maybe he had, but he certainly didn't have a patent on it. Or something.

Shimada was less sanguine, but kept his opinion of the new pajama boy to himself lest he rub any more salt into Yoshi's wounds, even if Yoshi wasn't acknowledging those wounds. Covering the opening of a new megahotel on Maui when the Pajama Pursuit ads first came out, Shimada heard about the ads before he saw them. He got an earful on the subject from Seiji, but what could anyone do about them? Shimada finally had enough, "Seiji, you're running up my cell bill over nothing," he said. "Bitch at Takashi about it, but get off my phone." He knew he'd have to apologize for that later, but he wanted to run up some charges by calling Yoshi, who cheerfully said he missed him, to come home soon, and that he had to get back to work. Deciding to take a page out of Yoshi's book, Shimada cheerfully got back to work and finished his story in time to catch an earlier flight. At Tokyo airport, he bought one of the magazines Seiji had been raving about and there, lo and behold, was a slick, fucking brilliant two-page ad of a cute boy in pajamas being chased by a pack of crazed salarymen. Being a journalist, and unlike most consumers who would merely feel strangely compelled to buy a pair of these pajamas, Shimada didn't shy away from the logical next question this photo scenario posed: What if they caught him? What would this pack of men do with the scantily clad cute boy they were chasing if they caught him? "Whoa, that art director should get some counseling," he muttered, and threw the magazine away before he got home to Yoshi, who was continuing to behave as if he'd never heard of the new pajama boy, or pajamas or advertising or running or anything connected with the subject.

"You want me to do what?" Shimada asked the skinny editor standing in front of him a few days after he'd gotten back. He'd just finished a stupid story about a new line of sneakers for a cheap weekly teenybopper magazine with high circulation that paid obscenely well and he was eating a bowl of noodles to celebrate, or mourn, the brain cells such a story had cost him and the big check he could look forward to for it. And now this. "You want me to interview the Pajama Boy?"

"Yup, and layout needs the art and story by dawn for the next edition. I'll pay you double the usual rate." The skinny editor was such a kid, his voice broke on the last word. But he was a kid with money, so his voice could do whatever it wanted as far as Shimada was concerned. "Here's the rundown and where you can find him tonight," the editor went on, handing Shimada a folder. "It's a shoot, so you'll have to get him on breaks, but you're good at that. I've read your political stuff. You get people to say weird stuff by catching them off guard. We want the raw pajama boy for the next issue."

"The raw pajama boy," Shimada murmured, opening the file. "I hope I'm up to it." He skimmed the first page. "And by dawn...I can do this. Especially for double pay."

The editor smiled smugly and sauntered off in the direction of another victim, i.e., another decent, overworked, but well-paid journalist who needed the money.

Shimada finished his noodles and headed for a cybercafe far enough from the magazine offices that he wouldn't run into anyone he knew there. He emailed Seiji to scan half a dozen of the best of Yoshi's pajama boy pictures and email them to him. Then he set a mouth-watering scene of a midnight meeting with the original Pajama Boy, Yoshi Katayama, in a luxurious suite at the five star Hotel Sylvania, which Shimada had recently reviewed for an American travel magazine, completely paid for by the magazine. He'd had a suite, high definition TV, room service, a well-stocked mini-bar, whirlpool bath, a sauna, and Yoshi for an entire weekend. Just remembering it made him tingle all over again. But he was merely setting a scene for a heartfelt profile and an imaginary interview with the only Pajama Boy that mattered to him.

Ever a trouper, Seiji emailed six high-resolution tiff files of Yoshi's best Sleepy Pajama Boy shots to go with the interview, and a question: "And what are you up to, Ryuu?"

So engrossed in his beautiful fiction, Shimada didn't answer until after he'd delivered his story to the layout department in the wee hours of the morning and stayed, drinking coffee and shooting the breeze with the high-strung, over-caffeinated insomniacs who worked in production, until the issue was beyond recall, and then he replied to good old Seiji with two words: "You'll see."

Of course the kid editor hit the ceiling when he saw the article, but had to back down when it became that week's sensational fashion story. Who was this mysterious sleepy, dreamy cutie who claimed to be the original Pajama Boy and had such a condescending, but sweet, attitude toward the Johnny-come-lately hyperactive Pajama Boy? "I hope the poor thing doesn't wear himself out running all over Tokyo," was one much quoted line, and the other famous line, the one that elicited barks of laughter from readers was, "I sure hope they don't catch him."

This must have been galling to the Pajama Pursuit account manager due to the fact that the profile hit the streets the same time the ad with the other Pajama Boy being chased by mini-skirted school girls rolled out. The ads became a joke, but the word on the street was that Pajama Pursuit sleepware sales were steady.

Seiji and Takashi were elated. Shimada was as happy as his busy schedule would allow him to be. Yoshi was somewhat dubious about the whole deal.

"I don't remember giving this interview," he said, one morning when Shimada had been out all night on a story. Yoshi shook the dog-eared, week-old magazine a co-worker had given him at the exhausted reporter. His co-worker had been surprised Yoshi hadn't seen it. Poor Yoshi had had to pretend he'd forgotten about the interview because Fugiwara was working them all to death in the shop. So, on top of being overworked, never seeing his boyfriend, who was interviewing him in absentia, and this stupid subterfuge was making Yoshi a very cranky Pajama Boy.

"Honey, if you let me get some sleep, I'll have a nice explanation for you when you get home," Shimada said, falling on the futon.

"We're meeting Seiji and Takashi for dinner," Yoshi said, picking up his shoulder bag.

"I know, I know, I was planning to explain it before we got to the restaurant where they're celebrating it with us," Shimada said, fighting to keep his eyes open.

"I hope they're treating."

The bitterness in Yoshi's voice could have corroded iron and was not lost on Shimada. "Yoshi, cheer the fuck up!" he yelled. "Your sweet little face and pajama-wearing ass just kicked the shit out of a major ad campaign."

"You mean you did!" Yoshi yelled back.

"Yes! Yes! Yes! I did! And I loved every second of it! Thank you for being the one, true Pajama Boy so I could skull-fuck the ad industry with their own ego-sticks!"

"Wha-ha-ah-at?" Yoshi could barely get the word out for laughing.

"I don– oh fuck, I don't know." Shimada curled into fetal position. "Go to work, Yoshi, let me sleep before my guts implode. Or something."

Smiling, because he was unable to be angry with the man he loved, Yoshi leaned over Shimada and kissed his temple. "You crazy man, I love you," he sighed.

"...mmmm...alovyutoo..."

The silly argument had made Yoshi late, so he let the call on his cell phone go to voice mail. He'd check it on his break.

Shimada got to the restaurant on time, but Yoshi was late. "I don't know, maybe old Fugiwara made him work late," Shimada said, getting his cell phone out.

"Oh, there he is," Seiji said, returning Yoshi's wave.

"Sorry, sorry, I missed my train," Yoshi panted, leaning affectionately into Shimada's arm.

Takashi assured him everything was all right and the waitress led them into a private room, which impressed Yoshi very much. "We just want to celebrate you and Ryuu putting that upstart pajama boy in his well deserved place," he said, urbanely, and ordered lots of sake.

"Seiji helped," Ryuu said after the first toast to the one, true Pajama Boy. "He picked the best pictures for the inter–" Yoshi's huge eye-roll cut him off "–ah, for the profile."

"What?" Seiji asked, digging into an appetizer.

"Oh nothing," Yoshi said, sipping green tea and letting his sake cup go cold. He shot Shimada a wry look. "That interview was just so over the top. I sound so bitchy. But the pictures were great," he added hastily when Seiji's smile faltered.

"I didn't think it was bitchy," Seiji said quickly. "It was just, um, assured and, ah, actually, now that I think about it, it sounded more like Ryuu than you."

Shimada choked on his sake and Takashi began to laugh helplessly. "But the pictures were very nice," he managed to say between laughs.

"Has there been any reaction from the other side?" Seiji asked

Shimada, ignoring Takashi's giggling.

"From Kawazu, the other pajama boy? No, he refused an interview with the same weekly, so maybe he's pissed off," Shimada said with one last cough. "I'm told he gave a very bitchy interview to Moda de Mike that they wouldn't run."

"What an idiot," Seiji said dismissively and nodded to the waitress putting his food in front of him.

"There's been some industry reaction," Taksahi said, putting on his 'ad man' voice and then dropping it when Shimada scowled at him. "Some bullshit about dueling pajama boys."

"Kawazu...is that his name?" Yoshi asked, looking up from his own dinner.

"Yup, Koji Kawazu," Shimada said with a smile. "Feeling some kind of pajama boy species affinity?"

"Ha ha. Look, Ryuu, I–" His cell phone cut him off; he dug it out of his shoulder bag. "Sorry, I thought it was off. Oh, not that guy again."

"What guy?" Shimada asked.

"Oh, some guy that wants to do pajama boy ads," Yoshi said, sounding frustrated. "He saw the inter– the profile, and he's been calling me all damn day."

"How'd he get your number?" Takashi asked.

"He said he got it from the art director at Nagato Fashions," Yoshi said, between bites of his very good meal.

"Just great," Shimada growled. "Now every wacko in the city will be calling you. What the hell does this guy want?"

"He wants me to come to his studio tonight," Yoshi said.

"The nerve!" Seiji snapped.

"Yeah, he wanted me to come this morning," Yoshi went on. "Like I would, and then he said come later, and I said I had dinner plans, and he said come after dinner."

"Persistent bastard," Takashi said, sounding amused. "Who is he?"

"Kenzu Miya–"

"–guchi?" Shimada and Takashi finished in unison for him and let their jaws hang open as Yoshi nodded that, yes, indeed, that was the name.

"That's him," Yoshi said cheerfully. "Y'know him?"

"Unfortunately, yes," Seiji said, rubbing his temples. "Did you ever see the Morango sports car ads?"

"Of course! I really wanted one of those cars, and I can't even drive!" Yoshi said, intrigued.

"Kenzu was the account manager on that campaign," Seiji said, sipping some sake. "He stole it from Shimada Miyagi when he sent

Asia Bugatti over to fuck the director of that line at KSN Automotive. It was something I didn't think of, which is why SM didn't get the account, and I left advertising not long after."

"Seiji, no one couldn't have anticipated a move like that," Takashi said, putting his arm around him. "Except Daitaro and he didn't offer Asia enough money."

"Who's Asia Bugatti?" Yoshi asked.

Takashi and Seiji looked uncomfortable, so Shimada answered him. "She's a porn star who models occasionally," he said. "Nice girl, I think she's retired now."

"She got HIV," Seiji said flatly. "I read it in a magazine," he added when they all stared at him.

"Which is why you should never do anal without a condom," Shimada said blandly, and neatly dodged the plate the waitress nearly dropped on him.

"Especially if you're a porn star who does anal," Takashi added.

"Ever," Shimada said, drinking more sake and ignoring his dinner and the nonplussed waitress. "Always and ever, sperm in the rectum is bad for your immune system."

"You're going to leave that waitress a big tip, aren't you?" Seiji nervously asked Takashi after she'd gone

"Absolutely!" he assured him cheerfully, as he and Shimada raised their sake cups to each other. "And then I'm going to buy a gross of condoms!"

"So, baby, where did old Kenzu say to meet him tonight?" Shimada asked Yoshi a little too casually.

"He didn't say," Yoshi said, frowning a little at his boyfriend.

"Call him, ask him," Shimada said, pouring more sake for himself and Takashi. He looked up at the ad man. "Let's go see him." Takashi nodded with an evil smile.

"You two are drunk," Seiji snapped. "And I–"

"Oh, hi...yes, it's Yoshi, turns out I can come to your studio tonight...in half an hour?" Yoshi looked up and got nods from Takashi and Shimada and a worried frown from Seiji. "Sure, where is it?" He repeated the address so Shimada could write it in his reporter's notepad. Shimada wrote something on the pad and showed it to Yoshi. "Make it forty-five minutes, I'm, I'm farther than I thought...okay, thanks, see you." Yoshi ended the call and slumped a little, but he was smiling. "I hope you two know what you're doing," he said, drinking a little more green tea.

"They're drunk," Seiji said loftily.

"We'll be sober in forty-five minutes," Shimada said, equally loftily.

"Forty minutes even," Takashi chimed in, stretching his upper body. "I could use a walk."

"Me, too, that's why I added fifteen minutes to the rendezvous time," Shimada said, reaching for his wallet and then graciously accepting Takashi's gift of dinner. "You're very kind," Shimada murmured under Yoshi's polite thanks.

"Oh, no, thank you, you two," Takashi said, dropping his American Express card on the bill tray. "I haven't enjoyed anything as much as Yoshi's interview-profile-whatever in a long time. And this is on SM, too," he added waving the gold card around. "Daitaro was greatly disturbed over that piece for some reason."

"Why should he care?" Seiji asked.

"I dunno," Takashi said, smiling at the happy couple in front of him and then beaming at the love of his life. "Ryuu's his brother, Yoshi's Ryuu's boyfriend, Ryuu's writing great stuff about Yoshi, and neither of them is under Daitaro's thumb and that bugs him."

"How the hell do you work for that jerk?" Shimada asked, drinking a little cold tea before rising steadily to his feet.

"I actually like my job enough to ignore Daitaro," Takashi said, leaning on Seiji, more for fun than support.

"Lucky you," Seiji and Shimada said in unison.

"Aaaand we're off!" Shimada said, draping an arm around Yoshi for their sobering walk in the lovely soft evening.

"What the fuckityfuckfuckfuck is this?" Kenzu asked when the quartet strolled into the nondescript industrial space exactly three and a half minutes late. "Why the fuck are you and Takashi here? Hi Seiji. And you're late."

"Yeah, thanks for waiting, big guy," Shimada drawled.

"I'm not the only one you kept waiting, Ryuu," Kenzu said, viciously.

Lights at the other end of the space came on and revealed a bare-bones photo set-up—a few lights and a roll of grey seamless—and a tall thin man with a thatch of unruly grey hair. He stared hard at Yoshi for a few moments and then moved towards him in easy, but powerful steps, glanced at Seiji, and then resumed his examination of Yoshi, who started back as if hypnotized.

"Shigeru Nakadai," Shimada said, somewhat in awe. "You dragged Shigeru Nakadai out for this. Who's your client, Kenbo?"

"Don't call me Kenbo, Ryuu, and you oughta know I'm not telling you who the client is," Kenzu snarled. "You've been out of the game too long, maybe you're out of your league."

"Fuck you," Shimada said coldly.

"Yeah, fuck you, Kenbo," Takashi said, speaking up for the first time.

"Later, children, let's take some test shots," Nakadai said, and grabbed Yoshi's arm. Yoshi reflexively jerked away. "Ah, so there is some fire in there. C'mon, beautiful, it's just pictures for uncle," he said coldly, advancing on the kid.

Shimada pulled Yoshi behind him and stood between the photographer and his subject. "Test shots, Nakadai-sensei?" he asked politely. "Is there a fee agreement for that?"

Nakadai drew himself up to his full height and snapped at Kenzu to deal with it. Takashi stepped forward to handle the minor transaction.

"Ryuu, who is that guy?" Yoshi whispered.

"He's one of the greatest fashion photographers in the world," Shimada said.

"Maybe the greatest," Seiji murmured from nearby. "Like the Richard Avedon of Japan."

Shimada told Yoshi to take his coat off and relax. He kept Yoshi close to him, but didn't block Nakadai's view.

"What are you up to, Ryuu?" Seiji asked.

"Oh, I don't know," the newspaper man said innocently. "Maybe a few candid shots of Yoshi by the Richard Avedon of Japan for the family album wouldn't be such a bad thing, would it?"

Seiji didn't have a chance to answer because Takashi turned to Ryuu and said, "Forty thousand yen?"

"How many shots?" Shimada shot back.

"Ten."

"Done! Go to work Yoshi," Shimada said, shoving his lover toward Nakadai.

"I–" Yoshi began.

"Come to papa." Nakadai took his arm and looked over his head at Shimada. "Ten shots, you say, I'll have to make the most of them."

And he did. He yelled at Yoshi, he coaxed, he praised, he yelled some more. Yoshi cringed, looked puzzled, looked dubious, looked scared, appealed to Shimada for help (Shimada just told him to hang in there, which was kind of useless advice), got angry, yelled back, and nearly burst into tears. "Well, that should do it," Nakadai said, with the barest hint of a smile visible, but those who knew him, knew it was his version of a broad grin. "You look like shit when you cry," he drawled at Yoshi and then turned away as if there was no one in the room.

"Fuck you!" Yoshi yelled and was ignored, so he threw himself into Shimada's arms instead.

"Where do I send the check?" Kenzu asked.

"Have his agent pick it up at your office," Nakadai said on his way out.

That was Nakadai's code for "Get me this model," and Kenzu slumped a little because the only one in the room who didn't know that was Yoshi. He straightened up to face down the predatory smiles spreading on Takashi's and Ryuu's faces. Seiji's face was unreadable, but Seiji had always been something of a cipher in the ad world. "So..." Kenzu said, handing out cards and receiving them from Ryuu and Takashi. "Say, ten tomorrow morning?"

"Make it three in the afternoon, Kenbo, I have things to do in the morning," Shimada said, knowing Daitaro would kill Takashi if he made a deal for anyone at another agency, especially SM's main competitor.

"Gone into the agenting business now, Ryuu?" Kenzu asked acidly.

"Just because this is short notice," Shimada said sweetly. "And as a courtesy to Nakadai-sensei. See you at three." Shimada turned and led his little party out of the building.

While waiting for a cab, Yoshi informed them all that he wouldn't have anything to do with Nakadai. "He makes me sick."

"Yeah, me, too," Seiji chimed in in support.

Takashi ignored Shimada trying to reason with the boyfriends and directed to the taxi to the Ur Bookstore. "They have a lot of magazines," he said mysteriously to the duet of "Going where? At this hour?" and "I'm really tired. I just want to go home." But Shimada supported him by saying, "Oooh, magazines! I love magazines!"

Takashi pointed out to Yoshi at least three current covers by Nakadai and then started opening fashion magazines at random, while Seiji followed Ryuu into the coffee table book section. "That was like a rape back there," he said when they were out of earshot.

"What are you on about, Seij?" Shimada asked, his attention on the glossy spines before him. "Ah, here they are."

"I said that was like Yoshi getting raped back there," Seiji clarified with some heat.

"Seiji, things that are like things are not those things and you're exaggerating," Shimada mumbled, carefully pulling books off the shelf. If only to spare Takashi from Seiji's wrath, Shimada turned his full attention to his ex-boyfriend when he heard a long, furious breath blown out. "Was it that bad, Seiji? It was rough, but Yoshi's not made of spun sugar," he said in what he hoped was an annoyingly soothing voice. "And he measured up. How many nineteen year-old models in the world have done that?"

"Quite a few, I think, but they all end up in rehab," Seiji replied in an equally annoying soothing voice.

"Oh, touché, Seij, touché," Shimada said, heading back to the magazine area. He stopped just before it. "But don't forget, pal, Yoshi has all three of us on his side, doesn't he? What bad thing could happen to him?" Knowing Seiji was momentarily, hopefully permanently, stumped on the subject of Yoshi's well being, Shimada spread the books on a reading table and he, Takashi, and even Seiji, who had been more of a fan of Nakadai's before he met him tonight, paged through to show Yoshi, sullen, but polite, what a genius he might get to work with.

"Do you want me to do this?" Yoshi suddenly asked Shimada, as if they were alone.

"Depends on the deal," Shimada replied blandly.

"He called me beautiful," Yoshi muttered.

"I'm sure many less qualified people have called you that," Takashi said gently.

"He also called himself your papa and that isn't true, so I wouldn't get all het up about everything he says," Shimada said less gently.

"You don't have to do this, Yoshi," Seiji said, staring Shimada and Takashi down. "You don't have to do anything you don't want to do."

"I know," Yoshi said, leaning tiredly against Shimada. He reached over to pat Seiji's clenched fist. "I think I'm just really tired now."

Shimada murmured, "We'll go home," into his hair and Takashi asked him which book he liked best. Yoshi pointed to one that had a lot of glamorous people standing around in wastelands with equally glamorous cars and electronics.

"Then we'll make this a present to you," Takashi said pleasantly. "To celebrate...something," he added, omitting that many of those pictures were taken for Shimada Miyagi clients. Neither Shimada or Seiji mentioned it as they followed him to the cash register with their own purchases: *The Economist* magazine for Shimada and a fantasy manga for Seiji. As a nice touch, Takashi had the book gift wrapped and then presented it so sincerely to Yoshi, hoping it would be good luck for all his future endeavors, that Yoshi, tired as he was, could not help but smile sincerely with his gracious, "Thank you."

It was nice for Shimada to have something to read when he got home with Yoshi. He would have rather made love, but Yoshi was too tired and fell asleep the second his head hit the pillow.

"Well, well, well, you've moved up in the world, haven't you, Kenbo?" Shimada drawled when he was led into Kenzu's corner office at the Mishima Muramaki (fondly known as MM) advertising agency.

"You're still an asshole, Ryuu," Kenzu said with a weary smile. "Tea? Coffee? Drink?"

"Nah, I'm on a tight schedule." Shimada looked at his watch. "I've been chasing a Peruvian general all morning and hope to get him this afternoon. My Spanish translator is waiting in your lobby." He waited patiently while Kenzu buzzed someone with a feminine voice and told that person to offer the gentleman in the lobby something non-alcoholic. "Thanks, big guy."

"Okay, here's the Yoshi deal," Kenzu said, and proceeded to lay out a fairly complex, but lucrative for Yoshi, ad campaign for Midoma, an elegant department store that only did top-of-the-line advertising.

"Huh, since when do they sell pajamas?" Shimada asked to buy some time to think up his negotiation. Kenzu's offer was on the generous side considering Yoshi's lack of modeling experience. Nakadai-sensei must have really seen something in those ten shots from the night before. "I thought Midoma was a purveyor of overpriced suits and shoes and stuff like that."

"Oh, they sell pajamas, but the campaign isn't for pajamas, per se, it's called 'Pajama Boy Not Included,'" Kenzu said.

"How lewd," Shimada observed.

"Ryuu, I swear, if I'd known you were anywhere within artillery range of this deal, I would have demanded the other pajama boy for it," Kenzu snapped. "As it was, the client saw Yoshi's profile in that hipster weekly you write for, liked the pictures a lot, and said they wanted the Sleepy Pajama Boy for these ads. Now that Nakadai-sensei's seen Yoshi, there's no way to switch him for Koji Kawazu, who is, I hear, becoming difficult to work with."

"Oh?"

"Oh, yeah," Kenzu went on. "Before he broke into pajama modeling, Kawazu was kind of a borderline hooker, high class, but still too many yakuza boyfriends. He only got the pajama boy ads at Shirane Normura because someone there pulled some major strings. And it's okay, Kawazu is fine at what he's doing, as far as it goes." Kenzu waved dismissively. "This 'cute boys in pajamas' thing is a fad. I don't know why it couldn't be cute girls in pajamas, but I'll be glad when the whole mess is over and we can get back to moodily lit cars, booze and electronics."

"Ah, yes, the soul of advertising," Shimada said. "Okay, let's talk about the deal." They haggled politely for a while and came to an agreement. Kenzu made the changes to the contract on his computer and printed out a copy for Shimada to take back for Yoshi's approval. Kenzu insisted that Yoshi come to his office to sign the contract in the presence of witnesses and Shimada agreed wholeheartedly. "After all, you wouldn't want me to railroad him into anything," he said. "Even if I would," he added, getting to his feet.

"Yeah, Ryuu, you're a saint," Kenzu said, rising with him. "This is a short, experimental campaign. If it's a success, I only want to talk to Yoshi's agent, not you, and not Takashi. Got it?"

"What about Seiji?" Shimada asked. "He was there last night, too."

"Yeah, I saw him, he looks a lot happier now that he's out of Shimada Miyagi," Kenzu said. "But if Yoshi's going to survive in the big time, he needs a Big Time agent. Find him one, Ryuu, find him an agent who's not going to sell him too cheap."

Shimada offered the merest hint of a bow and left Kenzu's office. On the way to the next attempt at ambushing the Peruvian general, he mulled over Kenzu's words: "Find him an agent who's not going to sell him too cheap." Yoshi's image was for sale now, and whether it was good or bad, it was a fact and it was up to Ryuu to find the right person to manage Yoshi's most saleable asset at the moment: his adorableness. But, it occurred to Shimada, Yoshi might refuse to model for Nakadai. Yoshi had been fairly adamant in the taxi that he didn't want anything to do with it. Of course Shimada would try his best to convince him to take the job because it was a short-term deal and the money was pretty good. And they could use the money. While Shimada's freelance work paid the bills and Yoshi's job at Fugiwara's shop covered their few luxuries, like movies and eating out occasionally, it would be nice to get a little ahead. But just then, Shimada caught sight of his Peruvian general and everything else went by the wayside. Luckily, when Shimada and his Spanish translator caught up with the general, he'd had a few drinks and was in a mellow, talkative mood.

After such a rough introduction, Yoshi was reluctant to work with Nakadai-sensei, but was finally swayed by the money Shimada had negotiated and the amount of effort he'd had put into it for him. Although Shimada never said anything directly, Yoshi could tell he was pleased his lover would be photographed by a master artist and it seemed to Yoshi it was the least he could do when Shimada was working so hard to make ends meet. And if it would make Shimada happy, that was even better. It would also be nice to have a little more money around, maybe they could even take a weekend trip somewhere that Shimada was not writing a story about. And after a little vacation, Yoshi could find another job because Fugiwara, the bastard, fired him when he asked for a few days off for the photo shoot.

The initial and ensuing "Pajama Boy Not Included" ad campaigns for Midoma Department Store were a huge success. There were one- or two-page ads in all the best magazines of Yoshi, appearing to be asleep in pajamas, being watched over and protected by a series of extremely well-dressed men and women. One ad had Yoshi sleeping on a park bench next to a man in an expensive trench coat holding an umbrella over him, another was in a crowded subway with Yoshi leaning against his protector, and another had him sleeping in an elegant hotel lobby surrounded by beautiful people in evening dress. All over Tokyo there were variations of these ads on billboards, most notably one of the pajama-clad, peacefully sleeping Yoshi leaning against a man in a tuxedo on the sixty-foot billboard directly across from Daitaro Shimada's office window.

Every day for several weeks Daitaro stared moodily out his window at his brother's beautiful air-brushed lover in one of the best ad campaigns of the year. He never said a word about it, even when Takashi tried to broach the subject, all Daitaro said was, "Billboard? What billboard?"

Takashi was very pleased with Yoshi's success and helped Shimada find a good agent, one they could trust, to manage Yoshi's career thenceforth. They settled on Renge Hirayama, their former colleague at Shimada Miyagi, who'd gotten sick of Daitaro's bullshit and gone to work as an agent at the gigantic Media Mondial agency. Renge took Yoshi as a client as a favor to Takashi and Shimada, who'd helped him find the courage to finally leave SM, and also assured him Yoshi's career would be easy to manage and short-lived because the pajama-boy-ad-craze could only last so long. At Shimada's request, Renge had agreed to field offers, but not seek them out. It made his job easier because he was already swamped with actors clamoring for work. A nice little model with a short career was all he could shoehorn into his workload anyway.

Not that he ever mentioned it to Yoshi, Shimada or Seiji, but in the midst of Yoshi's new success, Takashi got a call from the photographer Kurogane about the "Pajama Boy Not Included" ad campaign and how closely it resembled his original photos of Yoshi in pajamas. Taking the hint, Takashi got in touch with Kenzu at Mishima Muramaki and got Kurogane a gracious acknowledgement from MM and some money for having the brilliant germ of the Pajama Boy idea. It was more money than Kurogane and Yoshi had made on those original ads, but Takashi kept that to himself as well. Although Kurogane was completely mollified by the money and minor recognition, Takashi felt sorry for the old man because advertising was a dog-eat-dog world and even though Kurogane had discovered Yoshi, there was no place for him in Yoshi's good fortune.

Wishing only the best for Yoshi, Seiji was still somewhat concerned that Takashi and Ryuu had bullied the young man into working with Nakadai-sensei. But Seiji felt relieved that their old friend Renge would at least protect Yoshi from being taken advantage of financially. "But why don't you want Renge to get Yoshi more modeling work?" he'd called to ask. Shimada told him that Yoshi really didn't like modeling, but it was best to be prepared for jobs if they came down the pike—like the one from Mishima Muramaki that took them all by surprise—and neither Shimada nor Takashi had the time or experience to negotiate deals with vicious ad sharks, and that he was about to ask the Russian ambassador some embarrassing questions about gunships near some islands Seiji had never heard of and that he, Ryuu, had to go now, bye. Because Shimada and Takashi were, at that time, too busy to discuss Yoshi's career with him, Seiji decided to have lunch with Yoshi himself. "You look well," he said when they met at the restaurant.

"I feel pretty good," Yoshi said, glancing at the menu and ordering soup. "You know I got fired?"

"From MM's campaign?" Seiji asked in a shocked and hollow voice.

"No," Yoshi laughed. "They still like me. They hired me for more ads. I got fired from the clothes store."

"That huge, crazy place?" Seiji asked and Yoshi nodded. "Will you miss it?"

"Oh, kind of, but not really." Yoshi smiled over his soup. "I'll miss some of the guys I worked with, but not the store."

"Ah, I see. What are MM's new ads?" Seiji asked after a few bites of quiche.

"It's supposed to be a secret, but I'll tell you," Yoshi said, sounding annoyed by the advertising paranoia Seiji knew so well. "It's the 'Pajama Boy Not Included' thing again, but with cars and motorcycles."

"Oh my, how elegant," Seiji said, impressed and hopeful that the art director knew what he was doing. "Which motor company?"

"I forgot to ask," Yoshi said, as if it didn't matter. "And there's a stupid play they want me to do."

"A play?" Seiji asked.

"Oh, it's dumb, some bit part in a play that stars the other pajama boy," Yoshi continued. "I agreed, but only because I met Koji Kawazu and he said I was wrecking his career so the least I could do was bring in some audience while I was still famous."

"...WHAT?"

The play, "The English-Speaking Escort," started rehearsals before the next "Pajama Boy Not Included" photo shoot. There were a few days where Yoshi missed rehearsal due to shooting on location, but his part really wasn't very big and he was a quick study, so he didn't hold anything up. Koji was right, when the play opened it was a minor hit due to having both Pajama Boys it. And based on the buzz, Koji had gotten a major ad campaign as the Running Pajama Boy again for TK Sportswear. It was not as big or elegant as the Sleepy Pajama Boy for KSN Automotive, but his image, like Yoshi's, was all over Tokyo again.

TESE, as the cast and techs called it, was a fairly stupid romantic comedy with the plot being about an escort service that catered to Americans. Koji played the sexy escort whose cock-teasing antics with rich Americans run aground when he falls for a millionaire playboy businessman on vacation in Tokyo. The owner of the agency does everything to keep his best, English-speaking escort from retiring. Yoshi played the owner's secretary who's in unrequited love with his wacky boss. The script also managed to get Yoshi and Koji into pajamas in scenes in a luxury hotel in the second act. There was a lot of shouting, slapstick and Koji kissing a very handsome American actor every night. The play was sold out for weeks on end and the theater was packed mainly with women. But no matter; everyone was delighted, except Yoshi who was merely tired from credibly delivering his ridiculous lines and standing around looking convincingly cute on stage four nights a week and a matinee on Sunday. But he was not unhappy; he liked working as part of a group again instead of a solo model and the center of attention.

In the midst of the renewed Pajama Boy craze, an article appeared in a weekly magazine demanding to know if Japan had gone insane. What could be the possible attraction for a sleeping and running juvenile boy? Did these lascivious, licentious, degenerate ads all over the country limn an inchoate pederastic lust for somnambulistic sex bordering on necrophilia with the Sleepy Pajama Boy, and a voyeuristic joy in gang rape should the Running Pajama Boy stumble in his flight? Yoshi, after he looked up all the words he didn't understand, was, understandably, quite upset about the essay. "Why is it all about sex?" he practically shouted at Shimada, Takashi and Seiji one night after the play. At least one of them always made sure he got home safely, as some of Yoshi's fans were a little too enthusiastic at the stage door. Koji had an escort of tough guys with him each night, but occasionally he accepted a lift home in Takashi's Saab. However, that night only Takashi, Seiji, Shimada and Yoshi were in the car on their way to a late supper.

"Because everything is about sex, Yoshi," Shimada said wryly, and then smiled affectionately at his boyfriend's exasperated eye roll. "Actually, I think that essay is more about Daitaro."

"Huh?" Seiji asked.

"Y'know I was wondering about that," Takashi said. "That essay has three of his favorite words–"

"Lust, limn and inchoate," Shimada helpfully supplied.

"Yeah, and one or two I could let pass but three is awfully suspicious," Takashi went on. "Add to that he's been in an exceptionally good mood lately, I'd say–"

"We've found our Gigi," Shimada laughed and Takashi joined him.

"I'm glad you two think it's funny," Seiji said, sounding disgusted. "Daitaro's turned Yoshi and Koji into mental sex toys." He relaxed somewhat when Yoshi patted his shoulder and smiled at him.

"And what else is advertising?" Shimada asked.

"Oh, Ryuu," Seiji sighed dejectedly.

"I hear the play's sold out and extending its run," Takashi said. "I'm pretty sure that's not the result Daitaro intended, if it's his fault at all."

"Why does he hate me so much, Ryuu?" Yoshi asked as if they were alone.

"Because he can't figure you out."

Takashi decided to work late that night. He was escorting Yoshi home after the play, Ryuu was in Moscow on a story and Seiji was home sleeping off a minor head cold, so he was on his own, and there was no reason not to get caught up and even a little ahead at the office. He was happy to see Yoshi home after performances when Ryuu was unavailable. It was too bad Seiji wouldn't be there as he and Yoshi had become good friends. On nights when Seiji was free and feeling up to it, he and Yoshi often went out after the play. However, without Seiji, it would be an early night. Takashi would see the actor home and get home himself, probably well before midnight.

Daitaro was also working late and decided this was a good time to bother Takashi about Minoru Yamada's daughter, Yoko, who had a big crush on Takashi and wanted to open marriage negotiations. "I mean, c'mon, Takashi, the girl has a real thing for you. I mean, she's not even asking for a formal miai, just a nice meal in a five-star hotel with me, my wife, her family, your family, maybe one or two of her father's friends–"

"That sounds a lot like a miai, formal or no, Daitaro," Takashi murmured under the cascade of words.

"Also, you're great with women, they fall all over you," he said, sitting on his employee's desk. "And it's not like you're a married man."

"I'm pretty much married to Seiji, thank you, Daitaro," Takashi said, not looking up from the ad copy he was writing.

"And her father is way up the food chain of one of our hugest clients." Daitaro went on with his hard sell. "I mean if you really wanted to fuck me later, you could grab YKT Automotive and start your own agency."

"Ah, then I could do some huge ads of Yoshi sleeping on the hoods of convertibles," Takashi said, stealing a glance at the desk clock. "Tempting, boss, but no sale."

Daitaro made a disgusted noise and suggested they go have a drink.

"Can't," Takashi said pleasantly.

"Why not? What are you doing? Is it fun?" Daitaro could really be annoying sometimes. "I wanna come!"

Getting to his feet, Takashi put on a neutral expression. "Just a little chore–"

"I wanna come!"

"It's very boring–"

"I wanna come!"

"You'd be bored–" Takashi put on his coat.

"I wanna come!" Daitaro planted himself in front of the younger man.

"No?" Takashi suggested, cursing himself for staying late.

"Yes!"

Catching sight of Daitaro with Takashi at the theater, one of the stagehands yelled, "Goddammit, Yoshi, can't you leave us girls at least one attractive man in Tokyo?!" This got a general laugh and some mildly curious looks.

Yoshi gave the girl's arm an affectionate squeeze. She'd been one of the most helpful people in getting him up to speed on stagecraft, or whatever it was, so he didn't make a complete fool of himself in rehearsals. "Oh, that's just Ryuu's dad," Yoshi said coolly.

"I am not his dad," Daitaro fumed. "I'm his older brother!" This got another laugh. But Daitaro hardly noticed it, he was staring hard at someone behind Yoshi.

"I told you you'd be bored," Takashi said blandly, but was ignored because Daitro was wholly engrossed in staring at Koji Kawazu, who was strolling up to join their little group.

Koji and Yoshi had roughly the same lithe build, big brown eyes and luxuriant jet hair, but the resemblance abruptly ended there. Koji

109

was a few centimeters taller than his fellow pajama boy, his facial features were sharper, more masculine, and his eyes were not as large and dreamy as Yoshi's. He had fuller lips and a jawline one could break bricks on. Sleek, angular, and very sexy: Koji had taken his natural talents and added a graceful gait and tremendous poise to the already man-killing mix. He'd learned his composure in yakuza gambling dens, and he never intended on going back there. But it was a useful cool: a polar attitude that came in handy when sizing up a mark or a foe, while they stared, fascinated, by his approach. "You look a little like Shimada-san," Koji said when he joined their group and introduced himself.

"Does he make you call him -san?" Daitaro asked, shamelessly staring at him.

"He completely ignores me," Koji said with a pout. "But if I ever did address him, it would be respectfully."

"I'm a lot nicer than my little brother, Kawazu-kun," the elder Shimada brother drawled. "You can call me Daitaro."

"Oh, please call me Koji," the other pajama boy purred. And then asked if one of them could give him a lift downtown where he could catch a bus home.

Takashi and Yoshi hesitated but Daitaro had no problem volunteering Takashi's car for the job. "Too bad I didn't bring my Mercedes," Daitaro said smugly.

"Maybe not," Takashi murmured.

"Eh? I mean it's more comfortable," Daitaro went on. "And speaking of comfort, why don't we grab a late supper at Papa Elysium?"

"Oooh! Is it open?" Koji asked sweetly. "It looked divine in that magazine article on it."

"It should. We did the press and the club was designed by that trendy asshole architect," Daitaro schmoozed back.

"You don't call him that when he pays his bills on time," Takashi said, herding them to his car, wishing Yoshi would say he was tired and wanted to go home.

"Do you know Norboru Suzuki? I've read he's a very sexy person," Koji said, leering playfully.

"I can't say I've ever found him sexy," Daitaro said, simply leering. "But he's rich and builds sexy buildings, I'll give him that. Let's try it, Takashi. If they kick us out we'll go to Shakey's Pizza or something." This got a chuckle from Koji.

"I think–" Takashi began.

"I'm kind of hungry, Takashi," Yoshi said. "Could Seiji join us?"

Not only did they get the best table at Papa Elysium, but the trendy asshole architect, Norboru Suzuki himself, was there and made sure the management gave their party an enthusiastic welcome. He even sat with them long enough to be introduced to Yoshi and spend a few moments talking to Koji before he rejoined his wife and their party at another table. Daitaro took charge of ordering the food, so there was lots of caviar, smoked salmon, escargots à la bourguignonne, red pepper rouille, shrimp toasts, duck terrine with wine-glazed shallots, curried wild mushroom pate, duck pate, and champagne. Lots of champagne, maybe too much champagne, but certainly enough champagne for none of them to notice the mob of photographers having a field day with the pajama boys partying with two suit-wearing creative-types. Koji was often in the gossip papers, but it was a rare thing for him to be seen with Yoshi, let alone at a trendy new night spot.

Daitaro insisted on driving Koji home in his car, so Takashi, who was by then sick of both of them, gladly dropped them off at SM's office building. "Thank God they're gone," he said to Yoshi, watching them go into the crystalline lobby.

"D'you think that's a good idea?" Yoshi asked. "Koji's kind of...of fast and isn't Daitaro married?"

"Who cares at this hour?" Takashi asked, hoping that light in the sky was man-made and not dawn. The small noise Yoshi made in response sounded sad to him. "When does Ryuu get back?"

"Next week," Yoshi said. This meant Yoshi had a weekend to get through alone.

"Why don't you come stay with us?" Takashi suddenly suggested. "Seiji's over his cold and I have to work most of the weekend, so he'd probably love to have some company."

"Sure!"

Takashi pointed his Saab homeward. "We'll lend you some pajamas and you and Seiji can do whatever tomorrow."

"There's a show at a gallery I heard about..." Yoshi said, sounding sleepy, but happy.

Takashi let him doze for the rest of the trip to his and Seiji's apartment. After he got Yoshi settled in the guest room, he sent Ryuu an email telling him where Yoshi would be that weekend, but not mentioning the party at Papa Elysium with Daitaro. The next morning he had an email from Ryuu thanking him for looking after Yoshi. And by the time Takashi got to the office, photos of Daitaro sitting far too close to Koji were all over the gossip magazines in print and online.

But all Daitaro had to say about it on the following Monday was, "Damn, I take a good picture, don't I?" He was in an exceptionally good mood, which was, as far as Takashi was concerned, preferable to a bad mood. Takashi considered asking why he was in such a good mood, but Daitaro beat him to it by expounding on how wonderful the free publicity was for Papa Elysium, PRCK Architects (the trendy, asshole architect) and that it didn't hurt the world to know that Daitaro Shimada was not such a snob he couldn't be seen with trendy pajama models.

Takashi was inclined to accept this explanation and drop the discussion if only to get away from the blazing, blinding glare of Daitaro's rampaging ego searing everything within twenty feet of it.

Seiji and Yoshi had been amused by the pictures, and although Seiji said it looked like fun, he still preferred quieter, more intimate establishments for late-night suppers. He and Yoshi had such a good time in galleries and just wandering around Tokyo that weekend, they hardly had time to discuss the events of that night.

The only person Takashi had some qualms about seeing the pictures was Ryuu, since it was his brother and Koji who were the main photographic subjects. But Ryuu was exhausted by his Moscow trip and when he did recover and Takashi asked him what he thought about the photos, all Ryuu ever said was, "Damn, Daitaro takes a good picture, doesn't he? Maybe he should have gone into modeling. Oh yeah, and you and Yoshi looked bored out of your minds. Remind me never to go to that place."

A few days after Shimada got home and recovered from the Moscow assignment, Renge Hirayama insisted he have lunch with him so he could give him Yoshi's modeling checks. "I kept trying to give them to him, and he kept saying to give them to you," Renge said over a very dry martini. "Why the hell is that?"

"Now that you make me think about it, I think he doesn't have a bank account," Shimada said, chewing a nice fat, gin-soaked olive and perusing the menu.

"Well, do something about that, Ryuu," Renge said. He mentioned that the restaurant's Steak Diane was especially good and ordered it for himself. He also ordered another round of martinis. Shimada ordered lobster roasted with basil because the food in Moscow had nearly killed him and lunch was on Renge.

"Why is MM sending them to you?" Shimada asked vaguely. He was distracted by the huge sums on checks with Yoshi's name on them.

"According to Kenbo, Yoshi told accounting to send them to you and they had no idea who you were, so they sent them to me," Renge told him. "So that's the good news."

"There's bad news?" Shimada asked.

"There's weird news, and it's not my fault." Renge sipped his fresh drink. "It seems Yoshi verbally agreed to a three film deal with SKT Productions. One of their lawyers called me yesterday to work out the details."

"Oh, God..." Shimada looked down at the plate set in front of him. "Oh, lobster!"

Renge went on while his Steak Diane was flambé-ing and Shimada, at Renge's request, dug into his lobster lunch. "It appears that SKT is putting together a deal to make a film out of 'The English-Speaking Escort.' It's not a bad idea, really, and they're figuring there'll be enough juice from it to get at least two more films out of Yoshi from it. The SKT guy didn't say it, but I'm assuming they're making the same kind of deal with Koji."

"Did Yoshi sign anything?" Shimada asked and Renge, his mouth full of delicious Steak Diane, indicated that he hadn't signed anything. "Then you can get him out of it, can't you?"

"That's just it, Ryuu, I'm not sure I want to," Renge said, almost enjoying Shimada's comically shocked look. "It's a lot of money—"

"For a kid who's a fad, you mean," Shimada said.

"You know, pal, I really think we should stop thinking of Yoshi as a fad, because he's consistently defied all the fad pitfalls—no, eat your lunch and let me finish," Renge said, and Shimada obeyed because the lobster was superb. "We know Nakadai-sensei is a genius demon with a camera, but you can only get gold out of mud if there's gold in the mud. His work with Yoshi is some of the best work of his career. Yoshi comes right off the page with his eyes closed. How many established supermodels can do that? One or two. Somehow Yoshi does it naturally or learned it fast. I saw those first ads and they didn't give me much hope, but he's obviously a quick learner and inspired." He held up a hand to stop Shimada from interrupting. "It's faster if I finish and then you argue. Take this stupid play: who knew Yoshi could figure out how to cope well enough not to get laughed off the stage on the first night? And now this film deal. I say let's do it, Ryuu. I'll negotiate a bail-out if he's too horrible to make all three films. He's made some dough, and his movie career is over. If he's good enough, he can stop after three films, it's up to him. Movies are brutal, but so's modeling and theater work and he's aced them both, so I think he should at least take a shot at this movie deal. And then the money is too good to pass up, even you have to agree with that. I know he's just a sweet guy that you love with all your heart—even someone as jaded as me can see that—but since he's not a fad, he might just be a pot of gold. Now you can talk." And with that, he turned to his steak lunch.

"What is there to say, Renge? You've summed it up," Shimada said appreciatively. "If Yoshi really wants to do this, get him the best deal you can. I need to talk to him, though. He hasn't said a word about it to me."

"It happened while you were gone last week," Renge said, ordering coffee for both of them. "What have you been doing since you got back from Moscow?" Shimada merely smiled smugly at him. "Thought so. Well, if you can get out of bed, try to have a serious discussion before the weekend. I'm supposed to cut the deal or back out of it next week. I read your stuff on the Moscow/Tokyo trade meeting; you write like a novelist. I couldn't put it down."

"Thanks, I'm really digging the assignments I'm getting from News International," Shimada said, eyeing, but passing up the dessert cart. "Not only do they let me go out on a limb for a story, they back me up, too. I'm in Peru in a few weeks as a follow-up on General–"

"You know, I wonder if you shouldn't stick around more." Renge reached down for his briefcase, and not only for his wallet to pay the check. "Yoshi is too much influenced by Koji. He did the play for Koji and probably Koji talked him into the movie deal, too, because Koji benefits from those things as well, if not more than Yoshi. You did see those wonderful free publicity pictures on the web and the cheapo papers, didn't you?" Shimada said he had and thought they were wonderful free publicity and pretty stupid otherwise. "But what the hell is Yoshi doing running around with Koji? And goddamn Daitaro in the mix?" Shimada protested that Takashi had been there and it had never happened again. "There are rumors that Daitaro is fucking Koji."

"Really?" Shimada thought about it for a second. "So? Must be nice to have time to listen to idle gossip."

"It's part of my job."

"Okay, Koji's a slut, I had heard that," Shimada admitted. "It's his ass. So?"

"So, I think you should stay home more, Ryuu." Renge reached into his briefcase again. "Because anyone whose boyfriend looks like this, should be home to keep an eye on him." He handed a large envelope across the table to Shimada.

Shimada sighed and said, as he removed a photograph from its sleeve. "Ah, c'mon, Renge, I trust Yoshi comple..." The most beautiful Japanese youth in the world stared back at him from the glossy print. And it was Yoshi Katayama.

"Why can't you just keep them?" Yoshi asked. He was reluctantly filling out forms at one of the larger Tokyo banks, where clerks, tellers, bank managers, security guards and customers were flitting around to get a look at the Sleepy Pajama Boy.

"Because they're yours," Shimada said, checking the forms over and handing them to the nearly hypnotized New Accounts Manager.

"I'll give them to you!"

"And I took the afternoon off to do this boring chore with you, so at least humor me and deposit the fucking checks in your fucking new fucking bank account." Shimada smiled at Yoshi's giggling and ignored the New Accounts Manager's shocked gasp. There were a few other formalities and then Yoshi and Shimada were free to dodge the paparazzi by escaping out the back door into a waiting taxi. "Are they always following you around like this?" Shimada asked, watching the pack disperse after losing its prey.

"Not so much, unless they know I'm somewhere or I'm with Koji. They really hound Koji," Yoshi said innocently.

"I bet he loves it," Shimada said coldly, recalling Renge's words about Koji's influence on Yoshi.

"I suppose someone told one of them we were in the bank. The photographers, I mean. Hey, let's walk home from here," Yoshi suggested. He waited while Shimada paid the taxi and left a big tip for getting them away so quickly. The cabbie winked at Yoshi and said it was his pleasure to drive the Pajama Boy, and got a big smile from Yoshi. "I want to give you that money, Ryuu, I don't know what to do with it," he said as they strolled in the peaceful afternoon light.

"That's dumb, Yoshi," Shimada said dismissively. "Buy a car, a fur coat, diamonds, give it to charity, or better, give it to your relatives in Nagasaki. They'd love to have it."

"Oh...I meant aren't there investments or something I should do with it?" Yoshi asked, somewhat abashed by his lack of imagination and greed. "But I will send some of it to Aunt and Uncle and my cousin. That's a good idea! That's why I want you to have it, you know what to do with it."

"Oh, I see what you're saying, okay. I wrote about some ethical investors recently. Let's see what they suggest after you figure out what you want to send to Nagasaki," Shimada said, more kindly now that he understood.

"I want to give you half of it," Yoshi insisted. "After I send some to Nagasaki."

"Why don't you just pay the rent until the lease expires in December?" Shimada suggested. "I'm making enough for a bigger place, so we should move when we can." He draped his arm around Yoshi's shoulders. "And we'll see what the investor guys say about the rest. I'm not ready for you to keep me like a gigolo yet."

"Hmph, I've met a few gigolos lately. You'd never last, Ryuu," Yoshi said leaning sweetly into his lover.

"Yeah, well, how much time are you spending with Koji?" Shimada asked or rather, accused.

"Not much, none now," Yoshi said, completely missing the accusation vibe. "I think he has a new Sugar Daddy. He's been getting picked up by a hired car right after the show every night."

"'Sugar Daddy'? Where are you learning these things?" Shimada asked, amused, and all he got for a answer was a shrug. A very cute shrug, but a shrug nevertheless. "Now about this three movie deal, what's the truth, Yoshi? Do you want to do it or not?"

"I do," Yoshi said sincerely.

"Why?" Shimada asked.

"Because Koji says we're a fad and the movie money is good, so we should get as much of it as we can before we're history," Yoshi told him. "And it sounds kind of fun! Lots of work, but fun!"

Shimada looked into the earnest, loving, beautiful face of the man he was crazy in love with and couldn't find any arguments worth marshalling. So he just kissed him, and if anyone didn't like it, they could go straight to hell.

"Seiji, I'm only doing this—this thing to keep everyone calm and happy," Takashi said the evening he told Seiji he would not be having a miai with the Yamada family's daughter, Yoko, no matter how much it looked like one. "I have everything under control, just please be patient. I love you. Trust me for now."

Hiding his hurt, fear and terrible feeling of deja vu, Seiji said, "Yes, all right, I love you, too." Four years earlier, he'd heard something eerily similar.

When Ryuu's mother fell ill, Seiji could only wish her a quick recovery from afar. Ryuu's family hardly noticed him, and could never quite remember his name when he answered their calls at the apartment he shared with their younger son.

Well aware that Ryuu walked a tightrope with his family over him, Seiji was happy to be in love and in the background. He was never a spotlight kind of person; he felt best supporting Ryuu, who hadn't yet worked up the courage to tell his family he was gay and in love with another man, namely the one he was living with. After graduation, Ryuu had bowed to his family's wishes and joined Shimada Miyagi instead of taking up a career in journalism. Seiji had supported him in his filial obedience, and even joined him at Shimada Miyagi when Takashi offered him a job on his computer ad project. After a passionate, but futile, confession of love at university and another one after Seiji went to work for him, Takashi had finally settled for being Seiji's trusted friend. Ryuu never completely got over Takashi's admiration of Seiji and was wary of the other man, especially when Seiji went to work for him. But Takashi got into the habit of dating incredibly gorgeous models, and Ryuu's suspicion turned to a grudging respect. Ryuu could see how beautiful and sweet natured Seiji was, but he very much disliked it that Takashi had seen it. He didn't blame Seiji, who hid his radiance and fragility under a somewhat audacious and nervous façade, but it worried him that Takashi was sharp enough to see through it and worse, value Seiji for it, and even worse, try to take Seiji for himself. Being richer, taller, and more self-assured, Takashi was a formidable rival for anyone. Anyone who wasn't Seiji's first and only love. Nevertheless, there had been sharp words between Ryuu and Takashi over Seiji. Fortunately Seiji's sincerity and devotion to Ryuu had tamed Takashi into a happy friendship. It was crystal clear to all of them that platonic friendship was all Takashi was ever going to get from Seiji, so Ryuu and Takashi made peace over him. Seiji didn't have many friends and Ryuu was reluctant to deprive him of one of the few he'd made since they'd become lovers in High School. He was also mollified by Takashi's enthusiastic return to heterosexual hyper-normality.

Seiji had hoped Ryuu had a plan for eventually telling their parents about their relationship, but two years after graduation they were, as far as their parents were concerned, still just sharing an apartment in Tokyo. Apparently the fact that it was a one-bedroom apartment with one bed never roused either set of parents to ask who slept where. Daitaro, on the other hand, dropped in now and then, and took great pleasure in taunting them over the sleeping arrangements. He'd figured out they were lovers just by looking at them, and then, being thorough, Daitaro had them investigated to make sure. As annoying as he was, Seiji had mastered the art of flustering Daitaro by being unfailingly polite to him, no matter how much Ryuu's elder brother provoked him. The secrecy and subterfuge of loving Ryuu wore on Seiji's nerves, but he endured it and grew strong in it, knowing Ryuu would always be with him. He loved and trusted Ryuu because other than leaving him, there was nothing else he could do.

Ryuu's mother had been ill off and on for the past few years. Her ailment was something vaguely gynecological, so Seiji didn't pry, he just comforted Ryuu when he got stressed out about his mother's health. Due to being nearly invisible to Ryuu's family, except to Daitaro, Seiji was unable to offer any moral or physical support to his lover's mother. It came as a shock that Ryuu's mother was perfectly aware Seiji was her younger son's lover. The sick woman demanded that Ryuu leave him and move back to the family home while she recovered from her surgery. Daitaro swore he hadn't told his parents; he might tease his brother and Seiji about their relationship, but he was far from willing to stress his elderly mother and father over it. They later learned that Daitaro's selfish wife had told her mother-in-law about Ryuu and Seiji and what a poor example they were setting for her horrible sons.

"Look, I'm only doing this to keep my mother calm and happy until she's recovered from her surgery," Ryuu said the night before he moved back to his parent's home. "I have everything under control, just please be patient. I love you. Trust me for now. They know about us, so when she's recovered, we'll live together again. Openly as a couple and forevermore."

"But she must hate me," Seiji said, his voice shaking from shock and sadness. "And Daitaro's wife, too, if she told her. How can we–"

"You have to believe in me." Ryuu stared hard at him, forcing all resistance away.

Seiji lowered his eyes and said, "All right."

"We can meet sometimes," Ryuu went on. "The apartment is paid for until the end of the year. It's not that we can't see each other. They just don't want us to live together right now."

Seiji felt too exhausted to add "if ever" to the end of Ryuu's sentence; it would just cause another fight he'd lose and he felt he'd lost enough already. He was even too exhausted to respond sexually to Ryuu's advance on their last night in the apartment in which they'd been so happy. Seiji was not naturally cheerful or much of a fighter. There was nothing in his upbringing that could have prepared him for a closeted gay love affair, let alone falling profoundly in love with another man at barely eighteen years of age. Seiji had relied on Ryuu's strength and vision because it was what Ryuu wanted from him. And now Ryuu was leaving him, temporarily, but still leaving him to keep faith that he'd be back sooner than later and everything would be the same again. When Ryuu left that morning for work, he took his suitcase and said he'd be back for his books. He said this on their commute to Shimada Miyagi's offices, which made it even a little more painful.

Around noon, Takashi came to Seiji's desk in the less elegant area of the offices. Takashi and Ryuu were on the floor above in hi-tech work environments near Daitaro's office, whereas Seiji wrote ad copy and did rough layouts in a cubicle on a lower floor near the storage room. "Ahumm...Ryuu asked me to, ah, check on you," he said, sounding stunned. "I guess he's worried."

"Well, he has a lot to be worried about," Seiji said, managing to sound confident, but shaking inside, as he'd been since Ryuu said he was leaving, but only temporarily. "His mother is quite ill, and–"

"Oh, c'mon, Seiji," Takashi cut him off. "It's me, and Ryuu said he had to leave you."

"It's only temporary," Seiji said as firmly as he could. It helped being in the office, where his voice had to sound at least normal to his cube-mates. "Until his mother is well enough to stand the strain of Ryuu leaving the family."

"I know," Takashi said.

"I'm kind of surprised Ryuu asked you to check on me," Seiji said.

"I think he's worried about you, Seij," Takashi said, scratching his head over it. "I know he loves you, so I don't really underst–"

"I'm kind of busy right now, Takashi," Seiji said as politely as he could.

"Yeah, okay, I, uh, I just wanted to let you know if you need anything..."

"Yes?" Seiji prompted, touched that Takashi, a master advertising wordsmith, was at a loss for words.

"If you need anything," Takashi went on in a firmer voice. "Let me know. I'm here for you, Seiji, okay?"

"Okay. You're a good friend, Takashi, thanks," Seiji said with a weak smile and went back to work.

It was okay as long as Seiji could focus on work, but at the end of the day, the thought of going home to an empty apartment overwhelmed him. He called Takashi's cell phone and hung up when it went to voicemail. Very soon afterwards a winded Takashi was standing at his desk.

"I was on my way home," he gasped. "And I saw your missed call, so I got off the elevator...and ran up four flights." He paused to catch his breath. "I think I need more exercise."

"Why didn't you just call?" Seiji asked, impressed in spite of his looming depression.

"Um...because...I'm an idiot?" Takashi asked, still panting. "I didn't want to miss you."

"Thanks, Takashi," Seiji said softly, staring at the floor. "I was wondering...maybe...you know...we could..."

"Seiji, what?" Takashi asked, leaning his ear closer. "You're mumbling into your tie."

"A movie or something?" Seiji said, looking up at him.

"Oh...sure!" Takashi asked if he could use Seiji's computer and called up movie show times. He also made a call on his cell phone to break a date.

Seiji could hear an angry female voice that got angrier the more cheerful Takashi sounded. "Takashi, I didn't mean for you—"

"Oh, no, it's fine," Takashi said, shutting his phone off and waving it around. "I mean, you heard her, you're rescuing me for an evening of that." He suggested a new comedy/martial arts film from Hong Kong, which was perfectly in line with Seiji's taste in films. Further, Takashi picked a show time that would let them grab some dinner at a nearby café. If the circumstances hadn't been so dreadful for Seiji, it might just have been just another pleasant evening when Ryuu was working late and Seiji and Takashi were at loose ends. On those evenings, Ryuu would usually meet up with them somewhere late and go home with Seiji. But not that evening, and though Seiji did his best to enjoy Takashi's company, he couldn't completely forget that he'd be going home to an empty apartment.

"I feel kind of stupid," Seiji said. He was in Takashi's car and they were nearly to his place. "Helpless, too."

"Really? Why for?" Takashi asked. He was feeling pretty mellow because Seiji had managed a few laughs and smiles that evening. "This is a tough time for you and Ryuu. I just want to help out, Seij."

"I know, Takashi, thank you," Seiji said with a weak smile. "This is the stupid part, do you mind coming up and staying until I turn on all the lights? I forgot to leave one on, and I...I hate going into a totally dark apartment by myself."

"Sure, and we're lucky there's a parking space," Takashi said cheerfully. He looked up at the building rows of windows. "I'm not sure if that's your place, but it looks like there's a light on."

"Ryuu!" Seiji was out of the car practically before Takashi stopped.

Takashi caught up with him in the elevator and laughed happily at his blushing apology for running off. "I'm happy for you, Seiji," he said sincerely. "But are you sure that's your place?"

Seiji nodded, almost overcome with joy, and led his friend down the hall. He fumbled with the key, but Takashi noticed the door was ajar and pushed it open. Daitaro was sitting on Ryuu and Seiji's couch, an empty bottle of champagne in a bucket formerly filled with ice, now water, nearby indicating a long, but patient, wait.

"I was not expecting you, Takashi," he said, staring at Seiji.

Takashi pulled the devastated object of Daitaro's lustful gaze behind him. "What are you doing here, boss?" he asked, wondering whether to flee or stand his, or rather, Seiji's ground. "And how do you have a key?" he added at Seiji's whispered prompt.

"The deal with Ryuu was that I'd pay the entire rent until the lease expires," Daitaro said sleekly. "And if I'm paying the rent...I get a key."

The three were silent for a few moments and then Seiji stepped out from behind Takashi. "I understand," he said sadly. He looked at his wristwatch. "It's late, but I think I can stay at a friend's place tonight and figure something out tomorrow, I–"

"Well, if I'm so unwelcome," Daitaro said with boozy mock umbrage and getting haughtily to his feel. "I'll say good-night." And he swaggered out.

Takashi closed the door after him and leaned against it. "Ryuu's going to kill him."

"Ryuu should have been here to protect me," Seiji said dully, staring at the floor.

"I think Ryuu's doing the best he can under the circumstances," Takashi said, hoping he sounded reasonable.

"It's not good enough." Seiji looked up, his eyes dry, but very sad. "I can't stay here tonight. What if Daitaro comes back?"

"You have a bolt and chain on the door," Takashi said, looking it over. "That should keep him out." Takashi sighed and leaned his head against the door. "I could stay and sleep on the couch."

"What?" Seiji hadn't heard him speaking into the door.

Takashi turned around and said, "I said, I could sleep on the couch."

Without a word, Seiji walked forward and put his arms around his surprised friend. "You don't have to sleep on the couch," he murmured into Takashi's crisp white shirt.

"What?" Takashi could not believe his ears.

Seiji looked up. His eyes seemed warm with desire to Takashi, something Takashi had wanted to see for a long time, but just at that moment seemed a little strange. "I said, you don't have to–" Seiji began.

"I, ah, heard you," Takashi stammered. "I'm just, y'know, kind of surprised, I mean, I, you, you're not exactly yourself, Seiji."

"Yes, it's been a rough day. Finding Daitaro here didn't make it any better, Takashi," Seiji said reasonably. "But you don't have to sleep on the couch. You can go home. I'll be all right by myself." He stepped back from Takashi's embrace as if to prove it.

"Ah, I see," Takashi said, hoping he wasn't blushing. "I'll see you tomorrow then. Don't forget to lock these." He gestured to the inside locks. "And you have my cell if you need anything. Anything at all."

"I might need an escort home tomorrow," Seiji said with a sweet, platonic smile.

"It will be my pleasure," Takashi said, looping his arm around Seiji for a manly one-armed hug. "Good night."

Seiji locked up behind Takashi and made short work of disposing of the empty champagne bottle and putting away the ice bucket he'd never seen before. Daitaro must have brought it with him. In the bedroom, Seiji found a few other things Daitaro must have brought with him and was so angry and used such language, he was glad Takashi wasn't there to hear it. Or see the designer condoms and lube Daitaro had left on the nightstand.

The next day at work, after a halfway decent night of sleep, Seiji tracked Ryuu down and handed him a bag of Daitaro's condoms and lube. "Tell your brother I don't care if he's paying the rent, I want him to stay the hell away from me." The effort of keeping his voice steady made it all come out in a rush.

Ryuu stared into the bag, looking puzzled. "Where did these–?"

"When I got home last night, Daitaro was in our—I mean, my apartment—I mean, the apartment he's paying the rent on that I live in, waiting for me," Seiji said, getting angry again. "And then I found these—these things by the bed."

"Why would Daita–?"

"Take a wild fucking guess, Ryuu," Seiji hissed, furiously. "Or ask Takashi. He was there last night. He chased him off." He stormed off under Shimada's shocked look.

Figuring he better let Seiji cool off, Ryuu sought out Takashi, who confirmed Seiji's story about Daitaro being there, waiting for him the night before. "I see," Ryuu said sadly. "It's a good thing you were there, to, uh...to protect Seiji. Um...thanks."

"You're welcome. What are you going to do?" Takashi asked.

"What Seiji told me to do," Ryuu practically snapped. "Tell my brother to stay the fuck away from him." He blew out an angry breath. "And make sure Daitaro isn't there every night when Seiji goes home...what a fucking mess."

"I can help," Takashi offered. He stared pleasantly into Ryuu's assessing look. "I mean it, Ryuu, I want to help. Seiji's my friend, I don't want to see him hurt. By anyone."

"Okay, okay...thanks." Ryuu squared his shoulders and went off to confront his dreadful elder brother.

Thenceforth, either Ryuu or Takashi saw Seiji home and into the apartment. Takashi was pretty good friends with Daitaro's secretary and was able to get his after work schedule from her most days. On days when it was a mystery where he'd be, Takashi or Ryuu would call him to find out. There were a few suspicious evenings when Seiji and his escort got to the apartment and it seemed like someone had been there. Eventually Daitaro gave up and confined his Seiji harassment to the office in the form of impossible jobs and a mountain of work. As Ryuu's mother recovered from her surgery, she demanded more and more of his time in the evening, until eventually there were few evenings when Ryuu could see Seiji home and they could fall into bed for a few hours. Their express sex life made Seiji feel used and, he was sorry to admit, but only to himself, that he was glad Ryuu, his stressed-out, demanding, domineering lover, was too busy to see him very often. Seiji kept waiting, hoping, wanting to miss Ryuu, as in absence makes the heart grow fonder. But the person he found himself missing was easy-going Takashi when Takashi was not around, which was seldom.

So the time Takashi and Seiji spent together was more peaceful, but Seiji felt guilty for it being so. The stress Seiji felt was that Ryuu's mother was on the mend, which was good. But Ryuu was beginning to talk about leaving his family and settling down permanently with Seiji, something Seiji easily hid his lack of interest in, due to Ryuu never really listening to him anyway. He'd even lost most of his sexual attraction to Ryuu by then.

Ryuu had been as understanding as he was capable of being when Seiji seemed to lose interest in sex. Their sex life was awkward even under the best of circumstances. Seiji was shy and nervous and Ryuu was demanding and impatient in bed. He'd always been the lead in all his endeavors before and after he'd met and fallen in love with Seiji, so it never occurred to him to be on anyone else's schedule. Ryuu was, in fact, something of a bully when he didn't have the time or inclination to understand someone else's point of view. He knew he knew more than Seiji about most things and if he waited for Seiji to get around to figuring out how he felt about sex, they'd still both be virgins. Ryuu estimated he'd be able to come out to his family and leave it because they'd never accept a homosexual son, let alone one in a couple. He'd finally be able to quit Shimada Miyagi and he and Seiji could start a new life. They could even leave Tokyo as they had a university friend in Nagasaki Ryuu had been thinking of contacting about work there. It didn't matter what they did for money, as long as they could be together without any obstacles to their happiness.

So it was a great and horrible shock to him that when he outlined this difficult, but beautiful, future to Seiji, Seiji then broke up with him. "You're kidding...I'm willing to give up everything for you!" Ryuu yelled. "Why?"

They were standing on the street, so Seiji didn't answer him until they were sitting on a bench in a small, deserted park near his home, the one he'd formerly shared with Ryuu. "Because I can never trust you again," he said. He'd gone through this in his head over and over. There was nothing Ryuu could say to upset him. Except...

"I love you, Seiji, why are you doing this?" Ryuu's voice was raw with sorrow, fear and dread.

Seiji stared at his hands folded in his lap and didn't say anything.

"Why can't you trust me?" Ryuu finally asked in a more normal voice.

"If your family can break us up once, they can do it again," Seiji said softly. "I don't want to give everything up, I want to stay in Tokyo with my friends and family, with you...but we could never be happy, there'd always be some problem with your family. I'm tired of hiding how much I loved you. I–I guess I got so good at hiding it, I lost it. I'm sorry, Ryuu, I just don't love you anymore."

"Seiji, I promise, in the future–"

"What future, Ryuu? The one where we're poor and hate each other because we're all we've got?" Seiji asked bitterly. "Or the one where we just live together because we're too scared or proud to break up. Let's be brave and end it here. Please. Before I really start to hate you."

"You hate me?" Ryuu nearly yelped.

"I could, I really think I could."

"Seiji, I did the best I could," Ryuu said when he could control his voice. "What would you have done in my place?"

"Hindsight is 20/20, Ryuu, but I wouldn't have lied about our relationship for so long," Seiji said, almost brutally. "And if I–I ever have another relationship with anyone, I'm going to be honest with everyone about it from the very beginning."

"I couldn't hurt my family, they wouldn't have understood," Ryuu said helplessly.

"You didn't give them a chance to understand or accept me in your life," Seiji said with rising bitterness. "You didn't give me a chance to really be part of your life. It was like you were ashamed of me."

"I was never ashamed of you!"

"But that's what it was like," Seiji said, feeling very tired of everything, especially this conversation. "That's what it always felt like with you. That I was something you had to hide, like a bad habit or–or a crime or something like that." He sighed. "And that made us weak, so your brother, your mom, your sister-in-law, really anyone who found out about us, could break us up. And here we are now. I was never very strong in the first place, Ryuu, I thought if I just loved you enough, everything would work itself out. But loving you, or trying to love you enough, just wore me out, until I don't feel any more love for you. I'm sorry, I'm sorry, I'm just done, I'm sorry." Seiji swallowed hard, but did nothing about the tears streaming silently down his face.

Ryuu stared furiously in front of him. "It's Takashi, isn't it?" he demanded. "Isn't i–?" He turned angrily to glare an answer out of Seiji, but his rage was choked off by Seiji's tearstained face and empty eyes. Seiji just shook his head and stared at him. "I'm sorry," Ryuu whispered. He put his arms around Seiji's limp form and whispered, "I'm sorry, I'm sorry, I'm sorry," over and over until Seiji finally pushed him away.

"I can get home by myself, Ryuu," he said, getting to his feet.

"I have to check for Daitaro," Ryuu said.

"He's out of town with Takashi," Seiji said bluntly. "Good-bye."

Ryuu didn't exactly give up on getting Seiji back after this, but he had to proceed with great caution. His family was too busy showing him pictures of prospective brides to notice how distracted he was. They assumed he was just thinking about the wife and family in his future.

Work for Seiji at Shimada Miyagi became a nightmare. He was depressed, and then the horrific automotive campaign competition with the MM agency, that ended up with MM getting the contract, was the last straw for him. He quit and moved back to his parents' home and slept for the better part of two weeks before he could see anyone.

In those two weeks, Takashi came to his house every other day to see how he was doing. He introduced himself as Seiji's friend and former colleague, left his contact information so they could let him know if he could do anything for Seiji. In the course of these visits, Takashi impressed Seiji's rather puzzled parents with his devotion and made friends with the family dog. In those same two weeks, Ryuu, who was living only three blocks away, left messages on Seiji's cell phone that Seiji never returned, but he never once showed his face at Seiji's home.

When Seiji finally snapped out of his funk, he began to look for work and called Takashi to thank him for stopping by and being a friend. Takashi happened to be on his way to visit him, so they wound up having dinner and going to a movie. They did not talk about Ryuu, Daitaro, or Shimada Miyagi. The next day his mother asked him if the previous evening had been a date and Seiji said he wasn't sure. His mom then said something that astounded him. She said, "Takashi seems like a nice young man, your father and I just want you to be happy, so if that was a date, we understand." His parents were sincere and were always welcoming and pleasant to Takashi when he came to pick Seiji up for, well, for dates, some of which were as simple as a cup of tea and taking the family dog for a walk in the opposite direction from the Shimada family residence.

After weeks of odd jobs and interviews, Seiji was finally hired as a clerk at the National Archive. He'd always liked organizing things and had minored in information science at university, so he felt very much at home in his boring new job. His parents heaved a huge sigh of relief and invited Takashi for dinner to celebrate Seiji's new job. They were very happy to see their son getting back to normal; he'd become so withdrawn after he became friends with Shimada, they'd been worried, but now he was more his usual, low-key, slightly brooding, optimistic self.

One evening when they met for drinks after work, Takashi asked if Seiji had heard from Ryuu lately.

"No," Seiji said, wondering why, all of the sudden, Takashi brought Ryuu up after all the time that had gone by. "He...he stopped calling me after I didn't return his calls. Why did you ask me?"

"He's, ah, gone," Takashi said, signaling for the check. "He left Daitaro a note last night that he was leaving Tokyo and not to look for him. Daitaro asked me if I knew where he might be and to ask you."

"Do you think I'd tell Daitaro anything?" Seiji snarled. "Sorry," he said in a milder voice. "I, I don't know where Ryuu is or where he'd go. We didn't speak after that day I broke up with him."

They walked along awhile in silence and then Takashi said, softly, "I guess he gave up, then."

Seiji slowed down next to him. "I couldn't go on like that..." he said almost to himself. "It was too painful."

"I understand." Takashi put his arm around him and they walked like that to his car. When they got to Seiji's parents home, Takashi took Seiji's hand and pressed his lips to the palm. Seiji leaned over and kissed him lightly, more of a promise of kisses to come, kisses worth waiting for, than a proper kiss. Takashi did not come in to say hello to Seiji's parents, who weren't home anyway, and this was fine with Seiji. He had a lot to think about that night.

That weekend Takashi spent his Saturday obsessively cleaning his apartment and putting brand new designer sheets on his bed. Seiji merely packed an overnight bag and told his parents he'd be back late on Sunday. They didn't ask any questions, but didn't frown or scowl either. He arrived at Takashi's place in time for the simple dinner Takashi made for them.

"It's nice you can cook," Seiji said after thanking him for a nice dinner.

"I don't like cooking very much, but I like the challenge, and I like sharing it with people I like," Takashi said, feeling a little less nervous once they were on the couch with cognacs.

"It's been a long time since I've been here," Seiji said, looking around the comfortable room. "When you moved in, right? I helped you hang that painting." He gestured to a large landscape painted as if the view was from medieval castle walls. It included a parapet and a rushing river.

"Yes, and then I made a fool of myself," Takashi said, moving a little closer. "Sorry, thank you for forgiving me. I was out of line to kiss you like that. You...weren't mine."

"I couldn't like your kiss, even though I wanted to," Seiji said softly. "But this is now..."

"Yeah, now," Takashi sighed and drew Seiji into a kiss that rapidly escalated into a very passionate kiss. It was as if all the pent up love they'd had for each other burst into flame as they held each other close.

"I've always liked that painting," Seiji said as calmly as possible when he came up for air. "But could we go into your bedroom where I won't be distracted by it?"

"Yeah, I...think we'd be more comfortable there," Takashi panted, discreetly adjusting his erection in his chinos. Seiji, flushed and lovely, ruffled his hair and didn't help matters as he slid out from beneath him.

"Have you done this before?" Seiji asked as Takashi was carefully removing Seiji's clothes.

"Nope, only with girls," Takashi said running his hands over Seiji's lean flanks. "You'll have to correct my technique where you can."

"Tsk! I'm not going to comp–" Seiji frowned and then leaned up for a kiss. "It's like I haven't really done this before either. It feels so different with you, Takashi." He lay back in Takashi's arms and looked trustingly up at him.

"Your skin is so soft and warm," Takashi murmured, kissing his neck and letting his hands explore his chest, pausing to gently pinch one then the other of Seiji's hard nipples, and then lower over his taut belly and hesitating in his silky pubic curls. "Hey, why did you tense up?" he asked, making little circles with his index finger just above Seiji's penis.

"I, I don't know what you expect," Seiji said nervously.

Takashi took Seiji's hand and moved it to his own erection. "Something very similar to what I have," he said pressing Seiji's hand against his cock. "Does this seem sort of familiar?" Takashi asked, and when Seiji began to explore his manhood, he moved his own hand back to Seiji's beautiful crotch.

The truth was that Takashi was nervous, but he covered it well as he fondled Seiji's delicate arousal. It was warm, smooth, responsive. Takashi wasn't so worried about whether they'd be able to jack each other off; he was more concerned about fucking Seiji well, or at least adequately, without hurting him. He was slightly worried that Seiji would even want to go that far, but was encouraged when Seiji rolled on his back and didn't fight Takashi off when he pushed his legs apart. Nor did Seiji reject him when he nuzzled the head of his sweet cock. The desire in Seiji's eyes was the same as in the dreams Takashi had nearly given up on. "I, um, have...stuff..." Takashi mumbled.

"Stuff?" Seiji repeated vaguely. He looked on sultrily as Takashi drew a pack of condoms and a container of water-based lube from the bedside table. "Ohhh, stuff," he sighed happily and took up one of the condoms. "These are nice."

"I'm glad you like them," Takashi said, distracted by warming the lube on his fingers and not sure how to proceed. While still examining the condom package, Seiji helped him out by playfully draping an ankle over Takashi's right shoulder and tilting his hips up. Mentally thanking him, Takashi slid his slippery fingers between Seiji's smooth round cheeks and watched the younger man shiver with pleasure at the contact. Takashi leaned down for a kiss as, after a little exploring, he pressed his fingertip inside Seiji, who tensed a little. "Does that hurt?" Takashi asked gently, not moving.

"No, no, it's...it's just been a while," Seiji said, his voice breathy with desire. "Don't stop, okay?"

"Okay." Takashi kissed him again and pushed his finger farther inside. He leaned back to get a better angle to press another finger in beside it. Carefully monitoring how much Seiji was relaxing on his fingers, Takashi was impressed when on an inward stroke he brushed against something inside Seiji that caused his lover to arch with pleasure, his half-mast cock leaping to full hardness and a startled cry of pleasure bursting from his lips. Intrigued, Takashi explored the place inside Seiji again until Seiji was nearly incoherent with passion. "I'd always thought that was a myth," he said, surveying the splayed out, panting Seiji before him. He shifted his position between Seiji's legs and leaned over him.

"You'll need this." Seiji wasn't so out of it that he couldn't open the condom and carefully roll it down Takashi's erection and put some lube on the tip. "Um, I'm, I'm a little out of practice."

"I'll be gentle," Takashi said reflexively. Positioning the slippery tip, poised to enter Seiji's body, Takashi then had a moment of conscience. "We don't have to do this, Seiji," he said, willing to make the supreme sacrifice (that night).

"Yes, we do," Seiji said, teeth clenched with lust. "I want to, I want to very mmmmmuch." He sighed deeply as Takashi pressed the head inside and gently worked his cock in all the way to the root.

"Okay?" he asked when he hit bottom.

"Mmmmm." Seiji wrapped his legs around his waist and thrust up against him.

Unable to miss a hint like that, Takashi began to move in small pulses, not wanting to hurt the man beneath him. Eventually lengthening his strokes and encouraged by Seiji meeting his rhythm, or perhaps setting it in that telepathy happy lovers have, Takashi let waves of moans roll up from deep in his chest as he rose to his climax and felt the top of his head coming off. He held Seiji, thrashing in his own orgasm, against his chest, both of them getting their breath back in small, exhausted gasps, finally working up to long satisfied sighs of pure contentment.

"Did we live?" Seiji asked, smiling against Takashi's shoulder.

"I think so," Takashi said, kissing him, brushing Seiji's damp locks off his forehead. He shifted gently, this way and that, until his limp, but still condom sheathed cock slipped out. Reluctantly, he rose from Seiji's arms and disposed of the latex. "That was totally worth the wait," he said, relaxing back into the arms he'd left for too long.

"How long have you been waiting for this?" Seiji asked, sleepily stroking his hair.

"A few days after I fell in love with you at first sight," Takashi said softly. "I knew I was in love with you, I just didn't understand the desire part."

"I love you, Takashi," Seiji said, tightening his arms a little before dozing off.

"I love you, too, Seiji," Takashi said, making a vow before he slept. "And I will never leave you."

A few weeks later and with his parents' blessing, Seiji moved in with Takashi because they were very much in love. Because Takashi was honest with his parents about how much he loved Seiji, even before Seiji loved him back, Takashi's parents invited them over as a couple for family events and casual lunches and dinners. Their friends were simply glad to see them both so happy. Daitaro sneered, but Takashi had become so valuable to Shimada Miyagi, he mostly kept his opinion to himself. An additional benefit was that Seiji's new loving home was closer to his job and he felt so loved, so happy and so safe, it was as if he'd only been half alive before his life with Takashi.

So when Takashi said nearly the same words to him as Ryuu had said three years before asking him to wait out family events, Seiji's blood ran cold and his world withered before his eyes. The possibility of leaving Takashi, the way he'd left Ryuu, weighed heavily on Seiji's mind and was again a choice between this kind of hell and that kind of hell. But, hey, at least they'd been happy for a little while.

"And how did you find out about this mess?" Takashi asked, shoulders slumping. He was trying very hard to keep it under wraps until he could extricate himself from the Yamada daughter snare Daitaro had him in.

"Well, apparently Seiji mentioned it to Yoshi who mentioned it to me because Seiji is somewhat freaked out about it," Shimada said, sipping his very good martini and watching Takashi frown. "I've been in your place, Takashi. If you give an inch, they've got you."

"Got me? Oh please, Ryuu, this is a very different situation," Takashi said, snapping out of his funk. "For one thing, my mother's health isn't involved and Daitaro isn't my brother."

"But you are caving in to Daitaro, doing this miai with Yashimoto—"

"Yamada Minoro's daughter." Takashi ordered another round.

"Whoever's daughter, what's her name?"

"Yoko."

"Yeah, Yoko Yamada," Shimada said, rolling it around in his mouth with a gin soaked olive. "Yamada Yoko. I hear she's a little party girl hellion. That she has her eye on you seems odd."

"Yeah, thanks, I think," Takashi said, sipping his vodka tonic. "You seem well informed about her."

"She's been trying to run with the Jupiter Li crowd," Shimada said, a predatory gleam in his eyes.

"Should I know who or what that is?" Takashi asked.

"He's one of those Shanghai super zillionaires with a shady past that things happen around," Shimada drawled. "I have to find something to write about in Tokyo while I'm stuck here. Since I got tossed in jail for asking the right questions at the wrong time in Riyadh, the paper's keeping me close to home until the fuss dies down."

"That could take a while. And after your adventures in Riyadh, this Li character sounds more like a subject for the gossip columns than a hard-bitten international correspondent like you," Takashi said with a smile. He'd been hard pressed to keep Yoshi off a plane to Saudi Arabia while Seiji pulled strings he didn't know he had in the government. Shimada's paper and the Japanese State Department took a very serious interest in the matter, which had become an international incident. While Seiji did what he could from his government job, Takashi, Yoshi, Daitaro, Renge, Jun Ikoma, hell, even Kenbo, worked every angle they could think of to get Shimada out of the jam his apparently alarming questions to a Saudi official about his dead Filipina maid and the thriving sex slave trade between Saudi Arabia and the Philippines had gotten the reporter into. Takashi was touched to discover how many friends Shimada probably didn't realize he had in Japan. Ultimately, the Saudis decided he was more trouble than he was worth, and after three days in a cell with his translator at the main jail in Riyadh, banned them both from the country forever, escorted them to a New Delhi-bound plane and stood guard until it took off. In New Delhi they were met by an underling from the Japanese embassy, who put them on the next plane to Tokyo. In Tokyo, Shimada filed a story even his paper said was too much speculation, but Interpol was very interested in it. As far as Shimada was concerned, his involvement ended with Interpol's entrance, but the paper, after paying him as if he'd filed a major story, which translated to Shimada as a bribe to be good and stay local, kept him on the east Asia beat, mostly in Tokyo, until the name Ryuu Shimada ceased to cause diplomats to break out in flop sweats.

"Jupiter Li's interesting enough to try to be where he is and see if anything happens. That's something we newspaper people do on a regular basis," Shimada said. "We're funny that way."

"You mean that's what they do when they can't fly to foreign dictatorships and get in trouble," Takashi said, and smiled at Shimada's laugh. "I see. Well, I certainly wouldn't want to get involved with a girl in a crowd like that," Takashi said coolly. "That could be my way out of this mess."

"I don't think old Yoko's making much progress getting in with the In-crowd," Shimada said thoughtfully. "Especially since Li's been in Tokyo splashing money around, living large and chasing Koji Kawazu's ass since his second film came out."

"Koji wasn't bad in it," Takashi observed. "The film I mean, not his ass. It was a nice little urban gay artist in love with an urban gay married salaryman ill-fated romance story. Rather sad, but Seiji and I enjoyed it. I seem to recall you and Yoshi liked it as well."

"Yeah, we did. Yeah, it was nice I happened to be in town for both premieres, wasn't it? Even though I hate those kind of things, unless it's a news story. Thank the gods Yoshi's second film sank without a trace," Shimada observed. "And that he just can't act."

"I thought Yoshi was great in 'The English Speaking Escort'," Takashi said. "So did you."

"He was great, but he had a lot of time during the play's run to get good," Shimada said. "He didn't have that kind of time to get it together for the second film. He's not a good movie actor. I don't think he's much of an actor at all."

"Maybe it wasn't the right role," Takashi allowed. "I mean, he was playing a gangster's boyfriend and it was supposed to be a comedy, and there was that cool car chase, which was the best part, and then that awful shoot-out at the end and everyone, except Yoshi's character, dies, and–"

"Takashi, please don't make me remember," Shimada said, rubbing his temples. "Renge's trying to negotiate him out of the third film. Looks promising, keep your fingers crossed."

"He had some good moments–"

"Yes. He was cute in places," Shimada said firmly. "And this is not what I asked you here to talk about."

Takashi sighed. "As you must realize, I'm under a lot of pressure in all this," he said. "Daitaro is on me, my family likes Seiji, but now they wonder if it's a permanent–"

"Does he know that?" Shimada asked.

"Oh, God, no, my parents haven't seen Seiji since the Yamada clan contacted them about my character," Takashi said. "I never hid our relationship from my parents. They like Seiji very much. I even told my mother I was in unrequited love with him when I was."

"Yeah, before it was requited," Shimada said wryly, signally for another round of drinks.

"So, moving right along," Takashi continued briskly as he was sensing a certain tension in the air. "There's pressure at work, pressure from my family, and a certain amount of tension at home. It's like Seiji believes me when I say it's all a show, but then again, here you are."

"I'm here because Yoshi is worried about Seiji," Shimada said, trying his excellent new martini. "He might not be showing it to you, but according to Yoshi, Seiji is anxious and depressed about the miai. And it would be awkward for me if you and he broke up for any reason."

"We're not going to break up," Takashi snapped. "But why would it be awkward for you? Do you want him back?"

"No. And that would be awkward."

Takashi put down his drink. "Do you really think he'd want you back? After everything?" he asked, stunned and not looking at Shimada.

"Takashi, I don't know what he'd do," Shimada said, sadly, not looking at Takashi or the waitress because the last thing they needed was more liquor. "I thought I'd be with him for the rest of my life and he didn't want that. So as far as I'm concerned, there's no telling what he'll do if he feels threatened enough or hurt enough or any of the feelings he had when he decided to dump me for you, just when I was ready to dump everything for him." He sighed and took a sip of the martini he didn't really want anymore. "So, if you can wiggle out of this miai, do so. I think this is more of a make or break than you realize. When is it, by the way?"

"Thursday," Takashi said, pushing his vodka tonic away from him. "Unless I can, as you say, wiggle out of it. And it's not a miai, it's just a, a meeting or something."

"Yeah, right. I guess Thursday's the night Yoshi said he was going out with Seiji, now that I think about it," Shimada said. "I wasn't invited, but I suppose I'll live. Where are fashionable not-a-miais held these days anyway?"

Takashi named an elegant hotel that catered to a more mature, traditional type of Japanese. "Do you know what they're doing that night?" Takashi asked.

"I dunno, food, shopping, movie, galleries, whatever they do on normal nights out," Shimada said. "That's another aspect of this mess: I'd hate to see Yoshi lose one of the few real friends he has in Tokyo. He's pretty much surrounded by posers, losers, creeps, leeches and miscellaneous weirdoes lately. I really need Renge to get him out of that third film so he can go back to being a normal kid. The modeling jobs have tapered to nearly nothing, which is also great. I figure Yoshi can take a year off, go to school and we get back on track after this period of distraction."

"Well, some of it was fun," Takashi said, with a smile for Ryuu and waving his American Express card at the waitress.

"Yeah, kind of. Hey, I'll get this," Shimada said, holding up his VISA card.

"No, I'll get it," Takashi insisted.

"Thanks, Takashi, I said I'LL GET IT," Shimada said, raising his voice a little.

They eventually flipped a coin, and Shimada was allowed to put the tab on his paper's generous expense report to keep him happy in Tokyo, as opposed to Takashi's generous client-love Shimada Miyagi credit card, and all was well in the Hourglass Bar that afternoon.

The Hotel Arcadia, which Daitaro had chosen for the miai Takashi refused to admit was a miai, and hadn't been able to wrench himself free of, let alone wiggle out of, had a huge sunken bar and lounge in the middle of its lobby. Rather incongruously for such an elegant hotel, it was called the Impala Bar. Usually the Impala was a serene deserted sea of plush chairs, little marble-topped tables, tasteful lighting, and a long, long mahogany bar with a few well-dressed travelers scattered around it. One of the younger members of PRCK Architects had once suggested to the hotel's owners that his firm remodel the lobby, but this idea was politely rebuffed. The puzzled youngster later learned that the hotel really didn't want more traffic in the lobby than they already had, they were very happy with the reliable stodginess the hotel had achieved over the decades and they were loath to tamper with what they considered their own kind of perfection.

On the dreaded Thursday, Seiji didn't bother going home after work. He couldn't bear the thought of watching Takashi put on a kimono for the miai that Takashi refused to admit was a miai. It was upsetting to Seiji that Takashi was in so much denial about what was really happening, he wasn't bothering to fight it. Seiji was in denial, too. He didn't want to know a thing about the when, the where and the how of the proceedings on Thursday, beyond that it was on that date and he wanted to be elsewhere, having fun, if possible. He would have liked to support his lover in all this mess, but Seiji found it impossible to support someone who didn't realize or wouldn't admit how much trouble he was actually in. Takashi had never been in this kind of situation, with Daitaro pushing from one side and all of heterosexual Japanese tradition pushing from the other. How could Takashi survive all that pressure? Ryuu had caved in, and, in some ways, Seiji now saw that Ryuu was stronger than Takashi. Ryuu had left everything behind when he left Tokyo after Seiji left him. Not only had he survived and grown stronger, he'd thrived, triumphed and found a new love, a wonderful person, and they were happier than he and Seiji had ever been. That had never bothered Seiji before—that Ryuu and Yoshi were happier than he and Ryuu had ever been—but now that he felt on shaky ground with Takashi, it was gnawing at him. Not gnawing at him a lot, but just here and there, and then there was suddenly all this weird guilt for everything: hurting Ryuu, rebounding on Takashi, envying Ryuu's love for Yoshi while being friends with Yoshi. It all made Seiji just want to run away and sleep...forever, just sleep, and never have to worry about waking up. Seiji was so nervous all Thursday afternoon, fidgety and his stomach in knots, he almost cancelled whatever it was Yoshi wanted to do that night to distract him from what Takashi was doing that night.

"I hope you don't mind if we meet Koji for a drink later," Yoshi said when they met at a bar downtown. He was wearing a sleek black leather jacket, tight black jeans, a grey silk jersey t-shirt and dark magenta colored Italian loafers. Seiji felt elderly and dowdy next to him in his plain business suit and tie. "Koji's worried about you, he wants you to have fun tonight."

"Does everyone in Tokyo know about tonight?" Seiji said, sipping a little more of his humongous margarita.

"I guess I mentioned it," Yoshi said sheepishly. "Or maybe he mentioned it...I can't remember now. Doesn't matter, anyway, we don't have to go if you don't want–"

"Oh, no, I'd like to go," Seiji said quickly. "I, I appreciate what you and he are doing for me. It makes me feel less alone in all of it, sort of."

"Oh, Seiji, it's going to be all right, don't worry," Yoshi said. He put a lot into it because he wasn't sure he believed it himself.

"When did you see Koji?" Seiji asked. "I thought you two had gone your separate ways after the film."

"We pretty much did," Yoshi admitted. "Koji runs with a pretty fast crowd now, but I guess he figures you have to be nice to the people on your way up because that's who you'll meet on your way down. At least that's what someone said to me at the party for Koji getting cast as the star of 'The Occupation Boy'."

"Oh? What's it about?" Seiji asked.

"I'm not sure, I didn't stick around very long," Yoshi said, looking at his watch: they had another hour to kill. "I got sick of saying I was considering several projects when people asked me what my next film was. And the producer and production company of Koji's new film are American so everyone was speaking English and it really wears me out to try to speak and understand English for more than an hour."

"I bet Ryuu loved it," Seiji observed. "He loves speaking English."

"He wasn't there. He was on a story or hanging out with his newspaper friends," Yoshi said, somewhat sadly. "He didn't want to go with me. I guess I don't blame him. It was kind of a weird evening."

"Oh? How so?" Seiji asked.

Yoshi sighed, he didn't want to mention that the party had been at Papa Elysium's, where he'd gone with Takashi, Daitaro and Koji one night, nor that Daitaro and Norboru Suzuki the architect had been at Koji's party and had even had what seemed like an argument over Koji. It had been one of the main things that drove Yoshi home after an hour in that creepy crowd Koji currently had around him. "Just lots of high-strung people, some rough-looking guys. Jupiter Li and his body guards are a little scary, too."

"Really? I think I read he's building something in Korea with PRCK Architects," Seiji said. "He's incredibly rich. What's he like?"

"I don't know, I was only introduced to him once," Yoshi said. "And that was enough. He doesn't speak Japanese, so we said a few things through his translator, and then he just sat there all evening, talking to his body guards or talking to Koji through the translator. Koji really digs him for some reason." He didn't add that Daitaro and Suzuki had been very interested in Jupiter and Koji at the Papa Elysium party. "And, in addition to the Jupiter Li weirdness, there's always all these strange women with shrill laughs who drink too much at these parties. They get really intense over weird stuff, too."

"Like what?"

"Fashion and money," Yoshi said. "Oh and sex, like, who's having sex with who. It's stupid. I thought it was stupid before, but I really think it's stupid after Ryuu was in jail. I thought I'd lose my mind then. Thanks again for everything, Seiji, I don't know what I would have done without you and, and, um..."

"Takashi?" Seiji smiled wryly. "Yeah, he was great during that crisis." He ordered another drink. "What projects are you considering?"

"Eh?" Yoshi felt awful that he'd brought up just the subject they were trying to avoid.

"At Koji's party, you said you were considering your next project," Seiji said, licking salt off the rim of his glass. "Is it a film? Or TV?"

"Actually, it's nothing," Yoshi said with a grimace. "My second film bombed, so nobody wants anything to do with me and acting. I'm kind of relieved, films are too much work." He glanced at Seiji smiling sympathetically at him, which was good. "Oh, don't get me wrong, I don't mind hard work, but I never felt like I finished a thought when I was making the films. It was 'do this,' 'stand here,' 'look this way,' 'look that way,' 'smile,' 'frown,' 'cut!' and never a moment to think about what I was doing."

"I thought you were pretty good in the second film," Seiji said sincerely.

"You're a good friend, Seiji," Yoshi said, patting Seiji's shoulder. "I was terrible every time I opened my mouth. They should have just let me wander around in pajamas and tight jeans for the whole film, it would have been better." He was glad to hear Seiji laughing and they went on to talk about films and books and places and people they liked.

At seven o'clock they got a taxi to the Hotel Arcadia, where the party was already in full swing. "Oh my..." Yoshi said, looking around for a nonexistent corner of quiet.

"Well this should take my mind off of, uh, everything," Seiji said, blinking at the noise—Peruvian musicians, a Mariachi band, lots of shrill female laughter, and some kind of high pitched squealing in the background that might or might not have been a blender—and the collection of wildly dressed people milling about in a contained and controlled-so-far riot.

They hovered at the edge of the crowd until Koji himself, wearing a skin-tight black spandex cat-suit and thigh-high boots, rolled up to greet them. "Isn't this wild?" he said. "This place was made for a scene like this, yes, yes, yes!!!" He drew them into the throng and away from the pale and trembling hotel manager, who was torn between wringing his hands over the shocking, for the Impala Bar, goings-on in his hotel and serious amounts of money being tossed around that night, including a nice, big, fat tip for him in advance that other less sensitive people might call a bribe to play along. The manager was especially concerned because guests for an elegant miai would be arriving shortly and he was beginning to think it would be better if they were brought in through the back door. Unfortunately, a large group of people in kimonos had just arrived and were looking on the proceedings in the Impala Bar with great and pointed interest. This could be no other than the miai guests and the potential bride and groom.

"Oh! Oh!! Oh!!! There's Jupiter Li!"

Takashi glanced over at Yoko, whose delighted squealing could barely be heard over the din of the party. "Which one?" he yelled, wondering if he could use the chaos of the bar to escape. He'd been to this hotel in the past and never noticed how much the bar area looked like a cauldron before.

"The one in the big hat with the feathers...no, the white feathers, and shiny silver suit," she cried, leaning forward in desire. "Oh! And there's Koji Kawazu! And, and! And the other pajama boy!!! What's his name?"

"Yoshi," Takashi said dully. He'd just caught sight of Seiji, coatless, dancing with some guy wearing some kind of a sequined smock. Seiji sadly returned his lover's gaze and went back to his clumsy two-step. "Yoshi Kata–"

"WHAT THE FUCK IS GOING ON HERE?" Daitaro was red in the face with fury and practically on top of Takashi. He was, however, staring a hole in Koji, who was dancing with Norboru Suzuki, Jupiter Li's pet architect of the moment.

"Fuck if I know," Takashi said. "Excuse me." And he waded bravely into the crowd to find Seiji. "Seiji, what are you doing here?" he asked when he'd wedged himself next to his lover.

"Dancing," Seiji said, looking at the floor.

"Hey, samurai asshole, buzz off," Seiji's dance partner sneered.

"Shut the fuck up!" Takashi and Seiji said in unison, and then Seiji went on solo. "Takashi, I'm here to have a good time. You're here to do whatever it is you're here to do," he said, pausing to look pointedly at the little group of beautifully and traditionally dressed Japanese people being shepherded past the freak show of the northern hemisphere. "So let's both just get on with it." He smartly turned his back on him and swam into the crowd.

"Seiji!" Takashi tried to follow, but the tide of bodies was against him. He suddenly found Koji planted in front of him.

"Nice dress, Takashi," Koji snarled. "Is there one tie that unties for it all to come off?"

"Are you behind all this, Koji?" Takashi yelled, trying to get past him.

"I'd like to know that, too," Daitaro yelled beside him. "What the fuck are you up to, Koji?"

"You can both fucking drop dead!" Koji yelled. "Hey! Chang! These two are leaving!"

"We're going, we're going," Takashi yelled. "Call off your gorilla." He heard someone say, "Was that Takashi?" behind him, but didn't look around. He was thinking very very hard on what to do since he was out of his depth in this situation. "Um, I have to use the men's room, be right there," Takashi said when they got to the door of the private dining room, where the hotel manager was prostrate with apology and regret. Yoko was still trying to get away from her irritated father and mother to join the party, Takashi's parents looked concerned and puzzled, Daitaro's wife looked almost as angry as he did, and at the sight of all of them, Takashi fled for the Gents as fast as his zoris would carry him.

It wasn't much quieter in the bathroom. There were two, sometimes three men in each stall, but he found one that was unoccupied and locked the door and got out his cell phone.

Shimada was at the Murano Bar and Grill, a somewhat seedy hangout for all kinds of media types, but newspapermen were on the top of the heap. When his cell phone rang, he was halfway through his fifth martini and listening to a guy who'd gotten in trouble in Manila asking the same questions as Shimada had asked about money, murder, and who was really running the Philippine sex trade in Saudi Arabia.

This was a relief to Shimada, because he was starting to itch to work on the story that got him tossed in jail not so long ago. "Hey, Takashi...where the hell are you?" he asked, trying to hear the other man over some very strange echoic sounds in the background.

"I said you've got to help me!" Takashi yelled into the phone. "Seiji is in trouble!"

"What kind of trouble?" Shimada said from under the bar where the reception seemed a little better. "Where is he? Where the hell are you?"

"We're at the Hotel Arcadia," Takashi said desperately. "At the Impala Bar, it's a nightmare in there."

"The Impala? A nightmare of boredom," Shimada observed. "What are you doing–?"

"The–the–the, uh, meeting thing we discussed," Takashi shouted, starting to panic at Ryuu's lack of action.

"The miai? I told you not to do it," Shimada drawled, getting to his feet because he was having trouble finishing his drink under the bar and the bartender couldn't see him ordering another one. "Look, Takashi, I'm drinking with my colleagues. If you're gonna ignore my advice, you made your bed–"

"But Seiji is here!"

"–so you get to–"

"And Yoshi!"

"–lie in it. Of course Yoshi is with Seiji," Shimada said, taking a big sip of his fresh martini. "He's keeping him company while you do something stupid."

"And Koji is here!"

"So? Takashi this is boring," Shimada said, getting more irritated than bored. "I have world events to discuss here with serious journalists."

"Then I have a newsflash for you and your fellow newshounds, Ryuu," Takashi yelled. "Jupiter Li is hosting this party and he's here in the Impala Bar at Hotel Arcadia right now," and with that, Takashi hung up in Ryuu's ear.

"What a scoop!" Shimada thought. But, with Jupiter Li involved, he was suddenly on a mission to rescue Yoshi and Seiji from–from, something, maybe a Chinese billionaire or sex slavery or bad taste, or something, but one thing was certain: he would need reinforcements. Shimada poured the rest of his martini down his gullet, slapped some money on the bar and yelled to the assorted newsmen, paparazzi and gossip mongers in the bar:

"Jupiter Li is hosting a fag party at the Hotel Arcadia Impala Bar and both of the Pajama Boys are there!" He was at the head of the stampede to the taxi line.

Back in the men's room at the Hotel Arcadia, Takashi stepped out of the stall and was confronted with both Daitaro and Yoshi.

Daitaro merely yelled his name, but Yoshi was more civil. "I thought that was you," he said over the din. "Is your–your thing here?" Yoshi pushed away a drunk who wanted to know more about "his thing."

"I don't have a thing," Takashi blurted.

The drunk sighed, "Man, that's too bad."

"Yes, you do have a thing!" Daitaro yelled. "And we're going to it right now!"

"Oh, man, that's good news," the drunk mumbled, dropping to his knees. "Can I come with you?"

Yoshi stepped delicately around the kneeling boozer and followed the kimonos out of the men's room. "Takashi, I–"

"What kind of friend are you to bring Seiji to a thing like this?" Takashi wheeled and snapped at him. "Can't you get him out of here?"

Already feeling stressed and that events were spinning out of control, Yoshi lost his temper. "First of all I didn't know your stupid thing was here!" he yelled at the shocked ad men. "And second of all, why should I make him leave? And third, FUCK YOU BOTH!" He spun on his magenta loafers and ran into the crowd.

"Oh, shit," Takashi moaned and would have followed him but for Daitaro dragging him in the other direction.

"Takashi, please!" For Daitaro this amunted to begging, and got Takashi's attention. "Listen, please, just get through a half hour with the Yamada family and I'll work it out later and..." Daitaro let his sentence trail off. He was staring hard at something in the sunken bar.

Takashi considered pressing his advantage, but following his employer's line of sight, he saw Norboru Suzuki staring hard at Daitaro. Suzuki had his arm around Koji, who was looking the other way. Unable to ignore the rage being transmitted between the two men, for the sake of peace, Takashi decided to herd Daitaro away from there and into the banquet room. He vaguely heard a commotion at the front entrance, but he was too far from it and too distracted by what he now knew he needed to do, to really analyze what it might be.

What it was, at that moment, was most of the media talent in Tokyo bursting into the Hotel Arcadia and pouring into the Impala Bar.

It only took Shimada a moment to find the most normally dressed person in the moiling, sweaty, now slightly panicked, party crowd. "You're coming with me, Mr. Hayashida," Shimada said, latching onto a rather stunning-looking Seiji, who was being chatted up by a gigolo of some kind. "Scram, sharpie," Shimada growled at the overdressed over-charming young man. Ignoring Seiji's gasp of surprise, Shimada held fast to him.

"Ryuu! What are you doing here?" Yoshi asked, coming up beside Seiji in the now gigolo-free space.

"I'm the Cavalry, I've just come over the hill," Shimada said, not loosening his hold on Seiji, but grabbing Yoshi with his other hand. "Come! Let us lodge with my fleas in the hills! Or flee to my lodge in the hills! Or something!"

"You're drunk!" Seiji yelled.

"Yes! And the night is young!" Shimada cried, dancing a few steps as they were suddenly surrounded by the Mariachi band. "Oh, shit! And there's Jupiter Li and I don't have a free hand!"

In the private dining room, Takashi bowed to the assembled families, but did not sit down. Silently saluting Seiji and all the love he felt for him, he knew he would be brave, but didn't know if he'd be eloquent. He took a deep breath and looked directly into Yoko Yamada's feral little face. "Yoko, I owe you an apology," he said in a firmer voice than he thought was possible. "I've been wasting your time. I can't marry you. I'm homosexual and I'm deeply in love with the man I've been living with for two years." Takashi waited to for the room to explode, but all that happened was Yoko raised her eyebrows and nodded. Puzzled by this, Takashi decided to press his advantage while everyone else seemed to be in shock. "So, I apologize to everyone and I'll come around and apologize individually tomorrow," he said in a rush, backing toward the door. "But right now, I have something very important to do, so good night!" And he bolted.

Meanwhile in the Impala Bar, Shimada was still holding Seiji with one hand and Yoshi with the other. He ground his teeth and whined in frustration, "Gah! I've never been this close to Jupiter Li and now I can't do anything about it!"

"Well, you can let go of me anytime, Ryuu," Seiji said sharply. He'd given up trying to get away, it only made Shimada hold on tighter.

"I can't, I have to protect you," Shimada said.

"From what!?" Seiji yelled.

"Oh, I don't know," Shimada said, watching Li's body guards fend off the paparazzi. "Yourself, the unknown, whatever Takashi is afraid of for you."

"What?" Seiji asked, looking stunned.

"Yeah, like what?" Yoshi asked irritably from Shimada's other side. "Like what is Seiji in so much danger of that you and Takashi have to protect him?" There was such bitterness in Yoshi's voice, both Shimada and Seiji stared at him.

"Yoshi?" Shimada asked.

"Look, I'm really sick of all of this," Yoshi said, his voice rising in anger. "Will you fucking let go of me!" Struggling in earnest, he managed to wrench free of Shimada's grip and bolted, unfortunately right into Takashi.

"Ow," Takashi said, staggering against Yoshi to regain his balance.

"Fuck off!" Yoshi pushed free of him and ran into the crowd.

"You're on your own now, Takashi, old man," Shimada said, shoving Seiji at him and going after Yoshi.

"Well, excuse me," Seiji said, trying to get past him, but Takashi took hold of his arm. At least it was the other arm, and not the one Shimada had been crushing thus far.

Takashi sighed. "Look, Seiji—"

"I knew you were gay! Hahahaha!" Yoko yelled over the music at the not-terribly-happy-at-the-moment couple. "I couldn't figure out why you were doing all this marriage stuff. Oh! Look! Look! There's Jupiter Li!" She darted deeper into the bar. Her father was on her heels, but he paused to call Takashi a few unflattering names on his way by.

"Who was—?" Seiji began.

"Oh never mind, let's—" Takashi started to say.

"I CANNOT FUCKING BELIEVE WHAT YOU JUST DID IN THERE!" Daitaro yelled right next to them.

Seiji pulled the startled Takashi behind him. "DAITARO! FUCK OFF!" Seiji yelled as loud as he could.

Daitaro recoiled, and then was distracted by something behind them and ran farther into the bar area.

"Wow, Seiji, you chased him off," Takashi said in awe.

"I wonder," Seiji said, looking around Takashi and watching Daitaro head for Koji. "Takashi, I—"

"Seiji, listen, I'm sorry, this is a nightma—"

"Oh here you are, Takashi," Takashi's mother hailed him, as she and his father squeezed between some gaudily dressed bodies to get next to them. "Oh, and Seiji, too, that's good. We were worried."

"You were?" Takashi asked.

"Yes, this situation with the Yamada family doesn't suit us," his father said bluntly. "I'd frankly rather see you dead or with Seiji than married to a creature like Yoko."

"Gee thanks, dad," Takashi said.

Seiji looked at the floor. "Is this what your family thinks of me?" he asked his shoes.

"Oh, dear, no, dear, no, we like you very much," Takashi's mom said quickly. "But I think we should talk about this tomorrow. This is quite impossible. Come, dear." She took her husband's arm and they left the way they came.

"Seiji, we really need to get out of here," Takashi said, looking for the best way out of there.

"What's the point, Takashi?" Seiji said. "I think I'll stay—"

"I really hope you're happy, Seiji!" Daitaro's wife screamed at him. "Takashi just embarrassed everyone over you. First you ruin Ryuu's life, now Takashi's. What kind of a monster are you?" She didn't wait for an answer as she stormed off in the direction her husband had gone.

"Takashi! What the fu–?" Seiji began.

"I'll tell you later," Takashi said firmly, and put his arms around Seiji. "Let's dance."

Further inside the bar area, Shimada finally caught up with Yoshi. "What? What? What did I do to piss you off?" he yelled, keeping firm grip on his boyfriend.

"Nothing, go home, or go back to whatever you were doing!" Yoshi yelled, twisting away from him. "I'll stay here!"

Shimada pulled him into his arms. "I think not, Yoshi," he murmured, watching Daitaro and Norboru Suzuki squaring off, apparently over Koji, who was looking on and looking amused. "This place is about to explode."

Yoshi looked around Shimada's arm. "Oh my..." First there was Yoko Yamada arguing with her parents and Jupiter Li edging away from them. Not far from them, Koji was sneering and looking really flushed and sexy as Daitaro and Suzuki were shouting at each other about something. He felt Shimada tense and lean forward when Daitaro's wife entered the scene and Koji melted into the background.

A fight started behind Jupiter Li, and his body guards only made things worse defending him from it. There was a crowd surge: women screaming, furniture trampled, glass shattering. Shimada then did the only sensible thing: he slung Yoshi over his shoulder and ran for it.

Seeing Shimada carrying Yoshi and making a path to the front exit, Takashi grabbed Seiji's hand and followed in their wake. Originally thinking he'd get his car, he dove into the nearest taxi instead and told the driver to step on it. At the sight of crazed, stampeding party-goers, the driver didn't need to be told twice.

"What about your car?" Seiji asked, as he looked out the back window at the chaotic crowd behind them.

"I'll get it in the morning," Takashi said, and gave the driver their home address.

Back at the hotel's taxi line, Yoshi was yelling, "Put me down!" Shimada obliged by dumping him into the back seat of a taxi and barking their address at the driver.

"Sorry, driver, didn't mean to be rude," Shimada said. He was sitting on Yoshi who was yelling for the driver to stop the cab and let him out. "Crazy night, just ignore him."

The driver just nodded. "Never seen anything like that at the Hotel Arcadia," he said conversationally. "Very crazy night."

Yoshi went limp beneath Shimada. "D'you think you could get off me, please?" he asked and sat up when Shimada got off him. They rode the rest of the way home in silence.

"Well?" Shimada asked when they were upstairs in their apartment.

"Well, what?" Yoshi asked. "Hi Flounder." He bent down to pet the cat, who very pointedly walked into the kitchen. "Did you feed him today?"

"I must have or he would have torn hunks off of us when we came in," Shimada said, following Flounder to see that he did, indeed, still have dry food in his dish. "Are you feeding him more?" he asked from across the kitchen that was almost as large as their entire previous apartment.

"He wants smooshy food; I can tell," Yoshi said, dumping a small can of designer cat food in Flounder's dish, which was still on the cartoony fish placemat Seiji had given the cat as a housewarming when they came to Tokyo. Yoshi sighed, he scratched Flounder's furry head and then straightened up. "So...why were you there tonight?" he asked, leaning on the cabinets opposite those Shimada was leaning on.

"Takashi called in a panic when he saw Seiji in that freak show," Shimada said, puzzled by Yoshi's scowl. "I guess I owe him."

"It's not a freak show, I knew most of those people," Yoshi snapped. "And who do you owe what? Takashi or Seiji?"

"Takashi," Shimada said blandly, hoping Yoshi was either going to calm down or spin his anger out. "He's been very nice to us since we've been in Tokyo. They've both been very nice to us."

Yoshi sighed and rubbed his hand over his eyes. He looked very young and very tired at that moment. "I'm...I'm not like Seiji," he said softly.

"No, and thank God for that."

"But that's why you're with me, because I remind you of him," Yoshi said. He tensed when Shimada crossed the room and leaned very close to him.

"You did once, Yoshi," Shimada said softly, his face mere millimeters from Yoshi's. "But have you looked in the mirror lately? You're one of the most beautiful men in Asia now; Seiji doesn't come close."

"I'm not talking about my looks, Ryuu," Yoshi said, unable to meet his lover's eye. "I'm not from the same kind of people you and Seiji and Takashi are from. My family wasn't rich, I'm not going to university, I'm never going to have fancy jobs like you three do." A tear splashed on his shirt.

"Yoshi, so what? Being a graphic designer is a cool job, you'll be great at it," Shimada said, pulling him into his arms. "Or you can keep modeling and acting, if you want to, that's fine, too."

"I don't."

"Don't what?" Shimada asked, stroking Yoshi's hair out of his eyes. "Modeling or graphic design?"

"Modeling, I hate it," Yoshi said, sniffing until Shimada handed him a paper towel to blow his nose. "I can't act either. I could only do the theater thing because there were people to help me night after night."

"So, you can go to graphic design school like we planned," Shimada said, and then quickly asked if he still wanted to. Maybe Yoshi wanted to become a jet pilot or something, but the kid assured him he still wanted to do graphic design. "Okay, good. I know we got derailed when we came to Tokyo. It took a while to get back on track, but we'll be fine, Yoshi. Don't worry about anything, baby, it's all under control." Shimada held him tight and made a vow to himself that this would be true, and, nothing, not even Daitaro, would get in the way again.

Yoshi hugged him back and smiled as Flounder rubbed happily around their calves.

Seiji and Takashi didn't speak until they were in their apartment and Seiji walked directly into their bedroom without turning the lights on. Takashi followed and turned on the reading light on his side of the bed. Seiji was sitting on the edge of his side of the bed, staring out the picture window at the city. Takashi cautiously walked around the bed to sit next to him. "Look, Seiji, I really made a mistake tonight, I–"

"Your father really hates me," Seiji said flatly.

Takashi sighed. "My father says unguarded things when he's stressed and confused," he said carefully. "Remember the time at my cousin's wedding when he toasted the bride and groom with the wrong names?" Encouraged by Seiji's micro-laugh, Takashi put his arm around him. "Both my parents like you very much, Seiji. Tonight was a nightmare on a lot of levels. I'm surprised anyone could make any sense in that mess. What on earth were you doing there?"

"Koji invited us," Seiji said, leaning against his lover. "He said he wanted to cheer me up."

"And did it?" Takashi asked.

"A little, but...no, not really. Too much noise, too much confusion," Seiji said softly. "But it did take my mind off...off what you were doing....Until I saw you."

"And when I saw you, it focused my mind on what I was doing," Takashi thought, but said, "Yeah, it was a shock. I just wonder why Jupiter Li picked the Arcadia to throw that kind of party."

"I think Koji picked it," Seiji said, thinking back, piecing it together. "He said it was time to kick some life into the place. Or something like that."

"So he picks the one night I'll be there doing something really stupid," Takashi said slowly. "Did Yoshi know where the, the thing was being held?"

"The miai?" Seiji asked with heavy irony and Takashi could only nod. "No, he said he didn't know and I believe him. He wouldn't do anything to hurt us. Did you tell Ryuu?"

"I did, but Ryuu was as shocked as I was when I told him you were there," Takashi said thoughtfully. "I guess I owe Yoshi an apology. That is, if he didn't know and didn't set us up."

"Ta-ka-shi, we're talking about Yoshi and Ryuu," Seiji said firmly. "They're our friends. Didn't Ryuu come when you asked him for help?"

"He did, and I should have listened to him," Takashi said.

"What? When?"

"We had lunch earlier in the week," Takashi said. "He told me not to do– not to go to the thing, just say no, and I didn't. I thought I could handle it all, keep all the balls in the air, and it all came crashing down around me."

"Oh, Takashi."

"When I saw you in that crowd, I knew I could lose you," Takashi said, fighting to keep his voice level. "Not because I don't love you or you don't love me, but that you'd be swept away by events out of our control. We've been lucky so far, Seiji, we haven't had much opposition."

"Until now," Seiji said resolutely. "But I know better now, and I'm going to fight Daitaro with every last breath in my body this time."

"Well, I'm probably fired, so that's not something you have to worry about," Takashi said, and seeing Seiji's shocked face, went on. "I came out last night. My parents knew, but I told the Yamadas and Daitaro and his wife that I'm gay and I'm in love with you and I'm not leaving you. Ever. And it was easy, Seiji, at least easier than I thought it was going to be. The timing could have been better, but–"

Seiji's lips on his intercepted whatever else Takashi was going to say that night.

Upstairs in the best suite at the Hotel Arcadia, a pair of hands released Koji Kawazu's throat and dropped his lifeless naked body onto the bed.

"How's Yoshi holding up?" Renge asked over lunch a few weeks after the events at the Hotel Arcadia.

"He's still pretty upset about Koji," Shimada said, sipping a mineral water. He was cutting back on his drinking due to the stress of recent events. He neglected to add that Yoshi was sleeping ten to twelve hours a day and crying without realizing it. The doctor they'd consulted had diagnosed the problem as grief and shock, prescribed time and rest to cure it, and suggested they come back if Yoshi wasn't better in a few weeks. "They were more friends than rivals, after all. And between the police and the media, it's been a hellish mess."

"Are you two cleared?" Renge asked.

"I think so, we have each other as an alibi and our building security people saw us go in and not come out until the next day," Shimada said, recalling with distaste how relieved he felt that the building security was keeping those kind of tabs on him and Yoshi. "It's a nice building, that seemed to matter a lot to the police."

Takashi and Seiji had gone through the same unpleasantness with the police, but with less stress since neither of them were a supermodel or muckraking reporter. Although Takashi and Seiji had made up and had an even stronger bond after the unfortunate events with the Yamada family, they were still under more stress than usual. Daitaro had indeed fired Takashi from Shimada Miyagi, but Kenzu Miyaguchi had recruited him within hours of the firing for Mishima Muramaki. It was a small step down in status and money for Takashi, but a large step up in being out from under Daitaro's thumb. But Shimada wasn't worried; he knew Takashi would work his way back to the top in no time. Especially since most of his SM clients, including Mr. Yamada of YKT Motors, followed him over to MM.

Renge sighed and shook his head. "Seemed kind of inevitable Koji getting murdered like that."

"Murder is never inevitable, Renge," Shimada said, trying to keep the ice out of his voice. "Murder is a nasty, horrible thing that should never happen to anyone." He'd been furious with the line most of the papers had taken that Koji somehow had his murder coming, that his rise from yakuza sex toy to respected actor was something he didn't deserve and needed to be punished for. Shimada might have agreed that Koji needed to be reined in a little, something a better agent and a respectable, steady lover would have taken care of, but his death was a terrible thing that hurt everyone around it. Including Daitaro, who had had to admit that he was sleeping with Koji whenever he got the chance. In the course of the police investigation it had come out that Daitaro had told Koji where and when Takashi's miai was being held, but that he had no idea Koji intended to arrange that riotous party at the Impala Bar. Neither Daitaro, nor Jupiter Li, who was back in China and reluctant to answer police questions in Japan, nor Norboru Suzuki, who was also sleeping with Koji whenever he could, had been completely cleared. Jupiter Li had no reputation to damage, but Daitaro's and Suzuki's professional and personal lives were savaged due to the publicity.

"You're right, you're right," Renge said sadly. "I'm not used to this kind of thing happening anywhere near me."

"I've done the crime beat, Renge; no one gets used to it."

"I mean, I heard that crazy scene at the Impala was all a gay mad whirl," Renge said with a shrug. "The tabloids and webloids had a field day with it, made it gaudy fun. And then they found his body...you know no one's claimed it yet..."

Shimada recoiled mentally at this new piece of information and put aside whether he'd tell Yoshi about it. "Hey, Renge, what's up, pal? You didn't call me here to talk about Koji, and I'm losing my appetite."

"Well, you're really going to lose your appetite when I tell you the production company that had Koji starring in 'The Occupation Boy' have switched their sights to Yoshi," Renge said. "And, without a huge, expensive, media circus lawsuit you'll lose, I can't get Yoshi out of it. I've checked with Media Mondial's legal department about it and they said they won't even try to go up against this American film company."

Shimada looked up at the hovering waiter. "I'll have that martini now. Make it a double."

After an understandable initial resistance from Yoshi, Renge, without Shimada's assistance or opposition, finally convinced him to go quietly. Renge and Shimada were understanding when Yoshi compared taking that role to wearing the dead Koji's clothes or living in his house. But Renge finally put forward the argument that Yoshi could think of it as a memorial to Koji. The capper was when Renge said he'd insist the film be dedicated to Koji's memory.

Shimada had merely assured Yoshi he'd stand by him whatever he wanted to do. He'd patiently explained what damages and legal fees could add up to and what the tabloids would make of it. But he promised his lover he'd be there for him whatever decision he made. He hadn't been able to read the script or even a synopsis since there wasn't one, and he was trying to get a copy of the novel in English as it hadn't been translated into Japanese yet. All Shimada, Yoshi and Renge knew at that point was that "The Occupation Boy" novel was about a love affair between an American officer and a Japanese boy in occupied Tokyo. It sounded like an unappealing project, but the veiled threats already being made by the Japanese production company on behalf of their American partners were even more unappealing.

"Okay, I'll just do it and get it over with," Yoshi said in the car on the way to a meeting over cocktails with the production company. "It will be like, like going to the dentist."

"That's the spirit, Yoshi," Renge said. He was driving so he didn't look around at him in the back seat. "And I promise to keep you out of movies from now on."

"I don't like it that they're shooting in Vietnam, Renge," Shimada said, next to Renge. "I've never heard of this place they're going to."

"It's cheaper, Ryuu, at least they say so," Renge said. "There's studio facilities and, well, ruins. Not many urban ruins in Japan at this point."

"They could blue screen it," Shimada said.

"I tried that argument with the Japanese producer," Renge said. "They're going for authenticity. That's–"

"And shooting in Vietnam a Japanese and American movie about the American occupation of Japan is authentic?" Shimada asked, irony and awe dueling for top spot in his voice.

"That's what they tell me, Ryuu," Renge said neutrally. "It is why they say they're using a Japanese director and as much Japanese talent as they can."

"And that's why they didn't get a Chinese boy actor, eh?" Shimada asked with a little grunt of laughter. "That's what they did for that stupid geisha movie, all those girls were Chinese, and America didn't care."

"I don't think most of America could really tell the difference," Renge said.

"I thought you liked Michelle Yeoh," Yoshi piped up in the back seat.

149

Shimada smiled over his shoulder at him. "Honey, I LOVE Michelle Yeoh, but she's Chinese and it was supposed to be about geishas. But my Michelle was great!"

"I'm more of a Gong Li fan myself," Renge ventured.

"And Gong Li was great, too. Mmmmm, Gong Li!" Shimada nearly growled. "I really hate that other girl, the little crouching short skinny girl, what's her name?"

"Ziyi Zhang," Renge said. "Not my type either."

"Yeah, I hate her," Shimada said.

"You two are weird," Yoshi said. "Ziyi Zhang kicks ass!"

"She's short," Shimada said.

"She rocks!" Yoshi said.

"Eh, maybe," Shimada drawled, glad to have Yoshi taking an interest in something other than sleeping, crying and not wanting to do the upcoming film. Maybe later he'd get some Jet Li, Steven Chow and Jackie Chan DVDs and have a martial arts film festival...in their bedroom.

"By the way, I think Michelle Yeoh was born in Malaysia," Renge said, interrupting Shimada's mental list making.

"That still doesn't make her or the other two actresses Japanese," Shimada said, hopping back on the dreaded subject. "Much less geishas during the Occupation."

"We're here," Renge said, pulling into the valet parking.

"And why the hell is this party being held at the Hotel Arcadia?" Shimada asked, getting out of the car and opening the back door for Yoshi, who nodded vaguely at his question. "Hasn't this place suffered enough?"

"That's the thinking, Ryuu," Renge said, tucking the valet ticket into his breast pocket. "The American producer figured the Arcadia could use a little positive business after..." He glanced at Yoshi, who looked away. "Could use the business. Let's go."

The Arcadia lobby and Impala Bar were their usual muted selves again. Two men wearing smart business suits and a younger man in a tasteful kimono were hardly noticed wending their way to one of the smaller banquet rooms.

"What the fuck, Renge? Isn't that Hiroshi Matsui over there?" Shimada asked, not staring at an elderly man in a kimono listening politely to a group of Americans. "Isn't he short listed for a Nobel Prize in literature? What's he doing here?"

"They brought him in to fix up this mess of a screenplay," Renge said, nodding to their host and the director of the film, Yuu Tanaka. "It appears the original screenplay got the American and Japanese-

American aspects covered, but omitted the native Japanese angle. He's protecting our history and national interest," Renge added, his voice a little too bland.

"And maybe a whiff of nationalism," Shimada said under his smile.

"It is the 21st century, Ryuu," Renge said.

"Some things are timeless," Shimada sighed. "Come on, Yoshi, sooner done, sooner home." He gently towed his lover toward the group around Matsui for introductions.

Yoshi never quite got used to being examined by strangers; he still felt like a strange animal or a thing when it happened. He dearly hoped this would be the last time it happened, too. Yuu Tanaka and Matsui-sensei were at least discreet about looking him over, but the American producer, John Burton, was bold and rude enough to walk a complete circle around him.

"Perfect," Burton murmured in English, staring hard at him. "Simply perfect."

Yoshi lowered his eyes more in rage than modesty. Shimada drew him to his side, and said, "Yeah, well, I understand your script isn't in such great shape," in English and then they all waited for the flurry of translation to die down.

"We are lucky, Mr. Shimada, to have Mr. Matsui to help us," Burton said dryly in English and then introduced Yoshi to his American co-stars, Robert Hashimoto and Edward McAfee. They were both much more polite than Burton had been. Hashimoto's Japanese was fluent, but clunky, so he alternated between English and Japanese, although never in the same sentence. The American screenwriter, Norbert Waterbury, was doing a lot of talking, Shimada was doing a lot of answering, and Tanaka and Matsui-sensei were doing their best to ignore them.

Waterbury: "Everyone knows about Hiroshima, it's famous, but they forget about Nagasaki."

Shimada: "Not in Japan."

Waterbury: "But they're good at forgetting about the rape of Nanjing and the atrocities in Manchuria."

Shimada's jaw dropped. He was nearly recovered enough to say something sharp about the forgotten fire bombings of Dresden and Tokyo when Yoshi, poor kid, tried to come to his rescue.

Yoshi: "What was the rape of Nanjing?"

Matsui: "Something that happened in China in WWII."

Yoshi: "Is it a big deal?"

Trying to forestall an outburst from Shimada, Renge stepped in, and said: "To some people. For most of us it's just one more thing nobody can do anything about."

"Don't you study history in school, Yoshi?" Burton asked pleasantly.

"Of course," Yoshi answered. "But Asia has a lot of history to study." He smiled inscrutably and drew Shimada toward the buffet table. "These people are assholes," he said, not realizing Tanaka was within earshot. Shimada sighed and put himself between his lover and the director.

Tanaka laughed softly and looked around Shimada at his star. "Well, cheer up, Yoshi," he said. "Your English language skills will get a good workout on this film."

"Gee, thanks," Yoshi said, not even trying not to pout.

"If this Waterbury character is the level of American writing talent on this thing, I can't wait to read the script and the novel," Shimada said. "Why are you on this sick project? You seem like a normal person for a filmmaker."

"Oh, I'm in it for the money and the glory," Tanaka said with a straight face. "Unlike Yoshi, I didn't get threatened with a lawsuit if I didn't do this film. They just offered me too much money not to do it. And, to some extent, I've got the same issue Matsui-sensei has; I want to see it done right or as right as possible."

"Good fucking luck," Shimada said, smiling at Waterbury.

Tanaka glanced at the screenwriter. "Oh him, he's on a plane back to Los Angeles tonight," he said under his breath because Waterbury was heading their way. "He's done as much damage to a bad novel as he could; now it's up to our side to fix as much as it can be fixed."

"Uh, look, I'm sorry if I offended you," Waterbury said and smiled grimly at Shimada's noncommittal nod. "But Japan is weird," he went on, undeterred by the silence around him. "I mean, here you have a beautiful culture, but all American girls want to read are those dick-less gay comic books. They're crazy for them, what's that about? I mean, that's why Noreen Watson wrote the novel about the Occupation, to get in on the Japanese gay sex craze going on now in the US. And it sold like mad. It's well-written, she's a good writer, but she said in an interview that it's weird how American girls only want to read comics and watch cartoons about hot guys fucking each other nowadays. And the whole Japanese manga thing where no one looks, y'know, Japanese. She wondered if that's some kind of internalized racism to go with the internalized misogyny. Anybody know?"

No one did, and the party broke up shortly afterwards.

"Get him out of this freakshow," Shimada snarled as politely as he could at Renge in the car.

"Can't," Renge said, gripping the wheel tighter than necessary.

"Fuck the money," Shimada said, sounding very tired. "And the lawsuits."

"It will embarrass a lot of good people, Ryuu," Renege said, also sounding tired. "Matsui-sensei is involved, and Yuu Tanaka isn't exactly a lightweight either."

There was silence in the car until Yoshi spoke up, softly, but they both heard him, "It's only a couple of weeks of them, I can live through it for a couple of weeks," he said, looking out the window. "And my English isn't very good so I won't understand most of the bullshit they say."

Three days later Yoshi left with the production company for Vietnam.

> Food and shelter had been scarce for weeks in Tokyo. The Boy and his High School mates had been living in the ruins, scavenging as best they could, many of them died. When the Americans came they gave them food, sometimes without a hand job, usually in exchange for one. That wasn't all the GIs wanted, this much the Boy understood, but it was all he could bring himself to do to survive.

Tanaka thought a lot about the novel's opening paragraph when they got to the difficult part of the shooting. How long, he wondered, would Yoshi Katayama have lasted in the perverted postwar Japan that this crazy novelist envisioned? Probably not very long.

But Tanaka had one of Burton's assistant producers on location with them and on his back to get more out of Yoshi. In addition to a nagging-through-the-translator American AssProd to deal with, Tanaka had a bad script to direct into a good film and that alone was more than enough to worry about. That and doing justice to the poetic repairs Matsui-sensei had made on the Japanese language parts of the script. Tanaka planned to direct and edit as if it were some weird fantasy, which is what the book was and the script had become, instead of the gritty realism of the original screenplay. His intent when he took the project was either to kill it mercifully or just make some artsy pornography out of it. That became impossible due to Matsui-sensei's involvement, so Tanaka had to make the best of it. When the idea of a film of "The Occupation Boy" began to surface, the last thing the Japanese cinema community wanted was some music video director on his first film to butcher it if it could be salvaged.

While Tanaka disliked the project, he liked shooting it in this obscure part of Vietnam where no one could see him struggling with actors, the weather, Burton's AssProd, and his own conscience.

FADE IN:

RUINS OF TOKYO   DAY

BOY being chased by 2 GIs, running, looking over his shoulder, GIs catch him, rip his pants off, rape begins, BOY screams, is hit over the head, rape continues

SERGEANT run into the frame, reacts in horror and anger, runs to the rape scene.

SERGEANT
(in English)
You men! Stop!

GIs run off.

SERGEANT
Shit.
(lifts unconscious BOY and carries him out of frame)

FADE TO BLACK.

"Okay, let's do another take in five minutes," Tanaka said. "Yoshi, I need to talk to you."

Tanaka was a fine director and a fine person, but at that moment he had a film and reputation to save: not that it was all riding on Yoshi's acting, what there was of it, but the director was going to get something out of this difficult kid if he had to beat it out of him. It was obvious to everyone by then that Yoshi was on auto-pilot and just going through the motions. For a better actor, this wouldn't have been a big deal, but Yoshi wasn't a good actor and was holding back. Tanaka decided to try something the Americans called Method Acting.

"Yoshi, on this next take, I want you to remember a time when you were very afraid," Tanaka said. "And be that afraid for this scene."

"Why?" Yoshi asked. He sounded as tired as he looked, so his not unreasonable question came across as a defensive whine. He wasn't sleeping well and was on edge from it; that much was clear to everyone. But no one objected because it was the perfect look for the Boy he was portraying. Nevertheless, Yoshi was overreacting to Tanaka's suggestion.

Noticing Yoshi's body tensing in anger, Tanaka figured he could work with that. "Because you're doing a horrible job, Yoshi, all these people are depending on you–"

"To–to what?! Run? Get my clothes ripped off?" Yoshi yelled.

"Yeah, isn't that all you're good for?" Tanaka raised his voice, glad to see the kid seemed to be holding back tears of rage or frustration, but there was an emotion to exploit.

Yoshi threw a clumsy right hook at him. Tanaka's backhanded slap was only half as hard as it could have been. There was a gasp nearby and shocked looks from the small crowd they'd drawn. "We're shooting!" Tanaka yelled, dragging Yoshi, struggling and crying, into position. The director called over one of his toughest production assistants to make sure Yoshi stayed put and ran when camera started rolling. "You're scared, Yoshi," Tanaka said, shaking him. "You're fucking scared out of your mind. And we're going to do this until I get what I want."

> BOY POV coming to in a clean, white room.

>> DOCTOR
>> (in white coat, moving around the room with his back to the POV, looks over his shoulder, says in Japanese)
> Oh, you're up.
>> (crosses to BOY on cot)

>> BOY
>> (recoils from him, the BOY has bruises on his face and arms)

                        DOCTOR
            It's all right, all right, you're
            safe.

    SERGEANT enters frame

                        SERGEANT
                    (to DOCTOR in English)
            Hey, is he okay?
                    (to BOY)
            Are you okay?

    BOY   recoils   from   SERGEANT's
    uniform, DOCTOR notices and gets
    between them

                        DOCTOR
                    (to SERGEANT in English)
            Murdoch, I think your uniform is
            upsetting him.

                        SERGEANT
                    (looks down at his khakis)
            Oh, oh right, okay, I'll go. Tell
            me if he needs anything.

    SERGENT exits

                        DOCTOR
                    (to BOY in Japanese)
            He's, ah, he's okay, he brought
            you here.
                    (waits a beat for answer)
            Um, you were, uh, hurt and the
            other men are in, um, under
            restraint.
                    (waits a beat for answer)
            I treated your wounds and
                    (waits a beat for answer)
            Excuse me, you do speak
            Japanese, dontcha?

BOY nods

>   BOY
> But not the way you do.

>   DOCTOR
>   (laughs softly)
> I, uh, was raised in Los Angeles,
> I didn't know my Japanese was
> odd until I came here. With the
> Army.

BOY looks at him with fear.

FADE TO BLACK

The American actors, Hashimoto and McAfee, confronted Tanaka at the end of the day. "You were pretty rough on the kid," Hashimoto said, speaking for himself and translating for McAfee. "He was in tears and freaked out for most of the shoot."

"He can take it," Tanaka said neutrally and listened to Hashimoto relay that to McAfee, who looked slightly more pissed off.

"He's just a kid and you were a mutherfucker to him all fucking day," the big American snarled in English.

Tanaka held up a hand to forestall whatever Hasimoto was going to translate. "I got it, Bob, I got it," he said and sighed. "Whatever his mental state, Yoshi gave his best performances today. That's all I care about."

The actors stared at him with a mixture of disgust and incomprehension. "It...it didn't feel like he was acting, Yuu," Hashimoto said.

"I wonder, Bob, because you and Ed had good takes off Yoshi's 'not' acting," Tanaka said coolly. "Or whatever he was doing in front of the cameras today."

"He was killing himself," McAfee murmured, after the translation.

"That might be a bit of an exaggeration, Ed," Tanaka said and walked away while Hashimoto translated. Underneath his cool, Tanaka was elated. His actors were bonding in their roles even off camera. There might be something good about this Method Acting after all.

> Over the next few days with a safe place to sleep in an obscure corner of the Doctor's office area and being able to eat to

satiation, the Boy's aches lessened, bruises faded, and tears in delicate tissues healed. Rest and regular meals were doing the Boy good, too, he began to bloom under the Doctor's kindness.

Although the Boy was still nervous around the Sergeant, he was becoming more relaxed and accustomed to the big man's visits as long as the Doctor was somewhere in earshot. That the Sergeant usually had a small gift of chocolate or cigarettes seemed to help things along. The Boy was always polite, sitting up in his clean white bed wearing an oversized hospital gown and using his few words of English: please, thank you, hello, goodbye. This pleased the Sergeant a great deal and although his conversation was mostly one-sided and in English, the Sergeant was happier in those visits with the Boy than the Doctor had ever seen him.

Occasionally the Doctor translated a phrase here and there when it seemed important to the Sergeant. The Boy was well enough to not only correct the Doctor's clumsy Japanese, but also to laugh at it a little when they were alone. When the Boy got a little stronger, he began to help around the infirmary area. The Doctor moved his cot out of the medical area and into a corner near the Doctor's cot. They had long talks, the Boy about losing his family in the bombings, the Doctor about trying to practice medicine in the internment camp, enlisting in the Army and being sent with the Occupation forces to Japan. These conversations improved the Doctor's Japanese and taught the Boy a little more English. Eventually, the Boy regained his health and his strength.

The Sergeant waited at least that long before he asked the Boy to accompany him one evening.

> BOY and DOCTOR, BOY cutting bandages, DOCTOR mixing drugs

> > BOY
> > What does he want?

> > DOCTOR
> > You know what he wants. And you'll need someone to protect you while I'm away.

                    BOY
            (sighs, looks away)
        How long will you be gone?

                    DOCTOR
            Just a few days. Just to give one of
            the doctors at Nagasaki a little leave
            time.

        WIPE

        SERGENT leading BOY wearing a nice overcoat into a
        run-down building.

        CUT to interior, SERGENT picks up a key and guides
        BOY up a flight of rickety stairs.

It was an old room, in dire need of new tatami and a coat of paint,
but it was a scrupulously clean room. The Boy had avoided
rooms like this before, most of his encounters with GIs took
place in alleyways or bombed out buildings. The Sergeant took
the Boy's coat, the one he'd given him that very day...

The more Shimada read of "The Occupation Boy," the more concerned
and angry he became. This was the last straw and he was only half way
through the piece of pornographic trash. He hadn't heard from Yoshi
though he'd left several messages for him on his cell. But Yoshi was
good at letting his cell phone die and forgetting to recharge it. And
who knew where they were shooting; the town was just a name to
Shimada. If they were in Ho Chi Minh City or Hanoi he could have
called someone to do something, but they weren't so he couldn't. He
tossed the imported English book into a corner and called in a huge
favor at the Vietnamese embassy. They said they'd think about
expediting a visa. Then Shimada called Colonel Giang Tran and asked
for his help in rescuing his, um, friend who was in Vietnam shooting a
Japanese movie.
    Colonel Tran seemed to know all about it. "Oh yes," he said in
English, the only language he and Shimada had in common. "I heard
something about some weird American movie project north of here. I
didn't know you were involved."
    "I'm not, but I need to be sure my, uh, friend is okay," Shimada
said, trying to get the urgency across, but not give too much away.

"Is your 'friend' the beautiful Yoshi Katayama we see in magazines full of things we cannot afford?" Tran asked with a low laugh. "I think you share the same address, is that not correct?"

"You're extremely well informed, Colonel," Shimada said, casting around in his mental Rolodex for whom else he could call in Ho Chi Minh City with as much power, and coming up with nothing. "Why is that?"

"You came to my country looking for trouble, Mr. Journalist, and I didn't like you, so I had to study you," Tran said. "But what you dug up and wrote in your newspaper helped me. So now I'll help you."

"Thanks," Shimada said.

"And then we're even. You can pick up your visa on your way to the airport tomorrow. You'll be met at the airport."

> The Sergeant took the Boy's coat and not finding anywhere to hang it up, folded it and put it on a low table by the window. He did the same with his own coat. There was nothing to say, at least nothing the Boy could understand. The Sergeant stood close to the Boy, examining him like he'd never seen him before.
>
> "I never thought I'd want this," he said, putting his arms around the Boy and stroking his shiny black hair. "You're so beautiful."
>
> The Boy endured it, feigning shyness to hide his disgust. He let the Sergeant undress him and slip into the bed next to him. He let the Sergeant gently run his hands all over his body, and the Boy was more surprised, but less pleased, when the Sergeant discovered the Boy's cock was already hard. It only seemed normal for the Boy to spread his legs so the Sergeant could lay between them.

"Jesus, Ed, I hope we're back in America before Yoshi's boyfriend sees that," Hashimoto said when they looked at video rushes on Tanaka's laptop.

"Nothing happened, Bob," McAfee said, sounding guilty even so.

"It looked real," Hashimoto said, making eye contact.

"He was...he was really into it," McAfee said softly. "It seemed real, but it wasn't. It can't be, it's just a movie. I'm not in love with him."

"Neither am I," Hashimoto said. "It just looks like we are on film."

McAfee nodded and walked away. He'd be there the next day to watch Hashimoto's love scene with Yoshi, just as Hashimoto had made a point of being on the set for McAfee's scene. Knowing the other was on the set kept them from getting swept away by whatever strange magic Tanaka had terrorized out of the sweet kid who had once been Yoshi Katayama.

Yoshi had begun to dread waking up. Most of the time he could retreat into the robot-like mind he was using for the Boy. It was the only way he could do the things, even though they were pretend things, he was doing in the film. But the first few moments after waking, when he'd be back in himself and missing Ryuu with a piercing ache, were the worst of all the aches he was feeling.

The shooting was going well, or at least quickly. Yoshi had figured out early on that if he gave everything he had in each take, they could get done sooner. The love scenes were freaking him out the most and he was glad when there were a lot of people looking on. It made it easier to disassociate his body with what he was doing with it. He began to live for the word "Cut!" It was his blessed relief and liberation.

It was not lost on Yoshi that Hashimoto and McAfee were being incredibly nice to him, protective even, and this helped him get through what he was going through. Yoshi began to almost feel sorry for the Boy in the story who was torn between hating the Sergeant and needing him to survive. And all the while feeling sorry for the Doctor, and confusing pity with love.

Norbert Waterbury had arrived the day before and he was the happiest jet-lagged person on the set. He was elated that Yoshi, Hashimoto, McAfee, and the whole cast were, as he said, doing such a great job realizing his intentions, as he'd realized Noreen Watson's intentions. One of the Japanese cast had murmured that realizing bad soft-core porn is never that difficult and the only good parts of the script were the ones Matsui-sensei worked on. Yoshi managed to avoid Waterbury, but he felt sorry that McAfee got the brunt of the worthless hack's attention.

"What an ugly stupid script," Yoshi thought, going over the next scene, the one where the Doctor comes back from the atomic bomb site at Nagasaki and cries on the Boy's shoulder and then they have sex. Yoshi put the script down, put the Boy "on" and looked up to find Hashimoto, "wearing" the Doctor, studying him with a complex blend of compassion, rage, sorrow, and lust.

Tanaka barked and they went to work.

"You really don't have to do this, Colonel," Shimada said in careful English. He was sitting next to Colonel Tran in the back of a nondescript van being discreetly followed by an equally nondescript van full of armed soldiers. "I could have just rented a car and driven up there."

"I'm curious about what the Americans are doing up there," Tran said, offering Shimada a cigarette and smiling at his polite refusal. "One hears rumors. You offer a good route to find out what is true."

"Glad to help," Shimada said nervously. "It's mainly the Japanese production company up there, I think." He had a lot of respect for Tran, who was shrewd, wise and ruthless and devoted all of his talent and energy to making his country a better place. If that meant helping an upstart reporter on the trail of a murderous drug ring that dabbled in sex slavery get a story and run the bastards out of Vietnam and into Thailand, all the better. "I would have been happy to send you the novel," Shimada went on.

"Oh? You have the book?" Tran asked. "What's the story?"

"It's about the American occupation of Japan," Shimada said. "The story takes place in Tokyo."

Tran turned in his seat to stare at Shimada and made him repeat it. "The American occupation of Japan," Tran sighed. "The fucking Americans can't even let go of the wars they win."

Shimada cleared his throat and murmured, "So it seems."

"And what is your friend Yoshi doing in the film?" Tran asked blandly.

"He's, ah, he's, he plays a young Japanese man who, ah, befriends an American soldier, and...yeah..." Shimada looked out the window to collect his thoughts, which refused to be collected.

"Willingly befriends an American occupier?" Tran asked. Tran's English-speaking aide-de-camp glanced back at them from the front seat.

"Um, no, or yes, kind of," Shimada fumbled. "There's a rape, but not the man his character befriends. I think."

"It's possible," Tran said vaguely. "Japanese soldiers raped boys in China in the war."

"How do you know that?" Shimada asked, somewhat shocked.

"Japanese soldiers raped everything they could find wherever they went in that war," Tran said pleasantly. "Japanese soldiers did worse things in China, things that China is still angry about."

"Yes, that's true," Shimada said, wishing his English was good enough to change the subject without offending his host.

"But China has more problems than their history with Japan," Tran said with a chuckle. "Being outraged over history is a luxury in all the outrages of today." He looked carefully at Shimada to see if he understood and was satisfied with the reporter's gracious nod.

Tran's aide handed out substantial lunches. Shimada's breakfast wasn't sitting well on his stomach; he thought lunch might help.

They rode in silence until they reached the outskirts of some grim little town. They arrived as filming was winding down for the day.

Yoshi had just finished the love scene with Hashimoto and was trying to get the creepy feelings to go away. It was supposed to be an awkward love scene that turns lyrical, at least that's what the Waterbury thing harped on before the shoot. It had gone well: they'd gotten most of it in one take, and only one section—the beginning where Hashimoto had a long, passionate speech about death, war, love, hope, the future, etc.—had to be redone. Yoshi had changed into his own clothes and come out to get a drink from the caterers when he saw Shimada arrive. After a split second of hesitation, he threw himself into Shimada's arms and couldn't stop shaking.

"God, Yoshi, what have they been doing to you?" Shimada murmured, holding his emaciated, wild-eyed lover in his arms.

Colonel Tran looked on impassively and then turned his attention to the small group around a scrawny bespectacled Westerner, presumably an American.

Breaking off in mid-sentence to Waterbury, Tanaka thought, "Oh shit." He looked around for his Vietnamese intermediaries, who'd melted away at the first sign of the Vietnamese People's Army uniforms.

Poor, put-upon, exhausted Robert Hashimoto wound up translating Tanaka's Japanese into Engish for Tran and Tran's English into Japanese. Tanaka was desperately trying to think of some way of getting rid of Tran and his troops. He had another day of his assistant director shooting pick up shots and he'd planned to spend that day getting Yoshi Katayama's head back together. He'd been rough on the kid, but, damn, it was worth it for what they had on film. So, Tanaka was formulating his gracious brush-off when Waterbury had a brainwave.

"Let's show them the digital video!" the screenwriter cried, completely failing to notice Tanaka turning to stone next to him. "They've come all this way, it's the least we can do!"

"That would be fascinating," Tran said pleasantly.

While the video files were being organized on Tanaka's laptop, the catering staff pulled themselves together enough to serve tea and the last of the canned cookies they'd brought from Japan. Colonel Tran complimented them on their hospitality and said he looked forward to seeing what they were doing.

"You'll love it!" Waterbury enthused, waving his hands around and completely missing the bland menace in Tran's voice. "It's like a romantic look at the Americans in Japan after the war!"

"Romantic," Tran repeated blandly, turning to look at Shimada still comforting Yoshi. "How interesting."

"I don't think you want to see this, Ryuu," Yoshi said when they were called into the makeshift sound stage area.

"Why not?" Shimada asked, not removing his arm from Yoshi's shoulders.

"It's–" Yoshi began.

"Mr. Shimada! Thank you for bringing guests!" Waterbury enthused and took a seat next to Shimada.

"You're, um, welcome, I think." Shimada exchanged worried looks with Tanaka, sitting beside Waterbury, as the lights went down.

Ultimately the opening chase and rape scene would be edited into a smooth and seamless dreamscape that was almost sexy. Unfortunately the handheld video work was choppy and almost made the camera into one of the rapists. Shimada's breakfast and lunch and the heat and the jostling van ride hadn't really agreed with him, and now this vile thing he had to watch being done to the man he loved was simply too much for his already outraged digestive system. So when his gorge started to rise, he decided that Norbert fucking Waterbury's lap was the best possible place for it. He felt a little bad because some of the vomit got on Yuu Tanaka, but when he found out what he'd done to Yoshi on location, he was sorry he didn't puke more evenly on both the bastards.

While Yoshi was outside with Shimada, who was rinsing his mouth out with brandy, and Tanaka and Waterbury were changing into clean clothes, Colonel Tran and his men continued to watch the video. Tran was not amused, he was, in fact, infuriated by a story he'd consider disgusting in any circumstances. And the fact that it had been made in his country by foreigners just made him angrier. He sent his aide and most of his men to escort the film crew to the airport as soon as they could pack up. Tanaka started to object, but thought better of it. Whatever needed to be done could be done in Tokyo or with stock footage or not at all. Tran and his driver hustled Yoshi and Shimada into the van and drove off. "We will drive you to the airport," he said to Shimada through clenched teeth.

"Thanks," Shimada said, still weak from vomiting. He translated for Yoshi.

"Thank you, I want to leave," Yoshi said carefully in English to Tran. "Oh! But Tanaka has my passport," he said switching back to Japanese, which Shimada translated into English for Tran, who sighed and stared at Yoshi for a few minutes.

"Then if you don't have a hotel, you and your—your lover can stay at my apartment until the Japanese Embassy can issue a passport," Tran said evenly after he'd decided Yoshi and Shimada should not be anywhere near that vile film situation again.

Shimada and Yoshi were profuse in their thanks for the offer of hospitality but they were able to get a room at a hotel near the airport.

"I'll do what I can to expedite Yoshi's passport," Tran said as they were parting. "It is, however, up to the Japanese embassy how they handle it."

"There'll be a scandal, Colonel," Shimada said with a smile. "You just kicked a Japanese-American production out of Vietnam."

"I'll see them in hell," Tran said, and then smiled at Yoshi. "Take care of him."

"How did you know he's my lover?" Shimada asked, the newshound rising up in him. "You knew I was–"

"Homosexual?" Tran asked. "Of course. Don't you think we found out everything there was to know about you when you started asking interesting questions on your last visit?" Tran offered a microscopic bow and walked out of the hotel lobby.

"Who was that, Ryuu?" Yoshi asked in the elevator going up to their room.

"A great man," Shimada said softly.

They were exhausted, Shimada from his day and Yoshi from the filming. They took a quick, chaste shower together and fell into bed and immediately asleep.

Very early the next morning, Shimada's cell phone went off.

"Ryuu! Where the hell are you? Where's Yoshi?" Takashi was practically yelling. Shimada could hear Seiji in the background trying to calm him down. "Are you in jail or prison?"

"I don't think the cell reception is this good in Vietnamese jails, Takashi, but I've no personal experience to draw on," Shimada said blandly. He put his arm around Yoshi, who'd woken and started away from him. "It's okay, Yoshi, it's just Takashi freaking out before breakfast." Yoshi was more reassured than curious and went into the bathroom. "Hey, I get a question now: what's up with this call?" Shimada asked when the bathroom door was firmly closed.

"It's all over the news that the film crew was deported from Vietnam at gunpoint," Takashi said. "Aren't you watching the news?"

"No, actually, I was sleeping," Shimada said. "Unprofessional of me, I know, but there you have it."

"Ryuu! This is serious!" Takashi was yelling again. "No one knows where you and Yoshi are. The production company's spokesperson said you and Yoshi were taken away separately!"

"Well calm down, Takashi, it's hardly time to send money, guns and lawyers," Shimada said, watching the bathroom door and listening to the shower running. "Look, as you know the production broke up rather suddenly, so suddenly we left without Yoshi's passport. We're stuck here until we can get one from the Japanese embassy. I'll fill you in on all the details when I see you."

"Passport?" Takashi seemed stuck on this. "Is there anything I can do from here? At the Foreign Ministry or somewhere?"

"Thanks, I think we have it covered," Shimada said, noting that the shower was still running. "The most powerful man in Vietnam, possibly Asia, is working on it."

"Let me know if you need me," Takashi said, sounding somewhat mollified and certainly calmer.

"Well, I always need you, Takashi," Shimada deadpanned. "Hi to Seiji."

"I will. I'm hanging up now." And with that, Takashi hung up.

Yoshi was not a marathon showerer, so Shimada was disturbed to find him, eyes closed, head thrown back, just standing under the steam of water. Never one to be wasteful, Shimada stepped into the shower, bathed and turned the water off. "Okay," he said, pulling Yoshi in to his arms. "What happened?"

"I...I feel really dirty," Yoshi said limply against his shoulder.

"Why?" Shimada smoothed Yoshi's wet bangs off his forehead.

"You saw...you saw the film..." Yoshi was shaking in his arms.

"The rape? Did you get raped?" Shimada asked, momentarily stunned. "I'll fucking kill all of them, I'll–"

"I didn't get raped, I mean, not physically, I guess, um..." Yoshi looked up at him. "Could we get dressed and eat breakfast? I'm cold and hungry."

Yoshi seemed reluctant to talk about it until after their visit to the Japanese embassy, where they were promised a passport would be waiting first thing the next day. Colonel Tran's people had been there the night before and all hell was breaking loose in the Japanese press about the famous Japanese journalist and the supermodel being held/stranded/marooned/vacationing—depending on the source— somewhere in Vietnam. Even after Shimada's paper called for a statement that he and Yoshi were okay and would be back in Japan at the earliest possible moment, the Japanese diplomatic staff were anxious to get them out of Vietnam as soon as possible.

Another paper Shimada freelanced for called and asked, since he was there anyway, if he'd look into some rumors about toxic waste dumping in the Mekong. Shimada told them to get someone else. Then he turned off his phone and put it in his pocket. He and Yoshi were sitting in a park not far from the Japanese embassy, watching the midday street life of Ho Chi Minh City.

"Who was that yesterday?" Yoshi finally asked after a long silence. "The guy in charge? Colonel Pham?"

"Not Pham, Tran," Shimada said. "Colonel Giang Tran helped us out of there, although I now think he overreacted a little." He looked into Yoshi's stunned, haunted eyes and added, "On the other hand, maybe not." Shimada would have liked to put his arms around his lover, but he thought they might actually get arrested for it.

"He...he seemed like a strong person," Yoshi said softly.

"Uh, yeah, that's a good word for it," Shimada agreed.

"Um, maybe we should get him a present," Yoshi suggested vaguely.

"Yoshi, I think throwing those smug, arrogant bastards out of his country and driving away with you and me was the best present we could ever give Colonel Tran," Shimada said, trying not to laugh and failing. "I think that was the happiest I've ever seen Tran in my life," he blurted between giggles.

It was contagious; Yoshi started to giggle quietly and leaned against Shimada for support. Two Japanese men, helpless with laughter, drew a few looks, but otherwise were ignored by the busy city people. Pulling themselves together, they decided to go back to the hotel for lunch because it was easy. Shimada didn't have a translator on this trip and his English was good enough for the hotel. He was still tired and not up to any new experiences. And he was certain Yoshi wasn't up to anything more stressful than a cab ride back to the hotel, which had graciously written directions to and from the Embassy on their stationary for the travelers. They had lunch in their spotlessly clean room and although Yoshi ate, it wasn't with his usual gusto or conversation. Shimada was glad he had a magazine to read while Yoshi was silent and withdrawn. Reluctant to push him, Shimada figured there wasn't much he could do until they were back in Japan. The worst thing would be for Yoshi to have a breakdown in a foreign country. "Hm?" Shimada asked when Yoshi murmured something.

"I said, thank you for rescuing me," Yoshi repeated.

Shimada put down his magazine. "You're welcome. I'm sorry I had to, I should have come with you."

"They wouldn't let you," Yoshi said. "Remember? They said it wasn't a–a–a–"

"'A walk on the beach,' that's right, I remember now," Shimada said softly. "Yeah, I remember. I guess it wasn't a walk on the beach, was it?"

"No, it was like a bad dream," Yoshi said, looking at the middle distance and not at his lover. "It was like I had to feel all the fear and sadness I've ever felt all in one day, day after day. I just wanted to cry all the time, for my parents, my brother, Koji, those kids who killed themselves in Nagasaki, you know, you wrote about it, I—" Yoshi's pent-up tears finally spilled and he couldn't go on.

"Oh, baby, come here." Shimada drew him into his arms, noticing again how thin Yoshi was, while the younger man sobbed into his shoulder. "Why did they do that to you?" Shimada asked when the sobs died down to sniffles.

"I...because I couldn't do what they wanted unless I felt what the Boy felt," Yoshi said. "Everyone said it was brilliant. All I knew is that it was painful. How do people live through that stuff? I would die."

"I don't know, Yoshi," Shimada said, remembering when his world collapsed and how painful it was. Also reminding himself that Yoshi's world had collapsed once and the movie bastards had cruelly made him live a variation of it again. "I think you just take it moment by moment, until you're strong enough to go on with life."

Yoshi sat up and looked at him. "That's how the film ends," he said. "The Boy leaves the Americans and goes to work rebuilding Japan. That's what we shot a few days ago, I had to feel happy I was free, but sad to be leaving the safety or whatever I had with the Doctor and the Sergeant." Yoshi reached over for his cold tea and took a sip. "Um...nothing happened, I mean, really happened, it was all pretend, you know, the sex stuff."

"Like the rape?" Shimada asked and Yoshi nodded. "But it seemed real when I saw it. That's what made me sick, seeing that."

"I'm sorry," Yoshi said.

"It's not your fault, Yoshi," Shimada said, kissing his forehead. "And it was brilliant acting or whatever, but I love you and it freaked me out. And I'm a little freaked out that you suffered and I wasn't there for you. I just want to get us back to Japan where I can keep you safe and happy. That's all I want."

"I want that, too," Yoshi said, brightening a little. "I know you will; you always have. I'll never do another film, I can't, I won't." He started to cry again.

"You'll never have to," Shimada said firmly. "That much I can promise you. I'll fight for you. I should have fought for you—"

"No, you did...you did all you could." Yoshi laid gentle fingers on Shimada's lips. "I'll be okay, I did this, it didn't kill me, and now I can go on. I'll be stronger now, for both of us."

Shimada hugged him tight, fighting back his own tears. "Yeah...we'll both be stronger, for each other, than we knew we ever could be," he said.

Yoshi leaned back and kissed him, wiping both their tears away.

They were back in Tokyo the next afternoon. Flounder greeted them with fury, not from hunger or thirst because Shimada had discreetly called the building manager to make sure the cat was provided for those few days, but from sheer rage at being left alone for so long. Perhaps he was reminded of those terrible days before Yoshi adopted him in Nagasaki. After a can of cat food and some attention, Flounder settled down as if nothing had happened. It was, therefore, hoped that at least one of the three occupants of that apartment could get over the past and get on with the future.

However, there was the present to contend with. Tokyo media buzzed with various and ever more lurid versions of the events surrounding the filmmaking in Vietnam. The most outrageous had it that Yoshi had really been gang raped during the filming and that all the sex scenes were real, which made "The Occupation Boy" even more pornographic than it already was.

With the very able assistance of Takashi, Shimada, Kenzu, and even Seiji to some extent, Renge went on the offense with a media blitz that took Tanaka and his production company by surprise. They were even aided by the mysterious editorial writer who decried the work of perverse American authoresses who limned vile and inchoate lusts of repressed and demented modern young women who were so terrified of men and normal sex, they could only be aroused by men on men sexual violence. Neither Shimada nor Takashi nor Seiji had or wanted any contact with Daitaro, but Renge and Kenzu suggested they reconsider because the former partner in the now defunct Shimada Miyagi agency had been cleared by the architect Suzuki's confession. It had come too late to save Daitaro's marriage or career and he was eking out a living writing the same kind of tawdry news stories Shimada had written when he'd first some back to Tokyo. Unlike his principled younger brother, Daitaro supplemented his income writing porn and designing lurid ad campaigns for love hotels catering to women and sex toy distributors. This gave him particular insight into and ability to limn the inchoate lusts of repressed and demented modern young women with disposable income.

Although Daitaro's fall after Koji's murder had been spectacular, Suzuki, the actual murderer, had lost even more. He was facing life in prison, his wife had committed suicide, his daughter was put into the foster child system, and his parents disowned him. And just to pile on

169

the misery, Koji's medical records revealed that he was HIV positive, and Daitaro, Suzuki and, it was rumored, Jupiter Li, who was keeping a low profile somewhere else in Asia, were all now HIV positive.

This last fact had at least given Shimada pause. Should he contact his parents and let them know how bad Daitaro's condition really was? Should he look up his former sister-in-law and nephews? If only to ascertain whether his former sister-in-law knew she might have HIV? In the end he decided to leave all of them alone. None of them gave a damn about anything but themselves. They had, in fact done everything in their power to make his life unpleasant. He tried to exempt his father from this damning appraisal, but the best that could be said about him was that he didn't actively conspire against his younger son, which wasn't saying much and certainly not saying enough for Shimada to reach out to him. Maybe after his mother died....But in the present, there was no way his parents and his former sister-in-law could not know about Daitaro's stupidity and its effect: the most lurid details were splashed all over the tabloids and there was even a book being written about it by some hack journalist Shimada only knew slightly.

So Shimada put his family and the past behind him, because he certainly had his hands full in the present with Yoshi. Renge and Company did their best to present Yoshi as the victim of the yaoi craze as realized in America, that wretched land of excess and overkill. They planted stories indicating that Yoshi's delicate Japanese sensibilities had been overwhelmed by an American screenplay so vile that not even the great author Matsui-sensei could tone down its traumatic effects. Japanese history was not a vehicle for the lurid fantasies of strange American women with too much time on their hands. Yuu Tanaka struck back by hiring the Kimura Kano agency to make the argument in various media outlets that Japan was a powerful country able to endure the centuries and that if Yoshi Katayama was such a wimp, he was beneath art and history's contempt. Some of the attacks on Yoshi became so vitriolic, Media Mondial's legal department began rumbling about libel and character assassination. Renge arranged for an interview to surface with a legal expert questioning the legal rights and protections of Japanese actors working outside of Japan, and why it had been necessary for the Vietnamese police to deport Mr. Tanaka and his project from their country. The tone of the Kimura Kano-planted articles became much more civil after this.

"It wasn't the Vietnamese police, it was the army," Shimada said the next time he saw Takashi. They were on their way to meet Seiji and Yoshi for dinner.

"Was it?" Takashi asked, not even trying to hide how little he cared. "The army sounded too dramatic, like they're declaring war on us."

Shimada shook his head. "No wonder I hate advertising."

"Now, now," Takashi soothed. "How'd the loop sessions go?"

"Oh, fine," Shimada said, remembering how stressed Yoshi had been about seeing Tanaka or anyone or anything connected with "The Occupation Boy" again. Shimada was so concerned, he'd handed a primo story to another reporter in order to accompany Yoshi to the sessions. But surprisingly, once Yoshi was in the studio, he was all business. He overdubbed the dialogue where it was needed and they were done in half a day. Tanaka had sent someone from the post-production side of things, who'd never met Yoshi and couldn't care less about the scandal around the film, to supervise the recording session. "The actual, edited, cleaned-up movie is much better than what I saw. It actually looks pretty good, the little snippets I saw of it, but I can't..."

"Can't?" Takashi prompted after some silence.

Shimada turned and faced the man who'd gone from rival to enemy to friend over the years since they met at university. "I really love him, Takashi," Shimada said with raw honesty. "I can't separate Yoshi from the character, I can't know what he went through and then just sit in a theater or on a couch and watch him be abused for the amusement of the masses. Or something."

Takashi averted his eyes from the naked emotion in his friend's face. "I understand," he said quietly. "Kimura Kano is madly spinning this film as a great work of art. Something that provokes, enlightens and uplifts the soul as only a heartbreaking work of singular genius and the courage of post-war Japan as seen through the eyes of one of its victims."

"You. Are. Fucking. Kidding. Me." Shimada droned into Takashi's deadpan stare.

"Ryuu, I just won an award for the Uniflora Perfume campaign," Takashi said with a wry little smile. "But even I couldn't make up that much bullshit." He waited politely while Shimada laughed. "How's Yoshi?"

"He's good. You'll see at dinner." Shimada looked at his watch and they started walking again.

"How are you and Yoshi?" Takashi asked. "If that's not too personal a question."

"We're fine, we're getting back to what passes for normal for us," Shimada said neutrally. "We made it through this. We can make it through anything."

However, the larger picture of the Shimada-Katayama relationship had become somewhat more complex.

"You–you–you want to do what?" Shimada asked, clutching the sheets to his neck.

"I said I want to top." Smiling serenely, Yoshi tugged at the bedclothes his lover was holding like a shield before him. "It's wonderful; I've had a good teacher. I can assure you of that."

There wasn't much Shimada wouldn't do for Yoshi—cause an international incident, renounce his family, watch high school kendo matches—but he really wasn't sure he could let Yoshi fuck him. "I know that, but I'm not sure I'm ready for this," Shimada murmured, letting Yoshi kiss him. "I need to think about it."

"How long do you need?" Yoshi asked, tilting the bedside clock's luminous dial up.

"Are you on a schedule?" Shimada asked, mock horror mixed with laughter as he rolled around the bed with his lover, who was also laughing.

It was so good to have Yoshi snapping out of his funk. After they got back from Vietnam, Yoshi slept for three days. Not long after their return, a messenger from Tanaka delivered Yoshi's passport and luggage. There was also a letter from the production company's legal department expressing their profound displeasure with Shimada's actions and Yoshi's lack of resistance to them. Shimada forwarded the letter to Renge, who forwarded it to Media Mondial's legal department, who sent their own letter suggesting that Yoshi was being held against his will in Vietnam and Shimada had, with the very gallant Colonel Giang Tran's very able assistance, rescued a Japanese national from unlawful confinement. The production company's lawyers sent back a letter essentially saying, "You wouldn't dare," to which Media Mondial responded with a four page letter that boiled down to, "Do you feel lucky, punk?" and the matter was left there. However, on any and all contact Yoshi had with the production company, such as the overdubbing dialogue sessions, he was accompanied by a Media Mondial attorney. For all the saber-rattling on both sides, no one wanted "The Occupation Boy" affair to blow up into anything larger than it already was. They knew this because the Japanese government had told them so.

Yoshi pushed Shimada down into the pillows and held him there with a long, sweet kiss. Feeling Shimada's resistance dwindling and relaxing into the kiss, Yoshi pressed his advantage and was able to put his calf between Shimada's calves.

Breaking the kiss, Shimada asked in a husky whisper, "We're moving kind of fast, aren't we?"

"Shhhhh," Yoshi sighed. "At this rate, we'll be here until Hillary Clinton's second inaugural, if she gets the nomination."

Through Renge, Yoshi had refused to attend the Japanese or American premiere of "The Occupation Boy." The Japanese production company had made polite noises about the contractual obligation for publicity. Renge told them that Yoshi couldn't attend due to the psychological trauma he'd suffered at Tanaka's and Waterbury's hands during the principal photography. Furthermore, Yoshi would not even be in Tokyo for the premiere and then, through Takashi's and Kenzu's discreet channels let rumors percolate that Yoshi was recovering from his ordeal at a remote and exclusive mental hospital that was very much like an expensive spa. Not wanting any more bad press, the production company didn't press the issue.

Sliding his hand along Shimada's inner thigh, Yoshi eventually got him to relax enough to open his legs a little. While distracting the older man with playful nips to his neck, nipples, chest, and belly, Yoshi was able to wedge his body between Shimada's akimbo legs and lower his mouth to Shimada's erection. Yoshi ran his tongue over the head of his lover's cock before taking it in his mouth and pumping the base in the same rhythm as his sucking. Having planned for this and merely waiting for Shimada to be relaxed and aroused enough, Yoshi stealthily removed the tube of lubricant from under the pillow where he'd stashed there earlier.

"Okay, what's that?" Shimada asked, alert but not alarmed, and glad Yoshi wasn't stopping his excellent blowjob. He examined the container Yoshi held up for him in the dim light. "Oh, okay," he said with a dramatic sigh. "I love you, I trust you, you'll stop if I'm in agony, you'll—"

"Of course!" Yoshi pulled his mouth off so quickly, Shimada squeaked in surprise. "I wouldn't do anything you wouldn't do. I'd never do anything to hurt you, Ryuu. I love you. I just want you to be happy."

"Oh, touché, Yoshi," Shimada thought, but said, "I know." He gently stroked Yoshi's hair off his forehead. "I know, and, honestly, I've wondered what it was like for you...you know?"

"Well, now you can find out!" Yoshi began to cheerfully take the cap off the lube.

Shimada took it and recapped it. "It's not like you have a train to catch," he said, gently urging Yoshi back to his cooling erection.

The premiere of "The Occupation Boy" was a gaudy event in both countries. The film was gossiped about and admired for its artsy rendering of a badly written, lurid and titillating novel aimed at women who enjoy reading novels about men in love making out with each other. As a historical epic, it got a big horse laugh from what was left of the Greatest Generation, and was compared to "Hogan's Heroes," but not as funny, therefore not as good. Along with McAfee and Hashimoto, Yoshi's performance was singled out as rising above mediocre material and proving that he was more than just a pretty face. Nevertheless, Yoshi asked that his name be withdrawn when it was short-listed for a prestigious acting award. He wasn't an actor, he didn't want to be one, and he didn't want any more attention than he'd already had from the stupid movie. After a brief run in theaters, "The Occupation Boy" went into rental release, where it finally sank into oblivion except for the few die-hard yaoi fangirls who bought heavily discounted copies of the DVD before it sank completely below the pop culture radar.

Once Shimada decided to relax, he really relaxed, and Yoshi gently inserted a lubed finger. Shimada tensed and said, "Wow, that feels strange..."

"Bad strange or good strange?" Yoshi asked, stilling his movements.

"Um...good strange," Shimada said, and relaxed again under Yoshi's gently stretching him. And it was Shimada who eventually opened the condom and rolled it down Yoshi's beautiful arching cock.

No one who cared for Yoshi was ever able to sit through a complete screening of "The Occupation Boy." Not even Nakadai-sensei, who'd spent hours photographing him and, to some extent, terrorizing good pictures out of him. After seeing twenty minutes of the film, Nakadai contacted Yoshi through Renge to express his admiration for Yoshi's efforts in a bad film and sympathy for what he must have gone through. He also wanted to hire Yoshi for fashion shoot, but was politely informed that Yoshi had retired from modeling.

Pressing gently into Shimada's body, Yoshi was hypersensitive to every fleeting expression and sound no matter how subtle as he worked his condom-sheathed erection all the way in. He was spooned up behind Shimada so he only had his right profile to gauge his reaction to this first-time penetration. "Are you okay?" he asked over Shimada's shoulder.

"Mmmmmmmmmm."

Which was all the answer Yoshi needed and he began to gently fuck Shimada. Reaching around, Yoshi placed his hand over Shimada's and pumped his erection in the same rhythm. Neither of them lasted very long. Yoshi clung to Shimada's waist as he made one last deep thrust and gasped against his lover's shoulder. Feeling Yoshi's cock pulsing inside him sent Shimada into his orgasm with one or two quick strokes of his own hand. They lay in each other's arms as they came back to a more earthbound state.

Slipping out, Yoshi disposed of the condom and brought a warm damp towel back to bed. He wiped down the parts Shimada would let him, which were Shimada's belly and hands. "How was I?" he asked.

"You were great," Shimada said sleepily.

"I wanted you to come first," Yoshi said, curling into his side. "Sorry."

"Meh...next time," Shimada said, and dozed off as Flounder settled onto his chest in the loaf-of-bread position.

Shimada traveled the world as an investigative journalist getting in and out of trouble for a few more years. He eventually settled into an editorial position with a media conglomerate where he bailed out, scolded, and fought for journalists like himself writing top notch stories on the rights and wrongs of the world. Yoshi finally went to graphic design school, but ended up going into fashion photography at Seiji's and Takashi's suggestion. After all, they had reminded him, who thought up the Pajama Boy in the first place? Hearing about Yoshi's new career from Kenzu at MM agency, Nakadai-sensei asked to see his portfolio and liked it very much. He hired the former pajama model as an assistant and sent him clients when Yoshi set up his own studio.

The End